THE SUMMER SEASON

Recent Titles by Sheila Newberry

A CHARM OF FINCHES*
PAINTED SKY
THE SUMMER SEASON
TILLY'S FAMILY

*available from Severn House

THE SUMMER SEASON

Sheila Newberry

This first world edition published in Great Britain 2000 by
SEVERN HOUSE PUBLISHERS LTD of
9–15 High Street, Sutton, Surrey SM1 1DF.
This first world edition published in the U.S.A. 2000 by
SEVERN HOUSE PUBLISHERS INC of
595 Madison Avenue, New York, N.Y. 10022.

British Library Cataloguing in Publication Data

Newberry,   Sheila
    The summer season
    1.Love stories
    I. Title
    823.9'14 [F]

    ISBN 0-7278-5539-5

Typeset by Palimpsest Book Production Ltd
Polmont, Stirlingshire, Scotland
Printed and bound in Great Britain by
MPG Books Ltd, Bodmin, Cornwall.

This novel is dedicated to John,
who shared all the happy holidays afloat,
to family who were with us,
and not forgetting our constant companions,
two grey and hairy dogs.

"In my dreams I call out loud,
'How CAN we pass through all those locks
If we are fast asleep?'
While *Pili Pala* rocks . . ."

Preface

My grateful thanks are due to Mr R. J. Dommett of British Waterways and to the member of his staff who compiled such an informative set of notes on the kilns and quarries and the tram roads. Also for the song about the famous Crosha Bailey! British Waterways do a grand job in keeping the canal system alive and thriving again. The story of Ruth Owen and her family on *Pili Pala* was the result of all my dreaming on many a narrowboat holiday!

Our daughter Sara and her husband, Phil Holden of The Mumbles, who love to paint and photograph the area, helped greatly with my research too. As did Mr Dick Playle of the Music Hall Society. Thank you all!

The splendid canal books of D. D. and J. M. Gladwin (Oakwood Press) were also especially useful.

My canal is of course partly in my imagination, partly based on a real waterway which those in the know will no doubt recognise. As for the people, I do hope I have captured a little of that warm Welshness. We had the privilege of meeting a *real* 'Midnight Grocer', to whom my character, in a different time, pays tribute by 'borrowing' that name!

S.N.

Prologue

She remembered another chapel, another time. Not a simple meeting place like the mission, with flowers picked by the boat children in jam jars along the windowsills and sunlight streaming through the plain glass in the high windows, but a place with a great, arched roof, dark panelled walls, glorious stained glass and high-backed pews. On the lectern was a carved eagle with spread wings; on the altar a blue cloth overspread with fine, creamy lace.

This was Ruth Owen's first service at the College of Music, the first time she actually met Drago, although, of course, she knew him by sight and reputation as they both came from Brynbach, both lived alongside the canal though in very different circumstances. Ruth lived with her elder sister, Rachel Hughes, and her husband Davey: he was the lock keeper then and they had cared for her since she was six years old when her parents died of typhoid fever. Drago lived at that big house with all the steps down to the water's edge.

She was less than five feet tall with a childlike figure which belied her seventeen years and amazing dark eyes in that glowing little face. She had tiny hands with such a span over the piano keys.

Then, as always, Drago played the organ and Ruth Owen, the young student of music, was lost in the beauty of it all as the music soared to the rafters. She felt rising excitement within, for wasn't she, the scholarship girl, about to study piano with this marvellous teacher? This man was a living local legend.

She would have been amazed if she had known that the man so absorbed in his playing was also vibrantly aware of her presence, for she was but one student among many dutifully attending morning service.

"Don't be too much in awe of him," Rachel had advised quietly. "He has gifts yes, but so do *you*. Remember that."

"But to be taught by *Drago*, Rachel – that's always been my dream! Oh, but I'm going to miss you all . . ." She caught Meg's sulky sidelong glance – all this fuss! But she thought wryly that now Meg, Rachel's daughter, not far from her in age really, would be pleased to have the small bedroom all to herself. Could Meg actually be jealous of her success? She hoped not, being a kind-hearted girl.

They spoke, briefly, after the service, when he warmly gripped the hands of the new intake in turn and wished them well.

"I am—" she began breathlessly, as the others had done.

"You are Ruth Owen, of course. We are neighbours, give or take a mile or two of water between us . . . So, we are already friends, I hope?" He had a deep voice, an almost shy smile.

She was flattered, he was completely without side, so . . . nice. Middle-aged and married for many years, she knew that, but surely she could keep her hero worship hidden? She had this burning ambition, not only to play piano but to sing, for she had a lyrical Welsh voice; she intended to leave quiet Brynbach before too long and make her mark in a wider world. Drago, despite returning dutifully home at the end of each term, would, she knew, be the one to help her fulfil all her hopes and dreams. Who knows what heights he might have risen to himself, if he had not had the responsibility of an invalid wife?

In turn, the students were invited to Sunday tea, in Drago's rooms. All very proper, the girls were always in pairs with a lady tutor to chaperone, the boys, unaccompanied, in a group. Drago's manservant toasted muffins, served tea, and Ruth Owen sat fascinated, hardly saying a word, listening to Drago talking. He was always called 'Drago', never 'Mister Drago' or even 'Sir' and his darkness was as Welsh as that of Ruth Owen and many of the local young men and women whom he encouraged and inspired. Yet Ruth knew what they did not: that Drago had a foreign side to him. His paternal grandfather, a Spaniard, had been an engineer involved with the canal from its conception. He had married and settled in Brynbach, risen high in his profession and had built that beautiful house for his growing family. Drago, childless, was the last of that line.

Long letters home she wrote to her family for she dearly loved them even though she intended to leave them. She did not often mention Drago, remembering Rachel's words. In any case how could she explain the bond she felt between the two of them?

They were never alone together until the end of Ruth's first year was approaching. She had been his bright star at the end of term concert, singing to her own accompaniment, aware of his presence between the dignitaries seated in the front row of the audience. Such applause! The first of her dreams realised.

It was a day of mists and she walked by the lake in the college grounds, alone with her happy thoughts. He caught up with her, walked quietly beside her, merely catching her arm in his, respecting her day-dreaming.

It was then that the words were said: "I have patiently waited for this moment, Miss Ruth Owen – I have something I *must* say to you . . ."

That same night, full of anguish, Ruth had taken flight, her very first moonlight flit though there were many to follow – back to Brynbach, given a lift by a kindly carrier who knew her elder brother Ivor – back home to sob her heart out in Rachel Hughes's arms. "How *could* he?" wept her sister, hugging her so tight.

Three years passed and there was no time for day-dreaming. Ruth Owen was found a job in the canal office: quite the business lady she was with her hair piled high and her sober clothes. Rachel and Davey said they were proud of her, making a success of her life despite the bitter disappointment she had suffered.

There was Meg growing up now, almost fourteen, still resentful of her mother's fondness for her younger sister which made for awkwardness between the two of them and

3

quarrels over lack of privacy in their shared bedroom – "*Why did you have to come home like that?*" Meg raged once.

But there was also little Alun, born after Ruth's return, the surprise baby who brought such joy to them all.

"I'll *never* be happy sitting behind a desk, but *he* makes it bearable . . ." Ruth thought. She loved to let her hair down at the end of a tiring day, to whoop about the meadow at the back with the little boy on her back, to smother him in kisses when they tumbled, as they inevitably did, even though Rachel told her gently that she was spoiling him. Meg resented *that* closeness too. "*I* have to wash up the dishes while you're playing with Alun, Ruth," she said, lips compressed, eyes flashing.

Later, when things went wrong, she would wonder how she could have run away from her family, after all they had done for her to ease the shock and despair after Drago. Yet leave them she did, very early one morning; knowing how hurt Rachel would be, she couldn't even bring herself to write a note.

She had fled in her naïvety to London, trusting in that well-thumbed introductory card concealed in her purse, which had been presented to her by a musical impresario after that never-to-be-forgotten triumph at the college concert.

Amazingly, her hopes and faith in strangers were rewarded. Within a year she was enjoying modest acclaim on the concert circuit. Then she met the man she would eventually marry, Bayly Barley.

He was a handsome man with an imposing tall figure, a fine head of iron grey hair, waving at the back over his collar. As her career was beginning to take off, his was fading. He was quite a few years her senior. He had been married to Anne, who died following childbirth; he had a young daughter, Daisy, who lived with her maternal grandmother, who blamed him for the loss of her only daughter, and whom, it seemed, he never saw.

She had so quickly fallen in love with him, despite his initial lack of interest in her. There was a distant look, from the very first she was aware of it, in those narrowed, light-blue eyes.

She had tried so hard but she could never become remotely close to him, was unable to understand why he behaved as he did. Of course she was aware that Anne, tall and beautiful, had been the great passion of his life so she supposed that her loss had triggered Bay's instability, his excessive drinking. He was not cut out for responsibilities but she loved him nevertheless even though *this* love too had feet of clay.

She was destined when she cast her lot in with his to be classed as a third-rate performer. When at last she married Bay, her agent cut their ties. It was all downhill from then.

Would he have married her if she had not become pregnant with their daughter, Clemmie? Ruth doubted it. Soon after Clemmie's birth she had taken on Daisy when her grandmother died. "Of course she must come to us!" she cried to Bay, silencing his doubts.

In that gloomy house with dust sheets already covering the furniture Ruth Owen met Daisy for the first time. There were debts to be met from the sale of the property – Daisy's grandmother had lived beyond her means. Daisy had been bequeathed merely a few of her late mother's childhood possessions. Ruth learned that she and Anne had had something in common beside their love for a feckless man. Anne, also, had left home without a word, or a forwarding address. The first her unfortunate mother knew of Daisy's existence was when Bay brought the baby to this house.

Ruth Owen held out her arms impulsively to the bright-haired silent child, offering love and comfort to one who had grown up so far lacking both.

Over the years since, Ruth had discovered how very different Daisy was to her own Clemmie, who was the lively young Ruth Owen all over again, yet to her they were equally her daughters. She protected Daisy fiercely from the unkind indifference of her father. She had not bargained for the fact, she often thought ruefully, that Bay would become like a tiresome third child.

Those dreams, the ones which Drago had so cruelly shattered, they were long past. Yet often at night she would dream of Brynbach. Would she ever go back?

5

One

1897

There really was no need for The Singing Barleys to wait
for the moon to rise, for the gas lamps already flared
when they left the music hall after their disastrous evening
performance. The yellow light cast upon the uneven flagstones
seemed to dance round their hurrying feet.

This would be their last engagement at The Hippodrome,
Ruth Owen thought wryly, probably their last booking at any
provincial music hall anywhere: the reputation of The Singing
Barleys was well and truly tarnished. The moonlight flit from
the dingy boarding house in the back street of shabby houses,
as down at heel as the Barleys themselves, from the wrath of
their landlady was imperative.

Bay, with his unpredictable behaviour, his drunkenness, his
insufferable conceit, was certainly responsible for their present
plight. Even before their first appearance at this place he had
already quarrelled with the management regarding their billing.
He said imperiously that with his first wife he had enjoyed near
top of the bill status; now their name was in such small print it
was an insult.

"With your reputation," came the uncompromising reply,
"you may take it or leave it. Now, if Ruth Owen was to take us
up on our offer of a solo engagement . . ." Bay had stormed out
and as usual got raging drunk. Only Ruth's determination, her
persuasive powers, the attraction of her voice, had seen them
through that and subsequent performances.

Tonight Bay had done the unforgiveable. He had cursed the
ribald gallery when they cat-called at his slurred singing and

his stumbling on stage; such was his rhetoric the curtains had been swiftly lowered and The Singing Barleys were hustled into the wings and ordered to depart. Immediately.

Ruth, anticipating what was to come, had at last written home. She had addressed the letter to her brother Ivor, for surely he would act as go-between between herself and her family at the lock cottage?

The mention of this brother surprised the others. Ruth, so open and straightforward as a rule, was reticent regarding her past. At last, it seemed to Daisy and Clemmie, Ruth was willing to talk about the Owens who had been involved with the canal for generations.

"Ivor did well for himself, you know. Fancy! A wharfinger before I even left Wales – much older than me, you see . . . I have asked if we may use the old narrowboat, *Pili Pala* – that's Welsh, for butterfly – for a summer season. Oh, we'll travel along, we Singing Barleys, stop off here and there, put on a show, booked or impromptu, for don't my countryfolk appreciate good singing when they hear it? And," she concluded excitedly, "it will be *so* good to see my family again . . ."

Even Bay appeared amenable to this wonderful plan. The girls, Ruth knew, had been dreaming and hoping ever since. In this afternoon's post she had received a warm letter from her brother saying, 'Come of course! We'll make *Pili Pala* ready for you here.' It was fortuitous that Ivor had replied so promptly, Ruth thought, for naturally, yet again, they would be leaving no forwarding address.

In the darkened room, for they had doused the lamps to lull suspicion, Bay sat in the only chair, brooding. The shock had certainly sobered him up.

Daisy lay on the bed with her arms protectively around Clemmie, already dozing. She was only seven after all.

Ruth stood by the window, clasping Daisy's little, grey, hairy dog, peering at the road outside through a chink in the curtains. She would soon give the signal for them to make their move. Pompom's fur tickled under her chin; Ruth felt the dog shiver. Pompom sensed danger, excitement. Bay grumbled that the dog was a nuisance but Ruth realised how much the small stray meant to Daisy.

"Ready?" Ruth whispered at last. Daisy, well drilled, gathered up her sleepy sister. Ruth handed her the treasured guitar which had belonged to Anne. "Can you manage?" she asked softly. She sensed Daisy's nod.

Pompom whined. "Shush!" Ruth cautioned. It had been quite a feat she thought to smuggle the dog in and out of the boarding house each time they left for or returned from their engagements. Pompom must follow her mistress and not get under their feet.

She touched Bay's arm. "It's time," she advised.

Thankfully, the wide stairs were carpeted, muffling their furtive descent. The familiar smell of over-boiled cabbage and bacon fat cooked in the one pot assailed their nostrils, mingling with the musty odours of the shabby garments crowding the hallstand, for there were other, more respectable, lodgers: pale, listless clerks with shadowed, strained eyes who retired early to bed, eschewing the comfortless sitting room. There was no escape for *them*.

The street lamp immediately beyond the front garden diffused an eerie green light through the cracked, dusty glass panels in the door. The solemn faces of the Barleys, as they glanced at each other whilst Bay eased back the bolts, took on a sickly hue. Clemmie unexpectedly expelled a sighing yawn.

In return, from behind the closed door of their landlady's room, which was immediately off the hall, came a raucous snore followed by a grunting, then clearing of the throat. Stout Miss Prince heaved herself over with much creaking of her bed.

"I'm sorry," Ruth Owen mouthed silently in her direction, "you'll have the rent later, that's a promise!" Their landlady was most likely as impecunious as themselves.

They filed swiftly through the opened door which Bay closed carefully behind them.

On moonlight flits he invariably strode, unencumbered, ahead, intent on hailing a passing cab which would, of course, drastically drain any remaining resources.

"Please don't let him be in luck . . ." Ruth muttered to Daisy. She was acutely aware that they had just about enough to pay for the journey ahead. She would have to resort to the emergency reserve, that clever little pouch which Daisy, because her stepmother was a hopeless needlewoman, had sewn to her inner waistband. There would have been more if only they had lasted out until the end of the week.

Ruth struggled bravely with the hand luggage while Daisy sagged under her own burden. They blessed the left-luggage office at the station where they had left their larger pieces and where they were now headed. At this unearthly hour even the street cleaners had gone wearily home and the occasional lady of the night who sometimes greeted them on the corner had obviously given up too.

They huddled in the waiting room until dawn. Ruth remained sleepless, on her guard. She felt both sad and relieved that this part of her life was drawing to a close. Then she smiled as she recalled The Singing Barleys in happier times. She pictured Clemmie as a toddler dropping off to sleep in a rush props basket, covered over with one of her exotic shawls, clutching a feather in her fist, pulled from Ruth's ostrich-feather fan. In those early days Daisy, before the girls joined their parents on stage, minded the baby and carried on with her schoolwork in the overcrowded dressing room. Later, studious Daisy, now seventeen, had become her sister's tutor. Ruth had been wont to whirl in, gorgeous in bright silks, holding out to her girls hot pies in grease-spotted paper which she had hastily purchased in the interval. "Here you are, darlings – sustenance!" came the cry.

Once she had found Daisy obligingly struggling with the hooks and eyes which perilously fastened the satin frock of a plump artiste.

"Such *lovely* girls, Ruth Owen!" the lady said, bestowing carmine kisses. Ruth Owen glowed even more.

She felt her eyes closing despite her intention to keep alert. A great deal of water had flowed under the bridge since she abandoned her birthplace so precipitately, she thought drowsily. Metaphorically, maybe, regarding her life since, but literally under the bridges of the canal. Could her family really forgive her for that she wondered?

The bent old porter looked in on them. "The train will be here in five minutes," he told them. His rheumy eyes looked into Ruth Owen's. He knew. He had, of course, seen it all before.

Two

They did not stop off long at Ivor and Annie's house despite the warm welcome, but they were generously provided with a good meal there, their first in two days of travelling.

When Annie darted after them with a loaf and a pitcher of milk as they boarded *Pili Pala*, asking if they required any other provisions, Ruth airily replied that they would buy along the way. If Ruth Owen had a fault it was that she was not in the least domesticated; maternal, yes, but her family could not recall a single cooked meal served up by her. Bay had, surprisingly, made nothing of this for this culinary lack was the one thing in his eyes that Ruth had in common with Anne. He certainly did not realise that Ruth's singing was superior to that of the first Mrs Barley.

Ruth hugged her sister-in-law. "Dear Annie, we will see you again soon – I promise! But I *do* want to get on to Rachel's . . ."

"We understand," Annie whispered back.

Pili Pala had been lovingly kept in good order and Ruth Owen noted that the legend was newly gilded. The long boat was traditionally decorated with birds and cabbage roses and yes, there was its namesake, painted larger than life with delicate wings spread wide and clinging to a full-blown scarlet bloom.

She turned impulsively to her brother. Ivor was stockily built with a kind, plain face, more weathered than she recalled, embellished by a large walrus moustache. Here again were the striking, dark Owen eyes. "I do not deserve all this, Ivor," she exclaimed, "after the way I left!"

11

He patted her arm awkwardly. "We did not blame *you* Ruth Owen, never that."

"Who painted the name – freshened up the roses and the butterfly?" she asked touching them.

"Alun. He is quite the artist, Ruth, that won't surprise you, eh?" Ivor asked. "Well, if you wish to pass through the tunnel before dark . . ."

The girls were already wriggling on to the bench seat behind the table, next to the stove.

Ruth looked with delight at the dresser with its painted knobs, at the odds and ends of china Annie had thoughtfully provided: blue and white willow ware, made in Birmingham not China, from the local market, cheap and cheerful, some chipped, just as she remembered from the days she had travelled the canal in this very boat as a child. She pulled open the drawers. Worn silver cutlery from Annie's own kitchen table drawer, polished up brightly, with bone handles yellowed where knives had slipped into scalding washing up water. Saucepans were stacked one within the other, lids hung alongside pictures on the walls – faded old favourites, and one or two new. She wondered if Alun had painted these too. Cups dangled from hooks along the dresser shelves; there was a great, sooty kettle and a tall jar of rock salt. A lucky horseshoe was fixed above the windows, along with old brass ornaments. Storage space would be revealed presently inside the seats which, with the table, would double up at nights as the marital bed.

Seeing her husband's gloomy expression Ruth told them cheerfully, "See, although space is so confined we are just as well equipped here as in any of our rented rooms, and a good deal cleaner thanks to Annie! We won't need to have a bug hunt before we lay our heads down tonight!"

"Where are *we* to sleep?" Daisy asked tentatively.

Ruth at once put her mind to rest, she knew how much Daisy would dislike a communal bedroom. "On those bunks at the front – above the hold. They are very narrow, I'm afraid, but at least you'll have a little privacy until we are all out and about in the morning."

12

There had been several other boats tied up at the wharf when they arrived but now, it seemed, they were the only boat waiting to cast off. Old William, the horse, was submitting patiently to the harnessing by Ivor.

"Daisy and Bay will have to take it in turns to walk with the horse for I must manage the steering until they have learned the knack – I hope I have not forgotten how, Ivor," she said to her brother.

"It will soon come back to you," he stated. "No locks of course until you reach Rachel's cottage. There will be leggers lurking no doubt when you come to the tunnel, for I sent word that you were coming by the first boat to leave after the loading. Call your man up here, eh, I will give a little advice and then I will loose the rope. Good luck, little Ruth Owen!"

"Oh, I am so happy to be travelling the waterways once more – we had three boats, you know, when trade was still brisk, but I'm so glad Ivor hung on to dear *Pili Pala*."

"So are we!" Clemmie agreed cheerfully. She was petite like her mother, with sleek, dark hair drawn back into a single tight pigtail and again, those lustrous eyes. Perhaps it was a little unfortunate, Ruth thought, smiling back at her daughter, that Clemmie had inherited Bay's long, supercilious nose.

Daisy bent to stroke her dog, her reddish-blond hair, a lion's mane in which she had snapped many a cheap comb, dipping round her face. She pushed it back with one hand even as she parted Pompom's soft fringe with the other, revealing the dog's bright, knowing eyes. "Thank you for bringing us here, Ruth Owen," she said softly. "I feel as if we are about to make a voyage of discovery—" She broke off, embarrassed. Fortunately, her father was out of earshot, already walking the horse along the towpath.

Ruth understood. "We are, Daisy, I'm sure of that . . ."

They legged their way through the echoing, slippery-walled tunnel just before evening drew in, with the help of two obliging old hands and a lanky lad. Ruth steered steady and true while her voice soared in a fondly recalled boating song.

13

Daisy, on deck, hung grimly on to young Clemmie who, being a strong-minded child, had flatly refused to go below. The two of them were fascinated by the sinewy sidestepping as the leggers lay flat on their backs on the protruding boards, their stout hob-nailed boots pushing the boat onward in easy rhythm.

Ruth Owen, taking breath, was aware of the muffled tread of the horse's hooves as Bay reluctantly led this essential member of their team over the top to meet *Pili Pala* as she emerged from the tunnel.

The lamp hanging from the prow spilled patches of liquid light on the dark water below. In the cabin Pompom whined reproachfully, her paws scrabbling furiously at the firmly closed door.

Not far past the tunnel they moored up. "Isolated spot, I know," Ruth said, "but we are not permitted to travel the canal after dark."

Then the leggers took Bay half a mile along the towpath to The Navigator, with its tall, heavy wooden settles, roughly hewn, and unscrubbed tables reeking of spilled ale and sweating bodies. There was singing here too and when he was well oiled Bay's voice rose above the others. The company gradually fell silent, respecting the rich baritone of the trained singer. Then came spontaneous applause from Bay's companions. Later, his new friends brought him stumbling back to *Pili Pala* for Ruth to resignedly put to bed. She would have to reluctantly part with most of the remaining precious silver coins from the pouch.

She watched through the window until she saw the lantern swaying precariously along the darkness of the towpath; then she tiptoed past the sleeping girls and went as quietly as she could up the steps to the deck.

Bay almost missed his footing but Ruth Owen clung tight to his arm; his tipsy companions pushed, she pulled and he lurched aboard. "Goodnight and thank you," she told them firmly. She retrieved her own lantern from its hook and assisted him into their cabin, closing the door behind them.

She had made the bed ready. She would not attempt to

14

undress him. She merely pulled the blankets over him, leaving his feet protruding. He was soon snoring fitfully. She slipped off her own clothes, doused the light and lay beside him.

When at last she drifted into sleep, soothed by the gently swaying boat, she dreamed of the young Ruth Owen scrambling after Alun as he rolled deliberately down the steep slope of the meadow. She caught him, smothering him in kisses. "Are you all right cariad?" she cried.

"Of course!" and he pushed her away and rolled exuberantly the rest of the way.

"Wait!" she shouted in hot pursuit.

Rachel Hughes was waiting by the gate. As Ruth snatched Alun up she scolded as Mams always do. "Put him down, Ruth. He'll ruin your good clothes with his muddy boots." Such a boy he was!

She woke abruptly. The bunk was very hard and unyielding. She supposed rightly that the drink Bay had consumed last evening had rendered him oblivious to the discomfort of the sleeping arrangements.

In a few hours she would come face to face with Rachel again.

Three

D aisy could hear Ruth stirring so she tapped gently on the dividing door to let her stepmother know that she too was up and about.

A tousled dark head appeared round the door. Ruth Owen looked so tired – was it any wonder? Daisy thought, but, as always, Ruth was quick to smile. 'Ruth Owen' – everyone called her that even though she was Mrs Barley.

"I'm just going to sample the morning." Daisy kept her voice very low. "I thought I might freshen up in the river, the canal water looks so dirty. Do the boat people throw *all* their rubbish overboard? I feel so grimy after those hours on the trains. I shouldn't think there would be anyone about – would you? I'll say 'hallo' to the horse and I'll take Pom with me or she'll make a fuss and wake Clem up . . ."

Having nodded several times during what was quite a speech for Daisy, Ruth advised softly, "Don't go too far. Bay is bound to have a thick head this morning but we must make an early start. We ought to be at my sister's for breakfast; Ivor says she is expecting us by then. Anyway, I forgot to light the stove last night. Of course your father should have seen to it, but he wasn't capable, you know?"

"I know," Daisy said.

"She's a good cook, my sister." Ruth's thick-lashed eyes were misty with the remembering. "Fresh eggs it will be and her home-cured bacon cut thick and sizzling in the same old bent pan our grandmother used and yellow butter on her bread—"

"Stop!" Daisy pleaded, anticipating it all. "That bread-and-pullit seems a long time ago, Ruth . . ." A hunk of bread and a

16

glass of milk, courtesy of Annie, had been their scratch supper last night.

Clemmie still slumbered on the far side of the bunk they had eventually shared. Pompom wriggled out from the dark space below where she had been curled up on a thick coil of rope.

In the clear early light of that June morning damsel flies, tiny, translucent, bluey-green, flickered along the lush reeds below the towpath. Fish moved mysteriously, occasionally rippling the clouded waters of the canal. A cluster of ducklings, anxiously tailing duck and drake, sailed close to the narrowboat.

On the bank wild flowers grew in sweet profusion: poppies, forget-me-nots, tall, swaying yellow flags. Below the tangled brambles the meadow gently sloped away to the river. Like a painted backcloth, reminiscent of the ones before which the Barleys had so often sung, was the great mountain, brooding over all.

To Daisy, delighting in it all, it seemed as if at last The Singing Barleys possessed a home of their own even if, as now, she rocked the boat as she leapt from deck to dry land.

She ran bare-footed through the long, dew-drenched grass, Pompom alternately bounding ahead with her tail waving like a plumy flag, then rushing back to circle her mistress, barking her delight at being on firm ground again.

The old horse had not bothered to pull the slack of his tethering rope. He blew through his nostrils in a welcoming snort as Daisy, who adored all animals, finding them easier than people, slung her arm round his neck and gave him a pat. Animals did not reproach you for not living up to expectations, she thought, not for the first time, they accepted you for what you were.

Only Ruth's patient coaching had made something of Daisy's soft singing voice. She had fared better with the guitar for which she had a natural aptitude. She was well aware that Bay considered her an encumbrance and that, if he had his way, she would be shunted off to become a governess. It was Ruth Owen who pleaded for her to stay, boosting her very minor role with the act.

Pompom kept her distance from the horse, respecting those shaggy hooves. "Have a nice rest, old boy," Daisy said to her new friend, "for I believe Ruth plans a long haul ahead."

Cows were drinking at the rim of the river where it was shallow. There were flinty stepping stones, local rock tinted pink, stretching across to the far side. In the distance was the towering bridge.

Daisy shed her shawl, which she had knotted round her shoulders to preserve her modesty. She had rinsed her blouse, being fastidious, for their main luggage had not yet caught up with them. Ivor had promised to enquire daily at the station and to forward it to them by a following boat. Daisy had spread this garment to dry on the flat top of *Pili Pala*. She stood there by the river wearing a darned short chemise, her fair skin already flushed and freckled by a day spent in the open air, her hazel eyes gleaming at the lovely countryside all around. She could just make out, if she shaded her eyes, a twisting scar up the mountain where Ruth Owen said the tramroads ran. She imagined the workers toiling at this very moment in the limestone quarries. This industry was in decline, Ruth sighed, but despite the disasters and punishing working conditions this was a sadness to the local people for it was their way of life. "On the canals it was hard too you know," Ruth added quietly, "but not like *that* . . ."

Daisy walked some way across the stones then she stepped down into the sparkling, clear flowing water until she was almost waist deep. She flung her arms wide, gasping at the sheer coldness of the river, then she resolutely ducked down until her whole body was immersed. Here in Wales, she thought, among Ruth's rediscovered family, she was sure she would be happy. Her bright hair floated out around her like red weed.

Pompom swam energetically round and round, little grey head bobbing, paws paddling furiously. "Oh, *oh*!" Daisy cried out involuntarily at the cruel pleasure of her bathing.

Ruth Owen and Clemmie made do with a wooden bucket of water on deck.

"There, you'll do," Ruth said, releasing her daughter, who thought washing was a waste of time.

"May I go for a walk, pick some flowers?" Clemmie asked. All her short life had been spent in travelling from town to town. Flowers were bought, when Ruth was feeling rash, from flower girls with great baskets, not as here, free for the picking. Clemmie was on the towpath before Ruth had dried her face. These wild blooms smelled, oh, so heady, as Clemmie breathed in their fragrance.

"Not too far – and keep well away from the edge!" Ruth called anxiously to her daughter's departing back.

Here came Bay, distracting her attention, rumpling his hair. "What time is it Ruth? Not yet *seven*?" He looked at his wife with horror. "Just where am *I* supposed to wash and shave?" He glanced down now at himself with distaste. "Shame on you, Ruth Owen, to let me go to bed in my clothes!"

"Oh, *do* be quiet, Bay!" she sauced him. She could live with the fact that he did not love her enough because she knew he would be helpless without her. "It's not the first time, is it? You must soak your thick head in the bucket as Clemmie and I did; if you really must scrape your whiskers, you can do that at Rachel Hughes's."

"Good morning – Ruth Owen, is it?"

Startled, Ruth turned to see a young man standing by the mooring. She knew him instantly despite the fact that it had been fourteen years since she saw him and then he was only three years old. "Alun!"

He came aboard, smiling. "There's worried we were when you did not come last night, although Ivor did warn us it would most likely be today . . . So Mother sent me out to see if there is trouble like with *Pili Pala*."

"No trouble," Ruth said, embracing him impulsively. "Oh dear, Alun, how you have grown!"

"I imagine I have!" He hugged her back. "But you, Ruth Owen, are just as I remembered you . . ."

Belatedly, Ruth introduced the two men. "This is Alun, Bay, my sister's youngest – Alun, this is my husband, for my sins, Bayly Barley, who founded The Singing Barleys many moons ago: call him Bay, why don't you, for there's not much avuncular about *him*!"

Bay was forced to switch on his considerable charm. "So, you are the young artist who did such a splendid job on this old tub, eh?"

"I am glad you think so," Alun replied.

"Bay," she reminded him, "get washed now! Oh, I must run and fetch that naughty Clemmie back before she manages to lose herself – Alun, would you go down to the river for me? You'll find our elder daughter, Daisy, there: tell her to hurry back to the boat for we must cast off as soon as we can. Perhaps you could bring the horse back at the same time?"

Alun nodded. "I hope she is not as wilful a child as I was," he reminded her. "I never did a thing you told me to!"

Ruth's eyes twinkled. "Daisy is very obedient – she'll come if you say I sent you!" she said demurely. It was high time, she thought gleefully, for Daisy to meet a young man of just her own age . . .

Daisy splashed her face with water then clambered dripping back on to a large flat stone. Fool! she chided herself, you forgot to bring a towel! Her soaked petticoat clung to her body and she began to shiver uncontrollably; her arms and legs became all goosepimpled. She wrung her hair out as best she could, then made her way towards the bank, whistling Pompom to follow. The dog's method of drying herself was simple: she shook herself all over Daisy then wagged her tail disarmingly.

"Pompom!" Daisy shrieked.

"Did you fall in the water?" came a concerned voice, unexpectedly close by. "You were lucky not to have gone in further along, where it is treacherous and deep."

In a fluster, Daisy snatched up her shawl from the grass and hugged it round her shaking shoulders. Then she faced the stranger. "No, I did not fall in. Please will you go away?"

20

He had already tactfully averted his gaze from her, bending to caress the dog.

"I am so sorry to have startled you," he apologised. "I think you must be Daisy, although I thought you were younger, I really don't know why . . . You see, your mother is my aunt, I am Rachel's son, Alun. Ruth lived with us for a time when I was a small boy. I never forgot her. Great news it was to us when Ivor said he had heard from her again at last. I saw Ruth just now and she said you were down here by the river and would I fetch you. Shall I lead the horse for you? I brought his pail and his food, in case Ivor forgot like, for he is not much one with the horses." He turned away sensing that she was stricken with shyness now. "Don't worry, I will walk ahead. I will just say that I am quite used to young women in our house – well, with our Meg anyway. I have learned it is best to look upwards and whistle or to bury my face in a book, you see, at certain times." He added disarmingly, "It is a *little* house we have . . ."

'He's smiling!' Daisy realised, her alarm and annoyance evaporating immediately. She was so much more used to the company of women after all. First her grandmother, then her governess, followed by Ruth and the theatrical ladies. The only man she had real contact with, if you could call it that, was her father.

As she followed behind him she realised the resemblance to Ruth Owen: that same Celtic look, glimpsed briefly before he turned on his heel, those extravagant eyelashes, the high cheekbones. He was taller than his diminutive aunt, naturally, yet probably little more than her own height of five feet and seven inches. They must be of an age, she thought.

The Welsh voices fascinated her. Ruth Owen had never lost her lilt. Alun's accent was much stronger though. She fancied there was music in his speech.

They reached the horse and Alun loosened him, allowing Daisy to swiftly go past through the gap in the prickly hedge to the boat. Pompom, like a drowned rat, jumped nimbly aboard. Ruth Owen scolded and exclaimed a bit when she saw Daisy. "Oh, you are soaked!" She gave her a helping hand up on deck. "I thought you would just wash your face and hands, swish your feet in the river. You are a silly girl, you know, for it must have been *so* cold. June or not, this is the first real sun we have had. I shall call your father out, for the wretch is grumbling there is no room to swing a cat below, then you can go in the cabin to dry and dress . . . Daisy, did you see young Clemmie?" she added anxiously. She had caught sight of her but the girl had given her the slip.

Even as Daisy shook her head she spotted Clemmie way up the towpath but heading in their direction. "Oh, she's coming back Ruth – Pompom, fetch Clemmie!" she commanded. The dog bounded off.

Daisy retrieved her blouse. It was still damp but it would have to do. She dried herself as best she could on the towel already used by the rest of the family. Peering through the cabin window on the near side she observed Alun harnessing the horse. Then Clemmie sauntered up.

"You must be Clemmie," she heard him say. "I am Alun, your cousin."

"'Lo Alun," Clemmie replied pertly, "do take a bit of notice of Pom or she'll fall backwards in the water."

Alun obligingly bent towards Pompom who promptly leapt up into his arms and gave his face an enthusiastic washing. Laughing, he put her down.

"She was a waif and stray, you know," Clemmie informed him. "She must really like *you* 'cause she only licks people when she trusts them, Daisy says. We found her in Bradford. She was all ribs, you know, and ever so hungry. Just like *I* am right now! Anyway, Daisy saved her from a horrid man who was kicking her, she picked her up and took her away. That was two years ago and we've had her ever since."

Alun, smiling, called out to Ruth at the tiller. "Ready? May Clemmie ride the horse?"

Daisy, straining her ears, did not catch Ruth Owen's reply, but it was obviously 'yes' for Clemmie was hoisted on to Old William's broad, dusty back. Then Alun went to slip the mooring. Daisy had to smile at Clemmie's bemused expression as she turned her face in her direction. "Look, Bay, look at *me!*" she called to her father.

At least these two Singing Barleys were compatible, Daisy mused wryly. Bay indulged his younger daughter and she adored him.

Four

They glided smoothly along through tranquil light and shade, marvelling at the amazing reflections of the great trees in the water. Ruth still steered while Bay sat alongside, ostensibly to learn so that he might take his turn. He was silent, she thought, pale at the gills, not surprising after last night's excesses.

She glanced upwards, for Daisy sat up top allowing the sun and breeze to ruffle her hair into a tangle of curls. Ruth noted that her hands were linked round her drawn-up knees, her skirt demurely arranged to conceal her long pale limbs. Then she saw Alun, who was measuring his pace to the horse, look fleetingly up at Daisy too.

To Ruth it seemed as if the frantic pace of their life was completely slowed. She saw the wild things moving unconcernedly about their business: rabbits feasting in the fields, squirrels flashing up the oak trees, birds coasting over the water, a heron rising triumphantly with a silvery fish wriggling in its beak. Ahead of *Pili Pala* was a majestic flotilla of swans perfectly mirrored in the canal. It was all just as she remembered it, what she had regretted leaving all these years.

A lone donkey brayed as they passed, a skinny, ribby animal with buckled hooves and tail swishing endlessly against the flies. Old William's ears pricked up but he plodded obediently on. Pompom, running behind, gave a defiant bark then scurried to catch Alun up. "Strange how she has taken to Alun like that," she said to Bay. "I do hope Daisy doesn't feel deserted."

They passed a boathouse that almost appeared to be floating on the surface of the water but there was only a cottage or two, remote up the fields, until they came upon a large white house with rolling, smooth turf down to the water's edge and steep stone steps up to the entrance flanked by mossy, submissively crouching statues.

Ruth stiffened. "Ty-Gyda-Cerded," she said aloud.

"What was that?" Bay queried, startled.

"The house with all the steps," she interpreted briefly.

As they meandered past, the upstairs windows were flung up one by one, the drawn curtains billowing out in the breeze. Ruth thought bitterly that the grand lady of the house would be reclining still on a soft feather bed, yawning in her silken nightwear, receiving graciously the wicker tray set out with the requisites for morning tea. Which reminded her that she was very thirsty. "I'm parched, Bay. We really must get the stove functioning today so that we can at least boil water for tea – you might have thought of others before you drained the milk! We need to cook for ourselves too. Daisy has kindly offered to try her hand – we can't afford to eat at the pubs along the way . . ." It was imperative also to keep Bay away from the temptations of these, she resolved privately.

In the field they passed next at their dreamy pace she was pleased to see the long-tailed black sheep, then, leaning over the gate, watching them glide by, she saw a man with a beard just as black and woolly, his gold-rimmed spectacles glinting in the sun. He had not possessed the beard that last time she saw him. She hoped fervently that Bay could not hear her heart thumping. She did not expect to be so shocked.

"That chap doesn't look like a shepherd," Bay observed. "More like a foreigner in that light suit and panama hat."

The stranger raised this in greeting to *Pili Pala*.

Alun called out cheerfully, "Good morning, Mr Drago!"

She was distracted, for the next thing she knew was that the boat was jarring against the towpath and they were obviously stuck in the reeds. She felt foolish and, surprisingly for her, furious.

Alun steadied the horse and brought him to a halt. "All right, Ruth? Need any help?"

"No need to worry, Alun," she returned, but in some

agitation. "I can manage with the pole. His Lordship can take the tiller!" She called to Daisy, "Stay where you are, but hold on tight."

The man watched all this with unconcealed amusement. He did not move to offer his help and Ruth totally ignored his presence.

A few vigorous shoves with the pole and they broke free, were able to continue on their journey. The man was the first soul they had encountered since they set off that morning and there was not yet another boat in sight.

A three-legged dog, not at all concerned by his lack, defended the next bridge explosively. Pompom, tail between legs, leapt aboard as Bay, scraping the sides of the boat, steered them bumpily through. Then he relinquished the task in a huff to his wife who remarked on his lack of expertise. He caught the dog by her scruff and passed her up to Daisy. "Keep her out of trouble, will you?" he requested coldly. Pompom hid her head in Daisy's skirts, whining.

They had travelled barely two miles from their overnight mooring when the lock keeper's cottage came into view.

Alun advised that they tie the boat up at a safe distance from the lock so as not to hinder other users. "There will be a great deal of traffic during the morning," he said, as he hammered home the mooring pin. "It saves water when two or three follow on."

"What do the boats carry nowadays?" Ruth asked curiously. Even in her youth trade had been decreasing steadily, the railways being preferred, especially for the carriage of coal and limestone because of their speedy service and carrying capacity.

"Market goods mainly: sacks of grain, potatoes, swedes; the boatmen are willing to carry whatever the traders along the canal ask for, anything to make up a full load." Alun turned to Clemmie, still astride the horse. "Stay well away from the lock, Clemmie," he cautioned, "for it is awful deep. Didn't my own father almost drown in it once when he lost his footing?" It was important to teach the child proper respect for the canal and its dangers.

"Come and meet your Auntie Rachel, darling!" Ruth cried, lifting her daughter down. Holding her hand tightly she hurried along the path toward the cottage, calling back to Bay and Daisy to follow. "Do hurry you two! Can't you smell the cooking from here?"

Father and daughter walked together but there was the usual distance, coolness between them. Ruth vowed to herself that she would do something about that, Daisy deserved better. She caught the drift of their stilted conversation.

"Isn't it time you put your hair up, Daisy?" he asked, as if he couldn't address her without censure.

Ruth was startled and pleased when Daisy responded, "No, Bay! If I had my way I would shear my hair short – it's far too curly, thanks to *you*! – but Ruth Owen tells me I'll regret it if I do."

The cottage was indeed small as Alun said, two-up, two-down. Ruth exclaimed over the familiar, old-fashioned flowers crowding the tiny patch of front garden. In the rented field behind the house, which Alun kept now like his father before him, were a few sheep, a house cow, a growing pig in a pen for next winter's bacon and some scratching hens, who, no doubt, still laid in secret places, Ruth thought, and had to be cajoled into their coop at dusk. A piece was dug over for vegetables, and there were already beans twining high up their sticks – "Look, Clem, just like Jack and the Beanstalk, eh?" The scarlet blooms promised a rich harvest to come. It seemed to her that she had returned at last to Paradise, except why had she had to catch sight of Drago so soon?

Alun, having released the horse to the grass, caught them up at the front door, which stood hospitably wide. Before he could put a restraining hand on Ruth Owen's shoulder, she stepped straight into the living room.

There on a couch by the window lay the frail figure of Rachel Hughes. For a moment Ruth could not move, staring in disbelief. Then she was kneeling by her sister, arms clutching her convulsively, crying in great gulping gasps, "Oh Rachel, my dear – why wasn't I told?"

27

Five

The tinny clock ticked busily on the mantlepiece over the inglenook with its gleaming black stove. The kettle hissed and spluttered on the hob. Meg, obviously upset at Ruth Owen's reaction, forked bacon from the tilted frying pan on to the warming plates.

Alun touched Daisy's bare arm gently: she had rolled her damp sleeves above the elbow. She turned uncertainly. "Mam told Ivor, Annie, told me, not to say anything to Ruth . . ." he murmured, his breath lightly fanning her cheek.

Clemmie moved swiftly, suddenly to her father's side. Bay cleared his throat loudly. Pompom, ears twitching, sank back on her haunches on the step.

Still Ruth Owen sobbed. Then Rachel pushed her gently from her. Despite the age gap of sixteen years and the marks of suffering on Rachel's thin face there was a great resemblance between the two women. It was that Owen look of course. The silent Meg possessed this aura too. Ruth had not looked at Meg; it was as if she and Rachel were alone in the room together, unaware of any audience.

"No more crying, Ruth Owen." Rachel's voice was unexpectedly brisk and strong. "That's all been done with, long ago. There's no cure for the Infantile Paralysis, you see – you learn to live with what you have left when the disease has died down. And me – well past an infant when it caught me, eh? Thank goodness my dear Davey never lived to see me so afflicted. Meg and Alun fuss over me, so you see I'm quite happy with my lot . . ." She smiled at the solemn group by the door. "Now sit you down, all of you, at my table and loosen your belts for Meggie's really gone to town, the dear girl, over

28

your breakfast. However, she must hurry you along or she'll be late for her work. We'll get properly acquainted when you've eaten, eh?"

While she spoke Meg turned slabs of bread in the sizzling fat which made them all realise just how hungry they were.

Ruth Owen wiped her tears away on Bay's silently proffered handkerchief, stuffed it untidily back into his breast pocket, pulled out chairs and put her family into their places. This was her home. She wanted them so much to approve of it; she needed them to take to her relations, especially Clemmie, her own flesh and blood. She also needed understanding and acceptance for herself.

"Bay, you sit between Clemmie and me – Daisy will you sit here next to Alun? Watch out, for Pom's sneaking under the table . . . I warn you, my darling Rachel Hughes," Ruth cried, smiling now through her sadness at the unexpected, "that when we've eaten the talking will start and it may go on for *ever!*" Yet she could not look straight at her sister again, not now.

It was the best breakfast they had enjoyed in years for not only was there the crispy bacon and the fat bread, but soft-boiled eggs to dip deep into, and dark brown tea, well sugared, to wash it all down.

They were just wiping their plates clean with new bread, which Meg had baked earlier as Rachel told them proudly, when Alun saw through the open door that three narrowboats and a coal barge were lining up to pass through the lock. "You must excuse me – work to do." He pushed back his chair. "Why don't you come and help with the gates, Bay? The sooner you learn how to operate the lock paddles the better, I think. It is a man's work," he added, glancing at Ruth Owen.

"Can I come too?" Clemmie pleaded.

"You must stand in the doorway then and mind the dog like, keep a safe distance," Alun told her firmly.

"Daisy, will you watch her please?" Ruth Owen put in quickly. She was all too aware of Clemmie's daring nature.

She watched for a few moments over Clemmie's shoulder. The narrowboats contrasted sharply with *Pili Pala*, being blackened from the carriage of dusty cargo. "These are hardworking boats, not idling for our pleasure like *Pili Pala*," she observed.

The crew were equally grimy, forever toiling, but as cheerful as she recalled. Surprisingly, there were no children, for these were obliged to go to school nowadays and had been dropped off along the way. Some of the boat people resented this cut in their labour force but most would say that they were glad that their offspring were learning reading and writing even if their progress was upset by the constant changing of schools. The majority of their teachers were kind and helped the travellers to cope; however, in the yard at playtime some of the local children made them feel unwelcome.

Alun, to Ruth's unconcealed delight, kept Bay on the trot while he instructed him in the opening and closing of the lock gates, the dropping of the paddles, to enable the first two boats to steer within the lock. She felt the old fascination as she observed the level of the water rising as Bay and Alun hurried on to the far gates.

"Bay – actually doing some work!" Clemmie exclaimed.

"Clemmie!" Ruth reproved, but as she turned away she smiled to herself.

She followed Meg up the steep staircase which led directly into her old room. There was the big bed which she had shared with Meg and where Meg now slept alone. It was all the same: the plump pillows encased in starched white cotton, the darning she had laboured over so impatiently on the faded blue coverlet.

Meg, slight and ramrod straight, standing before the long mirror to put on her hat, might have been Ruth Owen herself all those years ago, wearing that long serge skirt, that prim white blouse.

Meg met Ruth's reflected stare. "So, you are back, are you, Ruth Owen?" she asked resentfully. "Mam told me the truth of it all when you were gone, you know. She told me all about Drago. I know *exactly* why you ran away. But because of you, *I* am still here. I am twenty-seven years old; what chance do I have of marrying now? I may not have your brilliance, but I took over your job, not fourteen years old I was, I surprised them all. When I've worked a full day I come back here and look after Mam. That should have been *your* responsibility . . . Mam is the lock keeper here, you know, in name, for the Company kindly appointed her so when Father died, but it is the boy who carries out her duties since she was struck down. *He's* like you, Ruth Owen, sooner or later – and it may well be sooner now he's met up with you, who spoiled him so when he was young, only to abandon him – us – with no word since – he will take off just as you did. What will happen to Mam then? Or will he wait for her to die first?" She stabbed her hat pin venomously through the cheap straw crown.

Ruth Owen winced. "Meg – how can you say that?" she whispered, her lips working as she blinked back scalding tears. Her happiness at being back here was so swiftly evaporating. "Forgive me, I never intended to hurt you . . ."

Daisy had come up the stairs a moment previously. She said, more loudly than she intended for the two were obviously unaware of her presence, "Bay's asking for you, Ruth."

"I'm off then," Meg said quickly, forcing them to step aside.

Daisy followed Ruth over to the window. "Please don't cry . . ." They caught a glimpse of a bicycle being pushed past the onlookers as the third narrowboat and barge entered the lock.

"She's going to work, Daisy, to the canal office where I was when I came back from college to live with Rachel and Davey again. They were so good to me, putting me through grammar school and making such sacrifices so that I could go on with my music."

"You didn't finish your course?" Daisy ventured.

"No . . . Alun was born then – maybe I stayed a few years because of him – I hurt them badly by running off; that's why I lost touch."

"Clemmie's telling Rachel all about The Singing Barleys – Ruth, Bay will wonder where you are."

"Let's find out what he wants then," Ruth said, getting a grip on her emotions. She gave Daisy a swift hug. "You're a dear girl – what would I do without you?"

As Ruth stacked the greasy plates, clearing a space on the

31

table for the washing up bowl, she chatted to Rachel, while Daisy went off to find Bay and to round up Clemmie to help dry the dishes, for the child had vanished at the very thought.

"I can't believe you are back home at last." Rachel smiled. "Soda? In the jar in the cupboard as always . . . Oh dear, it still frets me to be lying useless here, you know, while others do all the work."

Ruth swished the cloth in the water.

"Alun is so happy to see you again – ah yes, he cried for days when you were gone! 'You still have *me*!' Meg told him. 'She has gone to London, I believe,' I told the little lad, 'to seek her fortune with her singing.' How could I blame you for leaving, Ruth Owen? You were wasted here – such glorious talents you possessed!"

"I didn't make my fortune, though then I really believed I would – you see, I met Bay instead," Ruth told her impulsively, then regretted it, for Rachel looked anxious.

"Are you not happy then? Your husband is older than I expected, not that age comes into it, does it, for my dear Davey and I were much the same age and I lost him before he reached fifty," she sighed.

"I was so fond of your Davey. He was so kind to me, making me feel part of the family as he did. He never said to me, he *knew* but—" She broke off abruptly for Clemmie burst in, full of important news, followed by Daisy and Bay. She was amazed to see her husband so animated.

"I *know* I'm to dry the dishes but, Ruth – Auntie Rachel – The Singing Barleys have their very first engagement. Isn't that exciting? And it's all due to *him* for once!" Clemmie added artlessly.

Only Clemmie could get away with a statement like that, Ruth Owen thought ruefully.

"I shall appear with blistered palms from all the labour I've been put to," Bay said drily. "Let me elucidate. There is to be a wedding at the mission further up the canal this coming Saturday. *We* have been asked to entertain at the evening celebrations! I just happened to be chatting to the bride's mother . . . Outside in the meadow if fine, or in a nearby barn if it should rain."

"He's decided to grow a beard," Clemmie interrupted. "That's a good idea, isn't it? It will help to conceal his . . . *jowls* . . . that's a double chin, isn't it? Daisy always tells me, 'Increase your vocabulary', doesn't she, Ruth?"

They were all laughing now, even Bay, but he fingered his face vainly as if denying to himself that there was any slackness.

"I'm so glad," Ruth Owen said. "About the engagement, I mean, though I doubt you asked what we would be paid, eh, Bay? Regarding the whiskers, although I imagine they'll be grey – which *might* make you *look* more dependable, perhaps? – I think that it is an excellent idea! You see, my dear, if you wished to be shaving each morning life would soon be intolerable, for we can't be doing with fussing on the boat. When you've finished drying the dishes, girls, we need to go up to the village."

"Provisions, is it?" Rachel asked from her couch. "We can let you have eggs, milk, butter – don't you dare be too proud to accept, now! You might find the Midnight Grocer still abed but, as you'll remember, he always opens up if you knock loud enough."

Seeing Bay's intrigued look Ruth Owen enlightened him. "Eli has been serving here in that little shop for ever, it seems. He was never one to bother with the time of day. Should an order be requested next day no one is surprised if the groceries arrive by moonlight."

"Catch up with Alun feeding the hens first," Rachel suggested. "Ask him to let you have all the eggs he finds today. He'll make you up a boxful while you're up the shop. Why don't *you* go, Daisy?" she suggested slyly with a wink at Ruth Owen.

However, Clemmie wasn't going to miss out and Bay went too saying, "I want to ask the boy something."

Then Ruth and Rachel were left alone together again.

"Sit down beside me for a minute, Ruth," Rachel said quickly, "for now is my chance to ask if you intend to see Drago?"

Ruth Owen sank down on the end of the couch. Her face was very solemn. "I've already seen him, Rachel. On our way here, this morning . . . I guess the word was spread. Oh, don't worry, we didn't get to speak . . . Rachel, Meg has told me, before she left this morning, that *she* knows it all. Is it the same with—"

"Alun? No, my dear. What was the point? Meg was older – I *had* to explain."

"I've not told Bay, you know. We're happy in our way, Rachel, if that's a comfort to you, but I know I'll never live up to the memory of Bay's first wife, Anne, Daisy's mother, whom he adored—"

"Surely that can't be so! *He* called here after you left, asking where you were. Well, my Davey told him he had no right to know at all, indeed no . . . He just turned and went. Later we heard that he had left the college, gone right away. Another post, another place, folk supposed. Still, he came back here when he retired, to *her* of course, a few years ago now." A pause. "Why did you never write to me, Ruth?"

"I meant to, I really did. The longer I left it the more difficult it was to put pen to paper. You see, I'd let you down so badly. I'm really very lucky for I have my darling Clemmie, even if I never become famous, like you wished for me – right now we have no money at all but I don't care now I'm back near you – and I love Daisy just like my own. *She* took the place for me of Alun, I suppose. I missed you all, so much, all this time . . ."

"I'm glad." It came out as a sigh. "I always prayed all would be well with you. Don't be afraid, Ruth, when you and Drago come face to face and speak at last. The fault was always with him, never you."

"His wife is still living?" Ruth asked, rising and taking the pile of clean plates to the dresser. She had slipped easily into the old routine.

"I've not heard otherwise – still there, in the house with all the steps – don't I recall the cleaning of them," Rachel remembered wryly, "when I worked in Ty-Gyda-Cerded before you were born, me a slip of a girl? Very particular Eluned Drago was: those steps had to be as white as snow, even though *she* never walked up or down them. She'll be just as much the invalid as ever, I imagine. Fancy, *both* of us—"

"Rachel." Ruth Owen dropped to her knees again beside her sister. "If only I'd known, but I've come back to you now!"

"Don't be sad for me, Ruth Owen, I've accepted it, and so you must."

Six

Calling to the girls to follow her example Ruth Owen hitched her skirts up. They hauled themselves over the jutting stones in the craggy wall. They landed, in turn, with a jarring thump on the grass verge of the steep road which led up to the village.

As Daisy bent to rub her ankles ruefully, Ruth Owen remarked blithely, "We always used this short cut to the shop." She linked arms with her daughters. "Here, Daisy, Clem – you can pull your old Mam to the top of the hill. I don't want to be puffing and blowing when I meet the Midnight Grocer, now do I?"

"I'm not so sure *I* can . . ." Daisy teased.

"Well I can 'cos I can't wait to meet him either!" Clemmie grinned.

"Ah girls, he was a great friend of Rachel's Davey you know, for after a night out at the old Sheep and Cuckoo, Eli would deliver Davey home along with the groceries!"

"At midnight, I presume?" Daisy asked innocently.

"Of course! I wonder if he'll remember me?" It really was a steep hill. They had to pause to catch their breath.

Then Clemmie exclaimed, "'Course he will!"

Ruth gazed around her in delighted homecoming. As they struggled to the crest of the hill the view of the valley below was breathtaking. Sheep there were, of course, and cottages nestling in the dips, with purple slated rooftops; smoke wreathing up, despite the warmth of the morning, for how could you cook without the stalwart stove burning?

She gave Daisy's arm a squeeze. "Dreaming, Daisy?" Daisy, she thought, had been all moonbeamy since she met Alun. Romantic that she was, Ruth was pleased.

Daisy started. "I suppose I was . . ." But she did not enlarge on this and Ruth did not expect her to.

As Rachel had predicted, the blinds were still drawn across the bowed window of Eli's shop. His house was the first you came to when you reached the level path.

There was a cobbled courtyard before a stable door with a hitching post for horses and a water trough. A barrel had been cut down for the planting of flowers, and a pile of folded dusty sacks waited on the step, obviously returned by an earlier, disappointed customer who had failed to rouse the midnight grocer. Ivy twined through the letter box. On the side wall Ruth pointed out a boldly painted dragon. Above the lintel was tacked a lopsided board: 'Eli Pentecost, Not Just a Grocer, Brynbach.'

Ruth seized the yard broom when their knocking went unanswered. "Stretch this up, Daisy, there's a dear, for I'm too short, wasn't I always? Give a good tap or two to the upstairs window. Go on!" she urged as Daisy demurred.

Emboldened, Daisy much to her own surprise obeyed. But three thumps was all she managed before she thought better of it and let the broom slip through her fingers to the ground.

Clemmie jigged up and down in gleeful anticipation. "Midnight Grocer, *wake up!*" she shouted.

This was a signal it seemed for the occupants of the two other whitewashed cottages nearby to open their doors to see who was making all this commotion. Ruth Owen beamed and spread her hands wide to express: He hasn't changed has he?

"Surely – Ruth Owen, is it?" the neighbours said to each other.

The bolts shot back, the top half of the door swung open and Eli leaned his elbows on the lower half and poked his rumpled head out. Moon-faced he was with a sweet, huge smile which revealed a total lack of teeth. He had obviously pulled his trousers on over his nightshirt, but his thick wild grey hair had not met a comb. "Shop was it?" he asked sleepily, then: "Ruth Owen! Come in, come in – *Mam!*" he called. "Come down and see who's here!"

Now the door was flung open and Eli was shuffling behind his counter, sweeping off the bits of broken biscuit and chaff with one enormous hand.

"D'you think he went to bed with that bit of pencil behind his ear?" Clemmie stretched up to whisper in Daisy's ear.

"Clemmie, *shush!*" Daisy reproved, blushing deeply.

It was a shop which sold literally everything and anything from the formidable corsets in pink satin which encased an hourglass shaped wooden dummy with no head or arms, to sacks of potatoes, jars of sweets, mousetraps, matches and mothballs. There was scarcely room to manoeuvre between the boxes piled on the floor. Under a glass dome on a piece of marble, on the counter, reposed a great slab of saffron cake labelled 'Mam's Cake'. Squeezed between the barley sugar sticks and blue bags of sugar was a stack of hard-crusted loaves which looked as if they would snap the consumer's teeth (and had probably accounted for Eli's loss) with a pencilled card: 'Mam's Own Bread'. Along the shelves, next to jars of cloves and whole nutmegs, were glowing jars of pickles and jams, red, gold, green and rich brown declaring themselves to be 'Mam's Gage', 'Mam's Bramble', 'Mam's Relish', 'Mam's Mustard Pickle'.

"You see, girls, Eli is right, he's never been just a grocer!" Ruth Owen cried. "Doesn't the sight of Mam's preserves make your mouth really water?"

"Back on the boats, is it?" Eli's smile broadened, even though that seemed impossible. "Order now, Ruth Owen, and old Eli'll deliver later, wherever you may be."

"At midnight?" Clemmie couldn't resist it. Ruth beamed in return. She just knew Eli would think her younger daughter a chip off the old block.

"Shouldn't be surprised," he answered. He glanced toward the inner door. "Mam, where are you?" he called again; then added with a gusty sigh, "I'll have to rouse her – she'd hate to miss you, Ruth Owen, after all these years away. She's far too fond of that old bed!"

"His mother must be very old," Clemmie said candidly to Daisy.

"Shush!" her sister mouthed again.

Ruth enlightened them: "*Quite* old, I think – a tiny, dithering woman, as I recall, half the size of old Eli but she had as little sense of day or night as her son."

They all suppressed a gasp of surprise when Mam put in an appearance at last, propelled from behind by Eli. She matched his girth and déshabille with her cotton robe barely concealing her heaving bosoms for she was breathless and wheezing after descending the stairs, cream and roses her complexion. This was no elderly Mam but a young woman in her early thirties like Ruth Owen.

"Why, Ruth Owen!" "Why, Gwennie Jones!" Ruth and Mam cried out simultaneously. Then they fell on each other and embraced as best they could with the counter between them.

"Gwennie and I were at school together," Ruth told Daisy and Clemmie when she'd managed to cease laughing and exclaiming over their misapprehension.

"Two clever girls we were," Gwennie added, "the only ones from Brynbach to get the scholarship."

"So *you* are Eli's Mam, are you?" Ruth Owen grinned. "The one who makes all that cake and stirs up all those preserves?"

Gwennie nodded. She had a husky infectious chuckle and before they knew it, they were all laughing too.

"She had us all giggling away at school," Ruth gasped. "Always in trouble with the teachers, our Gwennie."

"That's why I left before time, why I ended up here in the shop with old Eli!" Gwennie's flesh shook alarmingly.

"When my old Mam went, I popped the question quick," Eli winked. "Being so well-known for all Mam's special lines like, I couldn't afford to wait. I knew Gwennie was a good cook for I'd been a regular visitor like at her house . . . and I soon found out the rest!" he added slyly. He patted his wife's plump arm to confirm that he thoroughly approved. Gwennie gurgled deliciously.

Into Rachel's basket went a loaf of Mam's bread and a generous portion of her cake, sliced by Eli with a meat cleaver for it was so packed with fruit. From the meat safe on the wall came chump chops which he wrapped in newsprint, then Mam's bulging herby pork sausages, ditto.

"I shall need to take you up on your offer to do the cooking!" Ruth murmured to Daisy, who nodded in reply.

The stub of pencil was licked, Eli squinted his eyes betraying a need for spectacles, and he began laboriously to make a list on a torn piece of paper. As he added up, Gwennie went on laughing and so did the others.

"Any family, have you, Gwennie?" Ruth asked as Eli displayed proudly as a sudden afterthought 'Mam's Cream Cheese'. Like clotted cream in that yellow dish, she fancied, instantly recalling the taste.

"There's a little chive in the cheese; makes all the difference, doesn't it? No, no family. We've not given up hope, you know, but then, I can accompany Eli and the midnight groceries whenever I feel so inclined, can't I? These two, these pair of gigglers, they're your girls of course?" She and Eli were a proper pair for winking. Now Gwennie wiped away the happy tears on her loose sleeves.

"Oh, didn't I say? Not that you gave me a chance to do so, eh? Meet Daisy and Clementina! Daisy is my husband's daughter from his first marriage but she's just like my own!"

"I'll bring the rest along later," Eli put in. He paused tactfully, then beckoned to Ruth Owen to 'bend her ear'. The girls knew what was said because Eli's whisper was more like a stage prompt. "On the slate, m'dear? You wouldn't be back on old *Pili Pala* unless times were hard, I guess."

"May I kiss him, Gwennie?" Ruth Owen did not wait for an answer – she did just that. "I hope we shall see you both again soon, at midnight, or any time between!"

As they went through the stable door Eli followed them with more audible whispering. "Thought you ought to know Drago's back at Ty-Gyda-Cerded."

"Thanks, Eli. I did know," Ruth replied.

"Let me know if you've any trouble like, being Davey's friend and Rachel Hughes's of course, you know . . ."

"I know. Goodbye for now," she said warmly.

"I wonder if they're going back to bed," Clemmie remarked artlessly.

Ruth exchanged a little smile with Daisy. "I shouldn't wonder," she said.

Seven

"Once you've been through the first lock you won't worry about the next," Ruth told her family with confidence.

She was amazed and pleased to see how quickly Bay had learned and that he was playing his part with the lock gates alongside Alun.

Despite her reassuring words, she noted her daughters' solemn expressions as *Pili Pala* sat within the towering walls then rose inch by inch as the water swelled steadily and pushed them ever upwards. Then they were gliding safely along the canal once more, waving a cheery farewell to the watching Alun.

The sun was high but Daisy laboured over the stove, which Alun had so kindly coaxed into reluctant life for it had been cold and unlit for so long while they were chatting at the shop. "Cook those chops well and long," was Rachel's advice, for Ruth Owen had no idea. Pompom sat by, nose twitching hopefully.

Ruth Owen, fastening a flagpole of washing (triumphantly achieved by Clemmie and herself dancing up and down in a tub full of suds on deck, bare-footed of course!) called down to Daisy, "You ought to see the dogged expression on Bay's face; he's really got the idea of the steering now."

Clemmie licked her pencil as Eli had his. "Ruth – Daisy, oh, *do* come up here for a minute! What d'you think of my poem?" Her mother had suggested that she might do a spot of schoolwork on her own as Daisy was otherwise occupied.

"Read it out, then we'll tell you, Clem." Ruth was fondly anticipating.

41

Sheila Newberry

> "We're The Singing Barleys,
>   We hardly ever wash
>   Except to soak our feet in suds
>   When we're feeling rather posh.
>   Oh, it's Bay Barley at the rudder,
>   Ruth Owen with the pole,
>   Dog and Daisy down below,
>   We're loaded down with coal.
>   (Poetic licence, eh, Ruth?)
>   We eat great lumps of bread and cheese,
>   Crumbs go floating to the fowl—"

Ruth now interrupted, improvising:

> "The wooded slopes slip slowly by,
>   At night we're cheek by (Wait for it,
>   Clem, here's that word again) JOWL:
>   Gliding through the sun and shade
>   We dream our days away
>   Steaming cups of well-brewed tea (Oi! Daisy!)
>   A dozen times a day.
>   So, it's Eli The Midnight Grocer-er—"

Bay had been listening after all for he broke in sardonically:

> "Who'll bill it on the slate
>   With a wife, I'm told,
>   As good as gold
>   And customers who'll wait . . ."

Daisy, coming up obediently with the tea tray, added the final touch:

> "In my dreams I call out loud,
>   'How CAN we pass through all those locks
>   If we are fast asleep?'
>   While *Pili Pala* rocks . . ."

42

"Take your tea," Daisy urged. "I daren't leave those chops cooking away on their own."

"Ruth, Bay, Daisy," Clemmie said in an injured tone, "I wasn't going to say any of *that* but I suppose it'll have to do . . ."

"We could set your poem to music, sing it as we go along!" Ruth felt warm and contented, they were having fun together just like a real family – how wonderful, she thought!

Later, as they tackled their lamb chops and potatoes, Daisy watched anxiously for their reaction to the first meal she had ever cooked.

Ruth, as always, was quick to reassure, speaking before Bay could open his mouth and say something cutting, for the chops were undoubtedly overdone. "Look" – she picked up her bone and nibbled at the dry meat still clinging to it – "you couldn't do this if it was all a-drip with gravy – delicious! I hereby appoint you Chief Cook and" – turning to Bay and Clemmie – "you two – Bottle Washers!"

"Ow!" Clemmie protested.

There were plenty of scraps for Pompom. However, Ruth was glad that Daisy had certainly mastered the art already of making a good cup of tea. 'Mam's Own Special Blend' turned exactly the right shade of brown and went down a treat with the yellow slab cake.

Ruth smiled at Daisy. "*You* look contented with your lot," she said softly. Bay and Clemmie had clattered up the steps to drink their tea on the bank while the horse was busy with his pail of feed.

"So do *you*."

"Oh, I am. And Daisy, we'll be back at Rachel Hughes's again in a few days' time, you know. *Alun* will be looking forward to that too!"

Daisy just had to give Ruth a quick hug. "I can't hide anything from you."

"I won't say anything to Bay – or Clem – you can do without her teasing," Ruth promised. Then the thought came to her that *she* had kept things to herself for so long – would she be able to bring at last old hurts into the open?

*   *   *

Their trunk caught up with them before they reached the mission, where the wedding was to take place, which was a relief for they couldn't perform to the best of their ability if they weren't wearing the right clothes. Where to stow the trunk was another matter. Ruth and Daisy tried to shift things around with Clemmie's help and Pompom's interference.

"Hear you're singing at the wedding party?" asked the boatman who heaved the hefty stage trunk aboard *Pili Pala*.

"We are," Bay agreed. "Not quite our usual venue, you'll appreciate," he added loftily. He wondered if the chap could read the bunch of handbills he had just given him 'to circulate'.

THE SINGING BARLEYS, TRAVELLING MUSICIANS
AVAILABLE FOR WEDDINGS, BIRTHDAY CELEBRATIONS,
DINNER PARTIES, DANCES &C.
APPLY PILI PALA, OR LOCK COTTAGE, BRYNBACH.
TERMS BY ARRANGEMENT.

Ruth Owen, who with Daisy had spent the previous evening penning these notices, thought that Bay really had no idea: how many of their fellow boat people would be having dinner parties, for instance? She considered privately that they might well be luckier with the bills they intended to post when they reached the town.

"There'll be a fair old congregation, with all the boats – I should get along there early if I were you, or you'll have a way to walk to the mission," the boatman advised, waiting around for a tip which seemed unlikely to materialise.

"Thank you, we will," Bay said dismissively. His pockets were empty, a fact he bemoaned every time he spotted a pub. These were frequent along the canalside, for the navigators who had strained and shovelled when carving out the waterway more than one hundred years ago, had, understandably, a raging thirst.

Ruth slipped her last sixpence into the hard brown hand. The boatman's bold eyes looked her up and down admiringly.

"We can manage now," Bay said sharply.

The trunk came bumping down the steps and Ruth and Daisy fielded it smartly at the bottom. They dragged it into the cabin. "It'll do as a spare seat," Ruth suggested hopefully.

"It'll need a cushion then," Clemmie said in her candid fashion, fiddling with the hasps, "or it'll be hard on our bottoms!"

"Here!" Ruth found the solution with a folded blanket for comfort. "Will that do? We'd better shake out and air all the clothes, Daisy—"

"Or they'll smell like Miss P's hallstand!" Clemmie wrinkled her nose and rolled her eyes up at the too recent memory.

They hadn't managed to get ahead after all and were forced to tie up behind a long line of boats on the Saturday morning. Firstly, Daisy led Old William to the Swan stables, Bay opted to remain in the cabin resting himself and his voice, and Ruth Owen, Daisy and Clemmie went eagerly along the assembly to see what was what and who was who. They were far less inhibited without Bay, of course.

Every boat was in the process of being well and truly scrubbed. Buckets of filthy black water splashed into the canal. Fresh water was drawn from the standpipe and brushes and soap were applied vigorously. Here were the young ones Ruth Owen had missed that first morning on the canal, freed from their school desks, shooting marbles on a dusty bare patch, scratching their tousled heads and grinning disarmingly at the newcomers. Torn cotton frocks and patched trousers, grimy hands and feet she knew would shortly be transformed, for wedding finery, like the Barley's stage attire was being shaken and aired. Gallons of water was being boiled for more scrubbing, of humankind this time, and ancient great-grandparents had been given the task of cleaning and polishing a vast array of boots. Smoke curled busily from stove pipes, also from the clay variety, clamped between both male and female lips; there was much shouting and happy cursing despite the proximity of the mission and the prominent sign displayed outside this squat, square edifice: 'Come Ye All And Be Saved!'

The bride and groom remained firmly out of sight in their respective family boats.

There was a trembling golden heat beating down on them and unexpectedly, from a mere streak of white cloud in an otherwise faultlessly blue sky, a brief scattering of rain. Clemmie touched the crown of her head wonderingly. "I just got a bit wet, Ruth Owen – did you?"

"You imagined it." Ruth kept a straight face. She held her palms upwards. "Where's the rain then, Clem, eh?" A lizard flashed along the footpath, over their feet, only seen, she marvelled, if you were not blinking at the time. Just like Clemmie's spots of rain.

Then one of the boatwomen was calling, "Ruth Owen – is it really you?" And the echoes came thick and fast: "Ruth Owen! Ruth!"

There was joy on Ruth's expressive face: she had returned, she belonged once more . . . If only they could stay long enough to put down roots, she wished.

"Daisy, Clem – come meet another old friend of mine, Juniper Kelly, someone with some good Irish blood mixing with the Welsh in her veins, you know, for she's descended from one of the first Irish navigators."

They gazed wide-eyed at the tall woman with her hair crammed up under a man's cap, whose muscular arms were folded across her narrow chest. She had a sack wrapped round her waist for the cleaning, and she wore men's boots too, possessing large feet for a woman.

"It's my daughter as is marrying," she told them proudly. "Sixteen years old today. We've been saving all year for a good wedding. So, you are singing for us are you? 'Twas your husband, was it, I met up with at the lock gates? I said to my Rose just two days ago, 'I've a notion we'll be meeting Ruth Owen again very soon!' Been on the London stage we hear – you'll do us proud, no doubt. And the preacher has asked Mr Drago to play for the service, it was not to do with me . . . You see my Rose has always been a good girl; she was 'saved', you know, when she was but nine years old and the preacher baptised her himself. We had a party then, too!

Always went to Sunday school and learned her catechism, did my Rose. Went to school as well. Puts me to shame: I never learned no reading. Though I knows bits of the good book by heart, mind." She had a deep, gravelly voice.

"You haven't changed, Juniper," Ruth said impulsively.

"I believe *you* have, Ruth Owen; oh, you look much as you did, yet . . . you've got over that business?"

Ruth interrupted quickly, "You'll see I am the same. Just older and wiser, that's all, I hope. These are my daughters, Juniper – Daisy born to my husband's first wife and Clemmie, our little one." She hoped the girls had not sensed her sudden agitation.

Juniper shook them gravely by the hand. Then she looked at them all for a long minute.

She can see into our souls . . . Ruth Owen thought, but the little involuntary shiver was not because she was afraid.

"Stormy weather ahead for all," Juniper stated. "And you, Daisy, will find that love brings as much pain as pleasure. Don't worry, sweetheart, for when you get through it all, and you will I promise you, you'll enjoy a long and happy life."

"Oh, I *do* hope so!" Daisy said fervently. Her life had been mixed so far, after all.

"What about *me*? And Ruth?" Clemmie demanded. "Are you a gypsy, Juniper? D'you tell fortunes?"

Juniper smiled. "Fortunes – no. I just sometimes see – what is to be. The time's not come for you to worry about such things, you just enjoy the present here and now. As for you, my dear old friend, Ruth Owen, you won't need to be warned to watch out for those who might bear a grudge . . . Anyway, you'll reap much happiness next spring . . ."

"Then *none* of us need to worry," Ruth put in quickly, "and, Juniper, I can see ahead too – to a wonderful wedding!"

Eight

It was cool and dark within the mission chapel. Ruth Owen, Bay, Daisy and Clemmie sat on a narrow hard bench at the back. There were the strong mingled odours of soap and polish. Just as Ruth had recalled so often the windowsills were decorated with simple jars of wayside and garden flowers.

Before the congregation, dolled up to the nines, were the young bride and groom, seated on a pair of plain windsor chairs. There was a small boy to energetically work the bellows for the black-bearded celebrity at the harmonium. From the stiff discoloured keys he produced throbbing chords which seemed to quiver and linger in the expectant hush, then finally fade away.

Ruth Owen was quite overcome with memories. She shook her head so that the flowers bounced on her hat and Bay tutted at her as if he were her father, not her husband, yet he did not detach his hand from her involuntary convulsive clasping.

It was strange, she thought: this place seemed to have cast its magic, just a little, on Bay. He had objected to attending the marriage service of course, but he'd no option. She so craved more affection from him; she wondered if she would ever be able to replace the long-lost Anne in his heart. She would not look over at Drago. Did *he* know she was there?

She was jerked back to the present, realising that the short service was over, that the young pair were now man and wife.

They walked hand in hand back up the aisle, beaming at friends and relations, blushing at the odd ribald remark which caused the following preacher to frown reprovingly at the culprits. "I would hope," he declared in ringing tones, "that

48

those of you who have taken the pledge of temperance will remember and honour that promise. I shall expect all the children here today at Sunday school tomorrow. Now may I be the first to wish every happiness to Rose and Huw?"

The Barleys waited until the rest of the crowd had filtered through into the afternoon sunshine before they, too, rose to leave.

Daisy, bringing up the rear, turned to find that Mr Drago was immediately behind their little party.

He smiled and held out his hand. "You are with Ruth Owen?" he asked. "One of The Singing Barleys? Allow me to introduce myself, for I have known Ruth, or of her, all her life – I am Raoul Drago, who was Ruth's tutor at college."

Blushing, Daisy returned, "I am Daisy Barley, Ruth Owen's stepdaughter."

"Ah, the little girl now – surely she is Ruth's own daughter?" Drago enquired. There were just the two of them now still inside the mission porch.

Daisy moved forward, stepped outside to be with Ruth. "Yes. Clemmie is her daughter. Goodbye, Mr Drago," she replied. But he followed her to the others waiting on the canal path.

"Welcome home, Ruth Owen," he said evenly. Then he walked past them and away. The wedding guests parted ranks to let him through.

"Who is he? The man we saw the morning you grounded the boat?" Bay's voice startled her with its sharpness.

"Drago. My tutor," she answered shortly.

"He was the man who watched us over the gate, wasn't he?" Clemmie recalled.

"So he was," Ruth stated. Then she added briskly, "Come on, back to *Pili Pala*. We must rehearse our repertoire for tonight and the next part is for family only, I believe."

They paused only to speak to Juniper, quite transformed in blue watered silk which hung loosely on her spare frame but imparted a graceful appearance. She wore a wide-brimmed hat, blooming with unlikely matching blue roses, but she had not compromised with her hair style, her raven locks being almost hidden as with the old cap.

"My daughter, Rose . . . Rose, this is Ruth Owen – you've often heard me talk of her, haven't you? She is Mrs Barley now and this is her husband who told me about their singing when me met earlier in the week . . . This is Daisy, this is Clementina, their daughters."

Ruth Owen found it hard to believe that the young Rose, tall and coltish in ivory silk trimmed with pink bows like cabbage roses, was younger than Daisy and already married.

Rose smiled shyly, and shook their hands in turn.

"My son-in-law, Huw," Juniper told them proudly. The boy was bolder, eyes sparkling with fun, his arm very firmly round his wife's tiny waist.

Ruth thought although they were not looking at each other it was obvious that Rose was very aware of their closeness. She imagined that Daisy already had experienced that feeling with Alun. Oh, she would be *so* happy if something should come of *that*.

"You will be with us at seven?" Juniper asked. "We shall make a circle for your performance. We have time to enjoy ourselves before the storm comes, I think."

"Storm?" Bay queried. "But there's a perfectly clear sky."

"It's on the way. I feel it." Juniper pressed something in Ruth's hand. "I will give you this now; it might be forgotten if we have to make a run for the boats later." She looked up at the spotless sky.

"Thank you. Seven o'clock it is." Ruth would not count the coins in front of her friend. They walked on briskly towards *Pili Pala*.

"You know absolutely *everyone*!" Clemmie marvelled.

While Clemmie took a reluctant nap after lunch with the promise that she could stay up until the very end after the singing, Bay sorted through the songsheets, putting them in order.

Ruth and Daisy walked the dog across the meadow. They discussed their costumes and the gypsy theme which Clemmie wanted, and bemoaned their lack of flatirons.

Ruth looked gypsyish already for Daisy had twisted her hair into rags which she had covered with a bright square of silk. "You are lucky to have such curly hair," she sighed. "Mine is straight as a poker."

"At least you can comb through your hair easily!"

"I believe your mother had hair the same colour as yours, even if the curl does come from Bay – in fact," Ruth added as they went swishing through the long grass with Pompom bounding ahead, "Bay said the other day, 'How like Anne she is.'" Ruth was not sure if if she had been meant to overhear what Bay had unconsciously exclaimed. She knew though that Daisy was hungry for information regarding the mother who had died soon after she was born.

"Why does he dislike me then?"

Ruth Owen linked arms with her stepdaughter. "I'm sure he doesn't, Daisy. It's just that . . . he's afraid, I think, to get so close to anyone again after losing her – he adored her, you see. That means we are both in the same boat regarding his affections, even though he does seem to unbend when Clemmie is around. You looking like his Anne can't help. It makes him remember too much." She hoped fervently that she had somehow said the right things.

"D'you think that's why he abandoned me, left me with my grandmother like that? She didn't love me either, I was always aware of it." There was pain in the asking.

"Perhaps. Though it would have been difficult for a man on his own, travelling around as we do, to look after a baby, Daisy."

They had come upon a little copse, a ring of trees round what had long ago been a garden. "Here it is," she exclaimed. "See, there was a cottage here, but it burned down before I was born. I always fancied this was a magic garden, with the flowers seeding and spreading, the fruit trees all unpruned so that the fruit is small, sour and scabby. Rachel and Davey brought us here sometimes for a picnic. I remember the tall flowers nodding around us and the buzzing of the bees . . ."

"It seems a magical place to me too, Ruth."

"Time to go back, I suppose, time to get changed."

*   *   *

51

Here were the Barleys, within the circle of straw bales on which sat the wedding guests, standing not on their usual wide stage but on the grass.

Ruth Owen, Daisy and Clemmie wore their hair loosened with flowers tucked behind their ears. Full black skirts with a froth of visible petticoat lace, tight scarlet blouses with billowing sleeves they wore and soft dancing boots with thin soles.

"We look more like *Spanish* gypsies!" Ruth whispered in Daisy's ear. How pretty and alluring she looked tonight; hopefully, Alun *would* come along tonight to see them as he hoped to do. She knew he would surely delight in Daisy's stepping outside her shy, introspective self.

She looked proudly at her husband. Bay wore tight black trousers, fastening just below the knee, white stockings and a white, ruffled shirt. She smiled to herself, acknowledging his vanity, knowing how appreciative he was of the admiring looks directed at him by female wedding guests of all ages.

She placed her fiddle beneath her chin, Daisy bent her head over her guitar, Bay took centre-stage, breathing deeply before making the introduction. Clemmie, her feet itching to dance, held on as instructed to Pompom's collar, which she had insisted on adorning with a large red bow.

The Barleys sang on and on as the evening progressed. Never mind that half the audience was constantly backing away towards the distant hostelry just so long as they didn't take Bay with them. As it grew cooler, a crackling fire of dry sticks was coaxed into a blaze round which the impromptu seating was rearranged. The rousing songs and dancing, the fast music gave way now to old favourites, sentimental songs by request. Finally Ruth sang her solo, in her own language, the Welsh of her childhood and growing up.

It was time for the singing to come to a close, for The Singing Barleys to take their bow. Room was made for them by the fire; Bay was presented with a tankard of ale, and the ladies with cups of tea, which they all consumed gratefully feeling suddenly exhausted. The singing had been so full of promise and passion.

As the moon rose, the Midnight Grocer and his Mam arrived. There was a cheerful jingle of harness as Eli helped Gwennie down from the cart. "They've been brought here by a moon-donkey," Ruth Owen said softly, for the sturdy grey donkey appeared silvery in the light of the full moon.

Someone else was jumping down from the cart, then reaching up to fetch a covered basket from the seat. Daisy smiled happily as she recognised Alun.

He came straight over to them. "Move up, Clemmie, make room for me between you and Daisy, eh?" Clemmie yawningly obliged. Pompom greeted the newcomer rapturously.

"So sorry I'm so late. Missed all the singing and music, have I? Meg made a bit of a fuss, said it was too late to go out when I have to be up so early in the morning, so I waited for her to go to bed before I slipped out—"

"We're glad you came," Ruth said warmly.

"'Specially me!" Clemmie wound her arms round his neck. "I *do* like having a cousin, so does Daisy, you see, Alun, we didn't know about you all here in Wales until we did our moonlight flit—"

"Not so loud, Clem," pleaded poor Daisy.

Ruth looked wistfully at them. When *she* was that age – but there, she thought, nothing had been straightforward for her, had it?

Alun felt in his pocket. "A letter for you."

"Oh?" Bay looked puzzled.

"It came by hand, from Mr Drago, not in the post."

Ruth watched Bay tucking the unopened envelope in the bag where they stowed their instruments. She bit her lip, wondering what Drago had seen fit to write about to her husband.

"We couldn't miss seeing the young ones set off," Eli was saying now to Juniper, close by. "Brought them a little something, didn't we, Gwennie? Where's that basket?"

Gwennie was engaged in hugging the bride and whispering in her ear, making Rose giggle. "Rose, my dear girl, how about this?" She released her and whipped off the cloth on the basket to reveal a real feast. Her joyous laugh attracted attention. "You may eat it under the stars, but no feeding the five thousand, mind – 'tis just for you two."

Pieces of cooked breast of chicken it was, with slices of Mam's honey-roast ham rolled in crumb. Hot potatoes were kept so, well-wrapped in napkins, but rather unfortunately warming 'Mam's Favourite Blackberry Wine'. Polished red apples were tucked in the corners of the basket for dessert.

"Oh, Gwennie, Eli, thank you – a midnight feast!" Rose exclaimed.

"Even Eve's apples!" her bridegroom teased.

The laughter caught on and continued as they went *en masse* to the canal bank.

"What's happening now?" Daisy asked Ruth, feeling emotionally attuned.

"They are going in the rowing boat – not far but out of sight and earshot. They'll moor up in a quiet spot: this is their honeymoon, bless them, just the one night alone together. Then Huw will join forces with Juniper and Rose on *The Molly Kelly* for she could not manage on her own being a widow like."

Bay was listening. "And a baby next March no doubt?" he remarked cynically. Ruth reproached him with an eloquent look.

Rose and Huw stepped down into the boat. Huw covered his bride with a blanket before he took up the oars. The crowd was still, quiet now, waiting.

Ruth Owen moved closer to Bay. Eli's arm went round his Gwennie's plump shoulders; Daisy dared to slip her hand in Alun's, while Clemmie clung to his other side. Pompom sidled off in search of scraps.

Juniper stepped forward, head high, fiercely blinking back the proud tears. It had been a wedding to remember. "Be gentle with my Rose, mind," she said to Huw.

"I will," he promised solemnly. She bent to untie the boat, and gave it a push. Huw dipped the oars. As the moonlight flooded the dark water it seemed almost as light as day.

A sigh trembled through the watching crowd. It was time for the festivities to end. Then came the first ominous rumble of thunder, followed by the rain.

"They'll get soaked!" Daisy cried to Ruth as the boat rounded the bend and disappeared from their sight.

"They'll shelter in the boathouse, I expect. And there's canvas for the boat. Well, we Barleys must make a run for it, eh? Bay, carry Clem, will you? She's just about asleep on her feet, never mind getting wet. Hurry man! Give me the bag . . . Daisy, Alun," Ruth added, far too innocently as the rain coursed down their necks and took all the curl out of her black hair, "you must find Pompom for didn't I just see her running after Eli, to see what tidbits he might have in the trap? You'll walk her back to *Pili Pala*, won't you, Alun?"

The boat was a haven from the storm. Rain rattled relentlessly on the cabin top, saturated the deck.

Clemmie was soon asleep in her bunk if still rather damp. Ruth did not think to towel her hair because such tasks had always fallen naturally to Daisy.

"We'll leave the lamp burning for her. She'll be back shortly, – you can trust Alun to see to that." Ruth thought that Bay, despite his disregard for his daughter, would disapprove if he realised that she had engineered the two going off like that together.

They peeled off their wet costumes, and hung them haphazardly to dry over the stove. Bay even remembered to stoke the fire. Ruth soon pulled the bed together.

Contented and weary she curled up under the covers. He climbed in beside her, not groaning as usual at the rigidity of the bunk. Unexpectedly, his arm went round her shoulders. She turned, pressed her face against his chest.

"You like my people then, Bay?" she murmured. "I knew you would."

Lightning haloed her long, shining black hair. His gaze was reflective. Bay tightened his hold. Anne seemed to be slipping away from him here in Ruth Owen's country. She was real, alive, warm and very loving. The summer storm excited him, stirred Ruth to say, "I do love you, Bay Barley, you old fool . . ."

It was a honeymoon night after all.

Nine

Alun took off his jacket and draped it over Daisy's head and shoulders. She experienced again that tingling as he tucked the rough tweed round the clinging folds of her wet silk blouse.

They moved through the crowd obediently as Ruth had insisted, toward the Midnight Grocer's trap even though they were both aware that Pompom had returned and was close on their heels.

"You want a lift back, Alun?" Eli asked as he hoisted his Gwennie aboard and fastened the tarpaulin as tenderly round her as Alun with his coat for Daisy or Huw with the horse blanket for young Rose.

Alun shook his head. "I promised to take Daisy back to *Pili Pala*—"

"When we've found my little dog," Daisy finished, unaware that Eli and Gwennie had spotted Pompom behind them.

"Ah well, that may take you some time . . ." Gwennie's laugh rang out once more. Then she tossed an apple to Daisy. "Not quite a lovers' feast, like the bridal basket, eh, but sweet to the taste, I reckon. Tell Ruth Owen we'll see you all again soon!"

There were screams at the brilliant flash of lightning, followed almost immediately by a gigantic roar of furious thunder. Along with the rest of the throng Daisy and Alun ran, in search of shelter.

"Not under the trees, Daisy – they might get struck!" Alun gasped. They were on their own now, running back up the meadow for everyone else was making for the boats. Why they did not go straight to *Pili Pala* neither of them would ever be able to explain.

They reached Ruth Owen's magic garden. They ducked for shelter between some bushes, flattening themselves on the ground as the storm raged directly overhead. Daisy was more exulted than afraid, for Alun held her firmly as they looked up in awe. Pompom whined and whimpered, hiding under Daisy's rucked skirt.

"We have the chance to talk now, Daisy Barley, to get to know each other a little more," Alun said softly. "We can't get back to the boat until the storm moves on."

Close up, his rain-wet face, his resemblance to dear Ruth Owen was even more startling. He stroked the drops so lightly with the tips of his fingers from her own wondering face.

"Yes, and no," Daisy replied at last.

He said regretfully, "See, Daisy, the storm is passing – that last rumble was definitely further away."

"My grandmother – my real mother's mother," Daisy told him, trying to postpone their going back, "used to turn the mirrors to the wall when there was a storm. It was my task to ensure that all the knives were away in the drawer. Because she was so frightened, I was petrified too. Yet, if the storm was during the night I never dared to creep into her bed for comfort – she was never one for hugging a child. I can't believe I wasn't afraid, Alun, out here in the open with *you* tonight . . ."

"I'm glad," he said simply. Then, "When did you become a Singing Barley, Daisy?"

"When my grandmother died. She never had a good word to say about Bay, she blamed him for taking her daughter away from her. She resented me too; she was forever reminding me that she never received a penny towards my keep. Then Ruth Owen and Bay came to fetch me. I don't know how they met, or how long they had been singing together but they were just married and, of course, I had the joy of a sister at last for Clemmie was a tiny baby. It was such a strange new world, exciting but also worrying for, you see, I'd led such a staid existence until then. Ruth is so warm-hearted, as you know, she accepted me straightaway, but I can't say the same for my father, I'm afraid."

"That's sad, Daisy – I still miss *my* father so much." He added perceptively, "They seem to rely on you a great deal."

"As your family do on you," she returned.

"Meg is so jealous – her cry when we were young was, I remember, 'I'll always be the oldest – the first!' Man that I am, Daisy, she yells at me now. If she knew I was here like this with you – well! – for she resents *all* your family because Mam is so happy to see Ruth again. Meg can't forgive Ruth for going off as she did. I believe she thought Ruth should have been the one to come back and care for Mam in return for taking her in all those years ago."

"What do you plan for your future?" she asked, delaying still further the moment when he would realise that his arms were still cuddling her close, and help her to her feet.

"I want to be an artist, but I can't leave and go to college – I have no money in my pockets, for Meg takes it all for the housekeeping. I have to ask for sketch paper, watercolour paints – oils are beyond the means of a lock-keeper-in-name-only. Our joint earnings go to keep our Mam as comfortable as possible, which is right."

"I would love to see some of your work," she suggested shyly. "Oh, I know you decorated the boat so beautifully, but—"

"I am painting a picture of *Pili Pala* just now." He smiled. "And I added the figure of a girl, sunning herself up top, this evening before I came out. It is for *you*, Daisy, when it is finished."

"Thank you."

"And you – have you any grand plans for *your* future?"

"Like you I have no money of my own. Ruth Owen has to hide what little we make because sometimes Bay drinks. He can't really accept our reduced circumstances. So here we are . . . I suppose I really just long for a *real* home, somewhere to return to when we've been travelling."

The rain had ceased as abruptly as it had begun. They sat up and moved apart. Pompom whined.

"All right, little Pom, we're going back to the boat now." Daisy looked at Alun, thrillingly aware of the tenderness of his expression. They had not even kissed, just clung together for the past hour, but she felt full of wonder and hope. "Oh, Alun. I *believe* . . . I love you!"

For a moment he seemed at a loss for words. Then, as they began to half-run across the slippery soaking grass she heard him cry out, "I feel the same for you, Daisy! I really do!"

Before they reached *Pili Pala* they became aware of the swish of bicycle tyres on the towpath. Towards them, then halting their progress, came Meg, her hair wildly blown about and saturated, her long skirts ripped where they had caught in the wheel spokes. Her face was deathly white, furious, her mouth working.

"Where *have* you been, Alun – sneaking out like that – and don't tell me to the wedding party for there's not a light showing on any of the boats, except the watch-lamp on *Pili Pala* . . . Is this what Ruth Owen encourages her daughter to do: to lead innocent young men astray? What have you been doing, or are you too ashamed to tell me?" she cried.

"Nothing Meg! *Nothing!* Just talking. There is no wrong in that." Alun faced up to his wrathful sister. Daisy pulled her hand from his clasp then she pushed past Meg and made for the boat, Pompom beside her.

"His coat – his good coat," Meg screeched.

Daisy stopped, wrenched the coat from her shoulders and threw it down weeping. "Alun, I'm sorry!"

She climbed aboard, rocking the slumberers, but they slept the sleep of the happy and content.

"Daisy! Wait!" she heard Alun call desperately as she bolted the door behind her.

She doused the lamp swiftly, let her clothes fall into a muddle on the floor which Pompom immediately settled upon and, shaking uncontrollably, she cuddled up close to Clemmie on the top bunk.

She cried silently, her tears falling on her sister's hair. So this was the pain of loving – as Juniper had said, so soon come true – this shock and despair, she thought sadly.

Ten

They were becoming old hands at dealing with the locks now. Through two more, as they slowly approached the town, and their turning point that Monday at noon. They were travelling in scorching heat, following on from the Saturday night storm. The water here was murky, the dappling masked.

Ruth was steering, Bay snoozing, Clemmie confidently leading Old William and Daisy, nursing a throbbing headache, was up top with Pompom on her lap.

When Ruth, wondering just what had occurred on the night of the wedding storm, for Daisy had been even quieter than she usually was ever since, smiled sympathetically at her, she averted her face. Ruth thought fervently, I hope Alun was not too forward. Had Rachel Hughes, she wondered, sat down with him a year or two back and spoken frankly and firmly of growing up? If only Rachel could have brought herself to talk of such things before Ruth Owen departed for college, her shock and betrayal at Drago's approach that day by the lake would have been diminished. It had been too late when, on her return, Rachel had rocked her in her arms like a baby and finally told her the truth. Ruth was glad that she had been able to explain such things to Daisy although she knew the girl would realise that she herself had not always followed a strict moral code . . .

Three factory girls lolled on the grass at the canal edge, dabbling their tired feet in the water, chattering away like artless schoolgirls, denying the cruel reality of toiling since dawn. In a heap behind them Ruth saw their discarded stockings and wrung-over cheap boots; their coarse skirts were hitched up revealing skinny white legs. They unwrapped thick dry bread from their lunch cloths, hurling the inedible crusts to the eagerly waiting ducks. Tepid tea was drunk straight from the bottle. Like the Barleys they were plagued by the gnats buzzing busily, irritatingly round their heads.

They look so happy, making the most of things despite the hardship of their lives, Ruth thought. She smiled to herself when she saw the lads creeping up behind the girls and she rightly anticipated the delighted screams as they were pounced upon. Much splashing of water ensued then and girls pursuing boys in mock indignation, tripping them up and wrestling playfully like puppies on the grass.

Even as *Pili Pala* began to distance herself from this scene she heard the shrill whistle from the factory and saw the girls seizing their boots and stockings, endeavouring to smooth down their crumpled garments and hair, making their reluctant way after the boys, back to the grindstone. She told herself that she must remember those girls and how they could only be young for such a brief respite each day, whenever she felt sorry for herself. She determined to help Daisy enjoy her dog days too.

"Cover your head, Daisy," she called, "or you'll catch the sun. Anyway, can you come down now and lead the horse? Clemmie must be tired and she ought to be poring over her books for a bit, eh? Bay looks as if he'll be non compos mentis for the next hour or so, too."

"I'm not sure that's the right expression, Ruth – well, maybe you are right! Of course I'll walk with the horse."

They had eaten earlier, 'on the hoof', as it were, because Daisy had confessed that she really did not feel up to cooking in this heat. When they stopped off at The Blinking Owl to rest and water Old William, Ruth had sent Bay in there for pies and, relenting, a jug of beer, hence his snoozing.

She eyed Daisy's pale face as she steered to the edge so that Daisy might jump off and to let Clemmie come aboard. "Sure you're all right?" she asked, concerned. She had thought Alun might call on them on the Sunday evening but he did not. They had stopped then at the busy public wharf with all the cranes, weighing machines, warehouses and stabling. Such a busy noisy place despite being the Sabbath. The Wharfinger had called in on them to enquire their business and to talk over old times with Ruth Owen.

A tall man, all in black, wearing a bowler hat, had called out to the boat people, "Temperance Meeting, the mission, six o'clock, supper will be served after the speaker. All welcome!"

He had distributed a sheaf of leaflets which were accepted with alacrity, for couldn't they be used for baser needs?

"Oh, let's go – *free* supper – and I do like singing hymns," wheedled Clemmie.

"Bay can take you: he's more in need of temperance talk than the rest of us," Ruth remarked drily. Anyway, she hoped for a heart-to-heart with Daisy.

To her surprise, Daisy suspecting this had put in quickly, "I'll come with you, Clem," before Bay could voice his objection.

"Yes, just a headache as I said," Daisy told Ruth now, obediently donning the proffered straw hat.

As they journeyed on they came to a much more urban area with rows of cottages and a rise of rooftops above the level of the canal reaching towards the town. But first, they had to cross the aqueduct. Just a modest one, nothing spectacular but still giving a good view of the river winding through the valley below.

Ruth and Bay tied up behind a long queue of boats and barges, waiting their turn at the final lock. Old William had his pail – Daisy saw to that remembering Alun's counsel when they first met. Pompom drank a dish of water. They spent the waiting time as usual in brewing tea.

They were drinking this when Bay suddenly remembered the letter Alun had given to him on Saturday. Ruth looked on guiltily as he slit the envelope for hadn't she held it in vain to the light to try to decipher the contents when she was briefly alone in the cabin?

She watched, biting her lower lip as he unfolded the sheet of paper, revealing a further envelope tucked inside. "This one is addressed to Daisy and Clementina." He sounded surprised. He handed it to Daisy. 'The Misses Barley' was written boldly on this envelope.

To Ruth's relief Bay read the other letter aloud first. There obviously was nothing sinister about the contents.

Dear Mr Barley,

The Singing Barleys are respectfully requested to provide the entertainment at a celebration to mark forty years of marriage between Raoul and Eluned Drago on July 5th next at their home, Ty-Gyda-Cerded, Brynbach. A fee of ten guineas is suggested. Time: six thirty p.m. for seven. You are most welcome to join us for dinner before your performance. Mooring: below the steps.

RSVP Raoul Drago.

Bay was obviously flattered. Things were really looking up. "Ten guineas, eh?" he exclaimed. "And we would have been quite satisfied with half that! Your old tutor must think very highly of you, Ruth. We'll be able to post off our acceptance whilst we are in the town—"

"I don't think we should go," Ruth stated flatly. He looked at her in astonishment.

"Think it's not quite the thing, is that it, Ruth? Don't be silly, you said yourself when you brought us here that we must be prepared to take on all kinds of engagements – look at the wedding, for instance, you were happy enough for us to entertain there. Naturally I shall accept." He made it quite clear that he was adamant.

The euphoria she had felt ever since their loving night evaporated. How could she explain her reluctance without revealing those things she still felt were too painful to talk about?

Thankfully Clemmie broke in impatiently demanding, "What's in our letter, Daisy? Oh, open it do!"

Daisy glanced at Ruth hoping that the contents of the letter she was about to open would not upset her too. She unfolded the thick sheet of crested notepaper slowly.

The Misses Barley are cordially invited to tea, any afternoon to suit them by Mrs Eluned Drago, who very much enjoys though seldom has the pleasure of the company of young people. No reply is necessary. I do look forward to your coming.

Eluned Drago.

Ruth Owen's expression was still stormy but she said merely, "It is up to you girls, of course, whether you accept."

"I see no objection," Bay put in smoothly.

"They sound quite foreign," Clemmie said.

"Eluned is a Welsh name; Mrs Drago, I believe, was born and has always lived in that house. As for her husband, who is her first cousin, he is of Spanish descent. His great-grandfather, I always understood, was an engineer who came to work on the construction of the canal. No doubt," she added shortly, "Mrs Drago will be able to tell you the rest."

"We'll see Alun again before we arrive back there, won't we?" Clemmie asked. "I wonder why he hasn't come along to see us as he promised!"

Ruth Owen answered quickly. "A lock keeper is expected to be at his post at all times, you know, a great responsibility for one of Alun's age. I imagine he can only get out when Meg is willing to take over." (And Meg, she thought ruefully, would be most unwilling.)

Forcing a more cheerful note to her voice she continued, "We can't have you going to tea with the lady in those old clothes, now can we? In fact, we will all need something smarter to wear to this . . . celebration. We badly need to earn some money while we are in town and to spend it on suitable finery like . . ."

"We can use those rhinestones we snipped from that old ball gown of yours which almost fell to pieces – remember? They would brighten up plainer, cheaper stuff," Daisy said quickly, before Ruth Owen got too carried away. Someone had to be practical or they would spend that ten guineas before it came into their hands! Ruth had sounded quite rash.

"Plenty of sewing for you ahead . . ." Ruth thought being busy would take Daisy's mind off Alun's non-appearance.

There was more excitement the other side of the lock when, as the cargo-less boat, they had to drop *Pili Pala*'s towline under that of a laden boat in order that it might pass the other way. Overtaking, though, of one boat by another was strictly prohibited, Ruth said. "So much for you to learn, you see. I expect you thought it was all quite simple when we took over the boat, didn't you?"

Thank goodness for the ever patient well-trained Old William. Pompom was much more of a liability in this busy stretch of waterway. She would need to be strictly confined below. There were far too many other barking dogs around. Besides, Daisy had whispered that Pompom would shortly be in season. As always this would present problems.

"Busking, Ruth – we could earn some money like that, couldn't we?" Clemmie jigged up and down, excited at the very thought.

"Clem!" Daisy exclaimed. "*I* certainly wouldn't be brave enough to do any such thing—"

"We're above *that* sort of entertaining, my girl," Bay reproved his younger daughter.

Getting her own back, Ruth refused to agree. "As long as we weren't recognised I imagine it could be quite exciting, particularly if we were showered with money!" She had cheered up. What was the point worrying about the inevitable meeting with Drago? she thought. She was adult enough to cope with that now, surely? Why else had she come back here after all?

Time to tie up, to stable the horse and to take the opportunity of using the privy at the back of The Angel, with its tarnished namesake gazing down impassively at the travellers from its perch on the sloping roof. They all disliked the primitive sanitary arrangements aboard the boat which comprised merely of a bucket in a dark corner.

Then they were off to explore the town.

Eleven

As they locked up and left the boat they were hailed by Juniper, who had followed them up the canal, albeit with several boats between.

"Will you join us for supper tonight? Young Huw had a bit of luck, caught a fine rabbit. We hung it like and my Rose has skinned it and prepared it for the pie dish – she has to get used to this, you see – but it would take more than the three of us to eat it all. You would be most welcome!"

Daisy, lagging a little behind the others, because she did not really feel like going to town, was not at all sure about rabbit pie. She had been entranced by the cheeky rabbits bounding about in full view of *Pili Pala* when they moored up in the evenings in the rural parts of the canal. Clemmie, too, made a squeamish face but Ruth said quickly, "We will be very pleased to come, Juniper, thank you." She would tell the family later that an invitation such as this should be considered an honour, to taste the cooking of a new bride at her table.

"I wonder if it was struck by lightning?" Clemmie murmured.

As the family moved on, Juniper put out a calloused hand, a fleeting touch on Daisy's soft cheek. "Don't fret, sweetheart, will you, for you'll surely be seeing *him* again very soon . . . Just remember what I told you. See how Ruth Owen casts her troubles behind her? That's the way for *you* to follow."

"I'll remember," Daisy said shyly. The tension and ache in her temples began to ease imperceptibly as she hurried after the others.

High above the steep winding streets of the prosperous market town – "Climb, climb, *climb* in Wales!" sang out Clemmie, urging them on – they could see the church spire sparkling on the one side and the imposing turrets of an ancient castle on the other. They paused to exclaim over the bustling shops which spilled their tempting wares over the cobbled paths outside, and to wish they could buy.

Daisy delighted in the atmosphere, watching the women with their deep baskets, their starched aprons over flowing skirts, summer shawls loose around their shoulders, with their glossy dark hair knotted simply. Their soft excited voices as they greeted one another was so pleasant to the ear, so different to some of the shrill tones they had heard in other town markets. She couldn't understand a word of the local conversation, of course!

They had posted a bill or two, including one at the canal offices and another in the window of the local dairy, when they came upon the grand entrance to a hotel. Bay stopped to read the menu in the glass-fronted case on the wall.

"More exciting than your friend's rabbit pie, Ruth . . . Ah, listen to this: 'Music played by the Valley Quartet, each lunchtime and dinnertime by popular request this summer season is unfortunately cancelled for a few days due to illness. Apologies from the Management.' Daisy – will you keep an eye on Clemmie out here while Ruth and I go to see said management to offer the services of The Singing Barleys?"

For once Daisy did not feel resentment at Bay's high-handed manner, at being treated as a person of little importance, a nursemaid to her sister; to her own surprise she was pleased that her tiresome father was taking charge and being enterprising.

Ruth Owen straightened her hat and followed Bay up the steps, where he held the door wide, as befitted a gentleman, with a flourish. When the heavy door closed behind them, Daisy turned to Clemmie. "Let's walk up and down a bit, Clem, we can't just loiter outside here, can we?"

They were looking at some pretty muslin dresses in a shop window and Daisy was trying to calculate how many yards at, say, one-and-eleven-three a yard of cheapest muslin she would need in order to make something similar for Clemmie, having in mind that bundle of blue satin ribbon in the trunk which would make a splendid sash, when she became aware of a tall figure beside them. Startled, she turned to see the young preacher who had invited them to the mission meeting.

"I am so sorry – I didn't mean to alarm you," he said, doffing his hat politely. "I tend to forget that my clerical attire can seem somewhat intimidating. It has its uses though," he added disarmingly, "as I hope it signifies I am a person to be trusted in time of need . . . You looked so absorbed – I could see that you were counting your pennies on behalf of your young sister."

Daisy said demurely, "Good afternoon." She thought it was strange that someone who could preach with such passion and exhortations to the ungodly to be saved from the demon drink should possess a sense of humour. With his hat off he looked even younger and he had a nice smile. His hair was prematurely grey but on him this was not ageing and he had decided dark eyebrows over kind, bright-blue eyes.

"I am glad to see you again," he said. "I couldn't help noticing, you see, at the service, that you both had such lovely singing voices. On enquiry, I discovered that you are a musical family and I instantly had the bright idea, if we should meet up soon as indeed we have, that I would ask you all to lead an evening of singing and praise at the mission should you happen to be in the vicinity on the second Sunday of next month? Naturally this would have to be a labour of love but the publicity would, no doubt, be not unwelcome? I wonder if you would be kind enough to put this proposition to your parents please?"

"You don't come from round here, do you?" Clemmie asked curiously.

"You are observant – I do not! But I *am* from the West country, from Bristol originally. I am Richard Bucktrout – now there's a surname for you to smile at, eh? Known to my friends as Dick . . . And I hope I recollect correctly that you are Daisy and Clemmie Barley, although I am unsure which is which?" Clemmie was indeed grinning at his name.

"I am Clemmie and she's Daisy!" she told him cheerfully. "And I'd like to sing for the mission – wouldn't you Daisy? – that was a very tasty supper you served up—"

"Clemmie, really!" Daisy put in, then, "I'll ask the others but I am sure it will be all right, Mr Bucktrout."

"I look forward to meeting you again then, Miss Barley, Clemmie." He replaced his hat, held out his hand to them both in turn, then went swiftly on his way up the street.

"I've been more to church, well, chapel, Daisy, since we came to Wales than I have in my whole life," Clemmie observed.

This was not quite true but near enough, Daisy thought ruefully. At her grandmother's, Sundays to the young Daisy seemed to smell of mothballs. It was the day she wore her best clothes, donned tight shoes and gloves and carried her mother Anne's prayerbook. Underneath the fading childish script: 'Anne Mary Collet aged seven 1862', Daisy had written 'Daisy Anne Barley aged seven 1887'. If her mother had lived she realised now she would have been only forty-two years old which was eight years older than Ruth Owen, who was thirty-four. Yet the ten years which separated Bay and Ruth seemed much more than a generation.

The small Daisy had felt close to her mother with that precious book clutched in her warm hands as she knelt in the privacy of the family pew. Since she had joined The Singing Barleys the prayerbook had remained unused, wrapped in tissue among her few personal possessions. It was certainly not a treasure to share with her father. Perhaps he had no real sense of family feeling, she thought wistfully now, because he had been adopted by a wealthy spinster when he was young and sent off to boarding school at an early age. He too had discarded family ties. Daisy knew very little of his background.

Clemmie was tugging at her sleeve. "Too hot to climb any further up the hill, Daisy," she complained. "I'm all of a muck sweat—"

Daisy rebuked her automatically. "Horses sweat; ladies merely perspire! Where did you learn that dreadful expression, Clem? At the hostelry? Let's make our way back to the hotel and see if there is any sign of Ruth Owen and Bay, shall we? Then we can suggest we go down to the dairy to buy an ice-cream—"

"And Bay'll insist we wait 'til we get back to *Pili Pala* before we eat it . . . I *hate* being ladylike, Daisy, and if you want to know where I heard 'muck sweat', well, the h'ostler said, 'If you don't give that poor old animal a rest . . .', well, *that's* what would happen! Here's Ruth – see – but where's Bay?"

Ruth was smiling widely. "Yes, at least two days' work, depending on the health of the leader of the Valley Quartet, nothing serious, we gather; liverish, the manager said."

"That's what you say is wrong with Bay when he's had too much to drink!"

"Clemmie!" Daisy and Ruth exclaimed together, but they couldn't help laughing. Clemmie so often voiced what they would like to say.

"Anyway," Ruth said as they approached the hotel once more, "I want you both to back me up for we could have started this evening; Bay was trying to persuade me we could give the rabbit pie a miss, but I said, 'Sorry, we have a previous engagement!'"

"Where is he?" Daisy asked.

"Still talking to the manager, giving a hopefully edited version of the recent successes enjoyed by The Singing Barleys. I said we'd make our way back to the boat for we'll need to organise ourselves for tomorrow if we are to be out all this evening. We'll have to come shopping here properly, when our pay is safely in our pocket. We might even still be here by Market Day – all sorts of things we might buy then, eh?"

"Threepence would buy us a large ice each," Daisy suggested, "and Clemmie wants us to be quite uninhibited and roll our tongues blissfully round 'em, all the way back to the boat."

"Why not!" Ruth Owen led the way to the dairy.

Juniper's boat was bigger than *Pili Pala*. The table was spread with an old lace cloth, beautifully laundered and lovingly patched.

Rose hovered anxiously over the pie which steamed deliciously through the cracked china funnel. Juniper shook the potatoes by the open window to flour them up. Huw had kept watch for the Barleys and now escorted them beamingly into the cabin.

"Hope you don't mind Pompom?" Daisy asked. "You see we had to shut her up all afternoon and she was howling when we got back from town."

"We like dogs," Juniper said. "Don't have one now for they can be a nuisance when they jump on or off, but she'll have to mind her manners with our fierce old cat."

The battered black cat leapt on to the dresser at their approach and glared balefully. Her tail flicked over the potatoes and Daisy knew she would have to steel herself to eat these if she was to mind *her* manners.

"You cut the pie, Mam," Rose pleaded, "I daren't."

Juniper sighed fondly but sliced into the pie confidently, spooning tender meat and gravy on to plates patterned with fading blue splodges. "My mother gave me these when I married. 'Tis theirs now – bluebirds for happiness, don't they say? Mr Barley, do help yourself to carrots – Ruth Owen-as-was, my dear, take more spuds – there's plenty."

Bay and Huw had the most meat, for men must always be fed well. Bay nearly blotted his copybook by raising his fork to his mouth just as Juniper said, "Will you say grace for us, Mr Barley, please?"

Daisy hoped that he would be able to think of something suitable. She could not know that the rabbit pie, the vegetables, had brought back vivid memories of his schooldays when his headmaster had presided over the long trestle tables at supper-time. 'Hands folded, eyes closed,' he had intoned while the hungry boys salivated over their full plates. 'Lord for these thy gifts . . .'

"For thy sustenance," Bay echoed that dry voice, "make us all truly thankful. Amen."

His womenfolk exhaled soft sighs of relief, then Clemmie exclaimed, "Ready, steady . . . Go!"

Yet she set them a praiseworthy example after all, after Daisy's little homily on good manners, by following the example of her hostess. She sucked the bones, dipped her bread in the gravy, licked her fingers and speared her carrots with her knife, as did Huw. Pompom was well rewarded with all the morsels she dropped under the table.

When the meal was cleared and the washing up taken away to the deck, to be dealt with after the visitors had departed, Juniper asked, "You will sing for us, we hope?"

"Oh, we always sing for our supper!" Ruth Owen smiled. "Bay, start us off, will you?"

Well past Clemmie's bedtime they sat on around the table, taking it in turns to suggest all the old songs. 'Billy Boy' was Daisy's choice. As they sang 'Where have you been all the day?' she thought wistfully of Alun. It would have been perfect if he had been here too.

As they strolled back to *Pili Pala* she wondered if she was hearing aright. Bay walked by her side and for once there was no awkwardness between them. "You are becoming so like Anne, Daisy," he said. She knew it was the greatest compliment he could have paid her and she exchanged a happy glance with dear Ruth Owen.

Twelve

The Singing Barleys stood discreetly behind the potted plants for they had been warned that they must provide pleasant background music only – for the hotel guests the excellent food was paramount.

On this occasion Ruth Owen played the mandolin, and Bay the piano as they began with 'La Troika', the Russian polka.

"This will see the diners through the hors-d'œuvres," Ruth murmured. The lively music encouraged both the girls to sway to the beat. Ruth guessed that Daisy felt more confident, screened by the glossy green foliage.

Their début at lunchtime had gone smoothly; given them all confidence for their later appearance. The applause at the end of each piece of music was spasmodic. Ruth could see that Bay was not too happy with this. He demanded attention, she thought wryly, even if of late this had produced a less than satisfactory reaction. Here, the diners showed their backs, and talked to their companions between courses, seemingly oblivious to the efforts of the group.

"They are certainly not as appreciative this evening," Bay said heavily to Ruth as they prepared to begin the next item. She had to remind him of their function and the importance of their promised remuneration.

Yet shifting slightly she could see through the mass of leaves that there was one table where the occupants were prepared to show their enjoyment, of their singing in particular, especially after their rendering of 'Sweet Violet'.

"*They* seem to like us," she whispered in Daisy's ear. "Look, the gentleman with the older lady – how fashionable she is in that mauve costume with those leg o' mutton sleeves!"

Even as they peeped, the lady smiled and gave a little wave as she became aware of their curious gaze. Daisy immediately ducked out of sight behind the palms.

"On to the Gilbert and Sullivan, I think," Bay muttered. Ruth took his place at the piano, where she would also sing. Bay, Clemmie and Daisy grouped around her. They went through their entire range of these catchy, immensely popular songs, coming to a close when they saw the coffee being served deferentially by the waiters. As the gentlemen lit their cigars and the ladies retired to the powder room from whence they would go into the lounge, The Singing Barleys straightened their sheet music and wondered if any refreshment would be coming their way, as it had at lunchtime, before they went back to *Pili Pala* where, no doubt, Pompom was singing *her* protest at being left too long.

"Good evening," Richard Bucktrout said. "May I introduce my mother? She very kindly provides the wherewithal for the mission suppers which Miss Clemmie enjoys and also, on occasion, insists on taking her son out to dinner to compensate for all his indifferent bachelor meals – Mother, these are The Singing Barleys, whom I have already mentioned to you."

Bay brightened considerably at the approach of such an obviously well-bred couple. He gave one of his exaggerated theatrical bows and clasped Mrs Bucktrout's proffered hand in its elegant purple glove.

"Bayly Barley, ma'am," he informed her smoothly, "my wife, Ruth, my daughters, Daisy and Clementina."

"You will join us for coffee in the lounge?" asked Mrs Bucktrout. "I am intrigued to learn more about you all. I understand that you will be singing for the mission soon—"

"Oh dear!" Daisy interjected, thoroughly embarrassed. "I meant to pass on the invitation . . . but . . . I'm so sorry!"

"We'll talk about it now, don't worry, Miss Barley," Richard Bucktrout said reassuringly as they walked together into the hotel lounge.

"Reverend Dick!" came Clemmie's voice all too clearly as she chattered artlessly to Mrs Bucktrout. "That's what we'll call him – Bucktrout's too long and too funny!"

To Ruth's relief Mrs Bucktrout agreed, laughing, "That's what I've always thought too – I only gained the name when I married, you know. By the way, Mrs Barley, you seemed to be singing one song specially for me – for I am Violet – I don't know about the 'sweet'; you'll have to ask my son about that. You may think of me as Mrs B, Clemmie, if you like, though of course *that* could also mean your mother, eh? Anyway, that's what they call me at the mission."

"My mother is usually known as Ruth Owen," Clemmie told her, "and you even *smell* of violets!"

Recalling what Daisy had imparted regarding the 'muck sweat' Ruth Owen thought they should be grateful for that.

They were charmed into accepting the assignment at the mission although Bay made it clear, "We are not particularly religious, Dick. Does that worry you?"

"Not at all," he replied. "All are welcome, especially those who have not yet found their faith. And we aim to feed the body and the mind as much as the soul. We are not all hellfire and damnation, you know."

Clemmie gave a little whistle. "Ruth gives me a wigging if I say damn."

They all laughed again. "Children are a joy, so honest!" remarked Mrs B. She opened her purse. "Here, Clemmie, take my card and persuade your elders to bring you to see me when you are next in town for I understand you are travelling up and down the canal between engagements? At any rate I look forward to seeing you all again when you sing for us."

Dick said directly to Daisy, "Will you be coming to our Sunday service?"

"We may be further down the canal by then," she replied.

Ruth reminded them, "Clemmie must get to bed, I'm afraid. Yes, I *mean* it, Clem! For don't you have a busy few days ahead with your schoolwork to fit in too? Thank you for the coffee, and your company, Mrs Bucktrout, Dick – we shall see you both again soon."

Daisy carried her sister back to the boat on her back. Clemmie pushed aside her hair to whisper, tickling her ear,

"Daisy, now you have *another* beau! I wish Alun would come and find us though, don't you?"

"Can't hear you . . ." she said unconvincingly.

"I can!" Ruth put in, teasing.

Pompom greeted them ecstatically, doing a great puddle in the process, about which Bay grumbled alarmingly having been the one to step straight into it. The mopping up gave Daisy a chance to avoid further questions from Clemmie.

"Into bed – *now*!" Ruth Owen ordered her youngest. "And stop asking Daisy so many questions."

"Ruth, d'you know, on Mrs B's card it says 'The *Hon*. Mrs Violet Bucktrout'. Does that means she's what Bay calls 'blue blooded'?"

"I imagine so, or inky-fingered like *you*, Clem – don't you ever wash properly?" Ruth asked in mock disapproval.

"Not often," Clemmie said honestly.

"Go to sleep . . ." her mother said firmly.

Bay waited until he and Ruth were settled in their bunk. "Douse the candle," he said. His hand strayed to the softness of her loosened hair. She waited, breathing fast. Affectionate gestures from him had been rare these last few years.

"Ruth – that is a very nice young man, eh? No money of his own probably but a mother who is obviously generous to her only son."

She was disappointed. "What are you implying?" She distanced herself from him, which was difficult, given the narrowness of their bed.

"Didn't you see the way he looked at Daisy? I have the feeling that he came specially to the hotel tonight in the hope of meeting her again. He must have read the new notice outside, realised that we would be singing. He is a few years older than she is, of course, and she is immature for her age but then, *I* am nearly ten years older than you."

Ruth Owen thought of Alun, the way these two young people had taken to each other. Oh, she liked Dick too, but: "Daisy must follow her own heart," she told Bay staunchly, preparing herself for an argument.

Then she could scarcely believe her ears.

"I have not been a very good husband to you, have I? But you've stood by me through thick and thin. I believed *I* was the strong one in my marriage to Anne: I cared for her so much. I blamed Daisy for her loss. I'm sorry for that. I was already going downhill fast when I met you. You have had the burden of a bad husband, one who drinks to drown disappointment, but you've never given up on me. I'm unworthy of you, Ruth. Now I want to try to make it up to *you*, at least—"

"And to Daisy!" she whispered. Her arms went protectively round him. She almost smothered him with her hair. "My old darling, I *do* understand – for I too have had my disappointments and there are things *I* should have brought out into the open years ago, and I will, soon, I promise, when certain matters are resolved . . ." She brushed the clinging hair from his face, sought his lips with hers and kissed him tenderly.

"There's not much of you but you've got a great heart," he murmured.

"Let Daisy choose for herself will you?" she asked again. "Clemmie is right: who would have imagined our shy young Daisy would have *two* strings to her bow, so soon after arriving in Wales?"

After some time he said, "Ruth, I *have* to know: was there something once between you and this man Drago? You seemed irrationally upset by a perfectly correct invitation. I must admit I have been wondering since—"

"There was nothing, *nothing!*" she answered vehemently. "I was drawn to him once but I was cruelly disillusioned. I don't think I can *ever* forgive him for that."

They talked quietly of other things, long into the still, summer night.

Thirteen

"M arket day, girls, you'll find is the same the country over," Ruth Owen said cheerfully.

"A lady left this envelope for you," the hotel manager had said when paying them off last evening. When Ruth Owen investigated, to their delight there was a generous tip. Five guineas!

"But who?" they wondered.

"The lady concerned merely requested that I give this to The Singing Barleys in appreciation of their most melodious singing. I do know who she is, of course, but she wished obviously to remain anonymous . . . I shall endorse this verdict if I am asked. I would be most happy to have you come again but I am afraid the season is now fully booked."

Not that they really minded, being ready for pastures new.

Back at the boat Daisy had asked anxiously, "We'll be able to pay Eli now, won't we, Ruth? And Alun for the coal?"

"Darling Daisy, we will – but let's be a little reckless too for once!" She counted out their total resources into neat piles on the table. "Here, a sovereign for you, Daisy, one for Bay – but not tonight, eh, while there's still time for him to spend it at The Angel? We really must give him credit for standing up to his enforced sobriety rather well . . . One for me – and d'you think Clemmie will consider a florin riches enough?"

When Bay returned from escorting Clemmie to the privy and from checking on the horse, it was all decided.

Now Ruth urged, "Off you go, Daisy, by yourself for once! I'll watch out for Clem – Bay's going to the barber to have his hair trimmed and washed and a little shape put into his new beard. We'll meet up in about an hour, say, here by the

78

china stall? I'll call in at the canal office to see if they have any enquiries for us; if not, we'll aim to turn round and begin the journey back." She smiled at Daisy. "Spend your money on *yourself*! I'll buy the muslin for Clemmie's dress and, hopefully, a pretty blouse apiece for the two of us. I might even buy Bay some new silk socks! I'm so happy to see that it's all the same here like."

The crowded stalls, heaped with bargains or the 'cheap and cheerful', the jostling crowds; the entreaties and jolly banter – even the smells were familiar, of rotting fruit and vegetables discarded in the gutter; fish, straw, live fowl in cages and, well, people, overdressed and odorous in the unexpected heatwave.

Daisy gave her an unexpected hug. "Did I ever tell you how nice you are, Ruth Owen?"

"You can tell me that as often as you like!" she twinkled back.

Gold to spend! Daisy felt happy anticipation. She knew exactly where she would head first, a shop she had noted that other day behind the market place.

It was cool in the long shop. Shelves were piled high with reams of paper, boxes of nibs, trays of pencils smelling deliciously of cedarwood; coloured inks in small bottles, india rubbers, rolls of coloured paper; Daisy walked slowly along the displays until she came to the section marked 'Tempera'. Here was absolutely everything for the artist or craft worker. Canvas, watercolour books, sable brushes, oil paints, boxed paints; palettes, charcoal sticks, gum arabic, coloured tissue. Alun, she guessed, would surely have been in his element.

For him she bought fine-tipped brushes, sheets of thick cartridge paper; for Clemmie, a fat notebook in mottled covers, ready-ruled and a supply of pencils, for Clem was always chewing them up. When her purchases were neatly parcelled up and tucked under her arm there was still plenty of change in her purse. It *was* fun being reckless! Of course she must treat Ruth and Bay too – and even herself!

Back in the busy market it was time to buy Pompom *her* treat, a meaty aitch-bone, wrapped well in newspaper to ward off the buzzing flies. There was music emanating from the top end and a crowd gathering – such a strident cacophony of sounds that Daisy was intrigued. She slipped through a gap between two gossiping matrons, receiving an indignant shove for her cheek which unexpectedly enabled her to have a front row view of the goings-on. Yes, she was right in her assumption. What a pity Clemmie was not with her for here was a busker: 'Jem, The One Man Band' proclaimed a tatty placard propped against a door post, for the performance was taking place in a space before a row of terraced dwellings.

'The One Man Band' was tied around with various instruments which were connected to his ankles and wrists. His clothes were torn and ragged but he sported a pair of large shiny boots, so maybe things were looking up for him, too, Daisy fancied. Marching up and down, the young coloured boy, who appeared to be in his early teens, clashed cymbals, marked time with his feet, blew lustily but somewhat haphazardly into a mouth organ, drummed relentlessly with one hand, operating clappers with the other, shook his mop-head of tight, dusky curls vigorously to a discordant jingle of bells which were fastened to his saucily placed cap. He even managed to dodge the farthings and screws of newspaper which the crowd aimed good-naturedly at him, though Daisy could see that he was marking exactly where the coins landed so that he could retrieve these smartly at the end of his performance. The choice of tune was rather unfortunate considering the present location, Daisy thought, amused, for she could just make out 'Ye Banks and Braes of Bonnie Scotland'. Perhaps the audience should be thankful the boy had no bagpipes.

She was shifting the parcels to her other arm when they, together with her purse, were wrenched from her grasp. For a moment she could not believe that she had been robbed and as she stood there aghast, the door of the house behind the energetic boy opened and a burly man came rushing out, seizing him from behind and bellowing, "Thief! Give a boy a bed for the night and he steals your boots!" He appealed to the crowd, "Get 'em off him, while I hang on to the young devil!"

Two youths sprang to his assistance, pulling the oversized boots roughly from the boy's filthy bare feet. There was jeering from the watchers while the boy sobbed and his instruments jangled with all the shaking. "I o'ny borrowed'm, honest – trying to earn a bit, to pay you back—"

"I'll pay you back all right!" the man shouted, clouting him viciously round the ear.

The scream of pain was enough for Daisy. Forgetting her own shock and loss, she dashed forward and pounded her fists on the man's restraining arm to force him to let go. "You *beast!*" she cried.

Ruth Owen, Bay and Clemmie had also been attracted by the busking and had threaded their way through the fast dispersing crowd. There was a warning yell: "Look out – a copper!" They were just in time to see The One Man Band scarpering and Daisy being well and truly clobbered back. She fell to the ground just as the policeman blew his whistle and her assailant slammed his door.

The rest was a haze of pain and later she had no recollection of Bay picking her up and carrying her through the now silent onlookers, through the market place, then downhill to *Pili Pala*.

Someone tweaked Ruth's sleeve. One of Daisy's parcels and her purse were thrust into her basket. "Saw what happened . . ." the man mumbled, then smartly made himself scarce.

Daisy came round on the bunk in the cabin. She struggled to sit up, but she was dazed still.

Ruth Owen adjusted the wet cloth on her head. "You've got a lump like an egg on the back of your head, where you fell—"

"And a *wonderful* black eye!" added Clemmie proudly.

Daisy winced.

"Don't worry about your parcel, it was actually returned by the thief; you even impressed *him* with your audacity, it seems," Ruth told her.

"And *I* found a parcel too – someone said it was yours. He'd thrown that away and I can guess why 'cos Pompom's being sniffing it hopefully ever since we got back!"

At the mention of her name Pompom's quivering wet nose sought Daisy's limp hand; her warm tongue licked it anxiously.

"Bay's rushed down to see if *The Molly Kelly*'s left yet," Ruth Owen said. "I know Juniper said they were delayed waiting for some goods to arrive – she'll know what to do for your head, she's as good as any nurse. *He* carried you back, you know," she added, in wonder. "I really thought he'd expire."

"Being so ancient," Clemmie piped up.

"*Bay* carried me?" Daisy wondered if she was hearing right.

"He certainly did," Ruth affirmed.

Juniper, wearing her old cap, bent over Daisy, looking intently into her eyes at the narrowing of the pupils. "A bit concussed. A day or two lying up in bed won't do no harm at all. Ruth Owen, dearie, my hands is too dirty: *you* rub this arnica gently in and round the swellings – 'twill bring out the bruises, soothe the pain . . . She'll do . . ." She patted Daisy's shoulder. "We'll be turning round shortly: why don't you make ready too and follow us down; then you can call on me, if you need me."

When Ruth returned from seeing Juniper off she saw that Bay was slumped on the trunk seat, still breathing stertorously. She looked searchingly at him. "You'd best rest up as well for a while, too. I'll fetch the horse and settle up the toll, Clem can take Pom for a quick run – on the lead, mind, Clemmie, and watch out for other dogs – then I'll ask Juniper if we can borrow Rose to help us get going."

Bay had been resting his head in his hands but as she spoke he straightened up and looked over at Daisy. To her amazement she saw that he had been silently weeping, his mouth was still working and tears coursed down his cheeks. "Bay, whatever's wrong?" she asked urgently.

"He shouldn't have carried me all that way—". Now Daisy was crying helplessly too.

Ruth Owen looked anxiously at them both. To her surprise, Bay rose, put his arms round her and hugged her tightly for a long moment. "You were right, Ruth," he mumbled. "I've never been fair to Daisy!"

"Wipe her eyes for her – *tell her*!" Ruth ordered. "And when you've done that I reckon you'll have recovered enough from your exertions to steer the boat after all, Bay Barley! I'll send Clemmie to keep an eye on you, Daisy, when she gets back with the dog. We'll cast off just as soon as we can."

Now there was a third one with tears in her eyes. She watched as Bay bent over his daughter.

Something good, positive, Ruth Owen thought, had come from misfortune.

Fourteen

The door was open. Rachel Hughes lay as always on her couch busy with her crochet hook. She dipped it in and out the fine wool which Meg had painstakingly spun after the sheep were sheared. That had been a job she had always enjoyed when she was strong and well. All those soft warm garments she had created to keep her family easy in the winter!

She wondered when *Pili Pala* would return. Such a brief visit, what joy to see Ruth again, but ever since Meg had been in a bad mood – oh, she had seen to her mother's needs as caringly as always but she had hardly spoken to the boy. It was a relief when she left for work each morning. There was something up with Alun too. She had sensed his instant attraction to Ruth's stepdaughter but something seemed to have upset things there before you could really say they had begun . . . He was a good boy, loyal to his Mam, but she had felt his restlessness increasing for some time now. He was too like Ruth Owen. They would not keep him here much longer.

"Mam?" he said from the doorway. "Are you awake? Someone to see you like."

Drago stepped inside. There was no time to tidy her hair, to retie the bow at her neck. She put her work down and looked up at him.

"What do you want?" she asked. "You know you are not welcome here – and why."

Alun was busy outside. They were alone together.

"I kept my word: I have not seen you since that day your husband showed me the door. You gave me no chance to explain then—"

"Nor will I now. Please go."

84

"Rachel, you of all people should know how I feel about Ruth Owen. You could smooth the way."

"She is a woman now. She must make up her own mind whether she sees you or not. You betrayed us, Raoul Drago. I will never forgive you for that. That day . . . you almost destroyed that young girl."

"Your illness has not dampened your spirit, I see. Perversely, I'm glad of that. But don't you admit I have a right—?"

"You have no right at all. Oh, if only Davey was here – he'd stand between us. He was a good man!"

"And I am not? It seems to me that once you thought the same of me."

"I said *go*."

"I still feel the same way, you know. That will never change. Goodbye Rachel. I don't imagine I will come again – there is no point to it."

"That is the truth at any rate."

She watched him go; heard him exchange a brief word with Alun.

Would he leave Ruth Owen alone? Did she want him to? Rachel Hughes picked up her work. The needle flashed in and out but she was not at all aware of what she was doing.

They had arrived back at the cottage. Daisy was glad that Meg would still be at work for she had witnessed more than they realised that day Ruth and Meg had confronted each other and she rightly deduced that her stepmother would feel the same way.

She looked through the cabin window and there was Alun on the towpath looking back at her and she knew immediately that nothing had changed between them at all. She could hear Ruth explaining what had happened in the town and he did not come to see her then for he was engineering their passage now through the lock to their old mooring place, further down the canal.

Surprisingly she must have dozed off while all this was taking place, for the horse was free, and the others were already in the house with Rachel when Alun spoke gently to her. "Daisy? Are you awake? Let me help you off *Pili Pala*; it is a good time – *Molly Kelly* was the last boat through, we were busy then."

"Hello, Alun," she said, sitting on the edge of the bunk for her legs were still rather wobbly. She knew she must look awful with her multicoloured eye and her pale face.

He sat down beside her. "I'm so sorry for what happened like, it was very wrong of Meg – we had quite a fight about it when we got back. I said my friends are my business! And I'm so sorry to think *this* has happened to you since." He looked closely at her eye. "You are a very brave girl."

"More praise! I must do it more often! Even Bay said I was spirited – just like my mother!" She endeavoured to lighten the intensity. "Alun," she felt under her pillow, "this is for you, just a little gift, you know, because The Singing Barleys did have some good luck, even if it doesn't look like it, and I thought you might find these useful."

He unwrapped the paper, the brushes, wetting his finger and pointing the bristles. "Thank you, Daisy," he said simply. "I never had such fine brushes before. I do have something to give in return: here – the picture of the boat and you up top, as I promised." He paused while she looked at the painting. Then, "It wasn't a dream, was it – the moonlight and us, talking through the storm, before Meg ruined it all?"

"No . . . I shall treasure this always, and one day I'll have it framed." Once more she acted on impulse and surprised herself. "Alun, hold me close again, just for a moment; there won't be another chance for a while, I think." Her pale face suddenly flooded with pink.

He clasped her gently to him as her arms slid hesitantly round his neck. Neither was confident enough to initiate a kiss. As they parted reluctantly from the brief embrace he said, "Mam said to ask you, Daisy, if you would like to sleep in Meg's room tonight. You must be still in need of rest after the shock like? *I* knew why you wouldn't want to, but—"

Daisy suppressed an involuntary shudder at the thought of Meg bending malevolently over her in the bed she had shared with Ruth Owen, in the middle of the night. "I shall thank

Rachel for her kind thought, of course," she said quickly, "but I'll make my excuses. Anyway, Pompom would whine and keep the others awake if I'm not here."

Hearing her name, Pompom, who had been keeping an eye on them, cocked head on paws, did indeed whine.

"Oh Pom," Daisy exclaimed, "my faithful friend, eh, staying on board with me when you might have been frisking in the meadow? Come on then!"

Alun kept his arm round her waist while he assisted her up the steps, for her legs were so weak, then along the gangplank to the towpath. He held her arm firmly as they walked to the cottage.

Ruth Owen was perched beside Rachel drinking a cup of tea.

"Here you are then," she said cheerfully to Daisy. "Meg is working late tonight, Rachel says, so she hopes we will stay and keep her company this evening." She smiled as she intercepted the happy glance between Daisy and Alun.

Bay was outside with Clemmie. She came rushing in to report breathlessly, "Bay says there's a flotilla of boats approaching, Alun! What does flotilla mean? That they're all floating?"

"I hope so, or we'll be grappling with the boat hook!" Alun pulled out a chair for Daisy. "I'd better join Bay. You can watch, Clemmie, but obey the rules, eh?"

"The girls have been invited to tea with Mrs Drago," Ruth said, watching for Rachel's reaction: "Ah . . ." said in such a way that it was apparent this statement had provided an answer to something. She continued slowly, "She never had children of her own: I imagine she is a lonely woman. It is a beautiful house as I recall it, though I have not been inside there for many years. There will be plenty to interest the girls. Shall you go with them, Ruth Owen?"

She hesitated. "I might. I'm not decided yet."

"It might be best."

"We will all be going there soon in any case: we are to entertain at a party to celebrate the Dragos' fortieth wedding anniversary."

"It must be all of that," Rachel said evenly.

Ten minutes or so later, when the excitement of the boats and the lock gates was over, Clemmie spotted Eli and Gwennie coming down the track from the wall which abutted the road, carrying a large basket between them. Ruth went out in response to her excited shout.

"The donkey wouldn't budge from his oats," Gwennie laughed, "and Eli said, 'Well, it's no hardship carrying a load downhill; we'll go up easy enough when the basket's empty.' Not midnight, you know, but we plan an early night; here are the groceries you ordered earlier."

"If you get up late and go to bed early then you don't need to make your bed properly in between?" Clemmie guessed.

Before Ruth could rebuke her, Eli, mopping his cheerful moon face, asked, "Aren't you going to ask us in for a nice cup of tea?"

Love shone between these two, Ruth thought wistfully, not the all or nothing that was her relationship with Bay. Eli and Gwennie were obviously such good friends as well as lovers. Unlikely as it seemed, it was a perfect pairing. It would be wonderful, she mused, if Daisy and Alun's fledgling romance proved as uncomplicated, but it seemed impossible: Meg might be absent right now but her presence was tangible.

Alun and Bay approached. "Yes, do come in," Alun invited. "Mam so enjoys a visit from you."

Seeing Daisy, Eli told her, "Met another admirer of yours today. We were collecting some goods up the canal like and the mission parson called on the folk where we were. He'd heard about your accident and was anxious so we were able to tell him we'd heard too but that you were recovering nicely and he said to tell you he hoped to see you soon, when you were up that end again, before you sing at that service he's got planned—"

"Thank you, Eli," Daisy interrupted.

"Who *is* he?" Alun asked.

Ruth Owen willed him not to be jealous.

Clemmie cut in with the answer: "He's nice, Alun, Reverend Dick I call him – his mother said I could – and she's nice too! We met him at the Tem – no-drinking! meeting before we reached town. Then we saw him again with Mrs B – that's what we're allowed to call *her*! – at the hotel where we were singing. Oh, we were a great success, weren't we, Daisy?"

She said, "I'm surprised he remembers us so well. The Singing Barleys are going to lead the singing at a special meeting next month, that's all."

"Oh, I know *him* all right. I met him at Ivor and Annie's a while back – he's a travelling preacher it seems." Alun sounded relieved.

Without Meg the gathering was much more relaxed. Ruth and Daisy rustled up some refreshments and, as dusk fell and Eli and Gwennie made no mention of their bedtime, Alun was able to relax his vigilance and there was much laughter and talking.

"I just love all your tales of when you and Ruth were girls, Gwennie." Clemmie gave a huge yawn.

"I'll take you back to *Pili Pala* and your bed, Clemmie – too many late nights, that's obvious . . . You look tired, Daisy, too – come on, both of you, say goodnight." Perhaps Bay was feeling a little left out of the story telling.

"I'll tell you some more of my stories another day," Gwennie smiled at Clemmie. She perched unselfconsciously on her husband's broad knees while he openly hugged her plump thighs. "And I might even bring up the time when Ruth Owen – at school you know—"

"That's quite enough, Gwennie!"

Soon after, Eli and Gwennie took their leave. That left just Ruth Owen with Alun and Rachel. The others had barely gone when Meg arrived. Her furious glance took in the untidy table, the cups and plates still unwashed, her mother still up despite it being past ten o'clock. "Alun, surely you and Ruth could have seen to Mam for me? Don't you imagine I am tired out after such a long day, all those columns of figures and my head spinning? . . . Well, you can see to things now for I am going straight to bed!"

Rachel Hughes turned her face to her pillow, her thin shoulders shaking. "Why is she like that, Ruth, why?"

"I love you, Rachel: please don't cry," Ruth Owen whispered tenderly, equally distressed. "You've shed too many tears over me . . ."

"You *must* go with the girls to Ty-Gyda-Cerded," Rachel managed, "but remember the Painted Room."

"How could I ever forget?" Ruth's voice was full of anguish.

Between them they saw to Rachel's needs. Alun carried that slight frame easily in his strong young arms to the room opposite Meg's. Her door was firmly closed. "I sleep so little I don't like to disturb Meg unless it is urgent."

"Where do you sleep?" she asked Alun.

"On the couch downstairs. Since I left Mam's bed, when I was grown too old for that."

At the door his voice betrayed the upset he felt at Meg's behaviour. "I'm so sorry, you know. Goodnight, dear Ruth Owen."

"Don't apologise," she murmured. Then she said loudly, hoping that Meg would hear, "We have to be on our way tomorrow, Alun, for I was thinking Ivor may have found us work by now. We should be at the wharf a few days. Then we'll go down to the other end, turn and come back to fulfil our bookings this end in a week or so."

He kissed her.

"Goodbye for now, boyo," she said fondly as he saw her out. "All these partings . . ."

She looked up at the moon as she hurried back to the boat. She would not allow Meg to destroy the young people's dreams, she vowed. She would be brave: beard Drago in his den on the morrow too.

He often walked at night when he could not sleep. He came slowly down the steps toward the water. He looked up at the house. There was a light in Eluned's bedroom window. She too was awake, full of thoughts as he was. But there could be no coming together for mutual comforting: over the past forty years they had been companions but not companionable. They had both accepted that. There was not that sadness, that aching any more. She knew, of course, of that past indiscretion. His fear now was that she might still desire revenge.

Drago walked quietly alongside *Pili Pala*. There was no light showing there. Did Ruth Owen lie close to her husband? Was there any significance, he wondered, in the fact that she had chosen an older man? She was still beautiful, still youthful but still implacable in her feelings against him. He couldn't blame her, he had been a fool, but her coming back here had greatly disturbed him. With Rachel hating him too what chance did he have to make amends?

There was a muffled bark from the boat. He moved swiftly on. He had the strong feeling that he would see Ruth tomorrow.

Fifteen

They climbed all the steps to Drago's house, Clemmie racing up nimbly ahead like a mountain goat. Ruth Owen held Daisy's arm, ostensibly to lend the girl support for she still looked wan, but drawing courage to herself by not walking alone.

The housekeeper bade them wait in the lofty hall while she announced their arrival to her mistress. Their attention was taken by the numerous paintings on the walls, of men with dark and brooding faces mostly bearded like Drago, the women stylishly dressed with enigmatic smiles and elaborate hair pieces.

"Here's Mr Drago surely!" Clemmie exclaimed, pointing out a wedding portrait which had probably been painted from a formal photograph. "He was really handsome then, Ruth – no spectacles or beard!"

"Clemmie, shush!" she cautioned her exuberant daughter.

They were ushered into the sitting room which overlooked the lovely garden at the rear. It was a sumptuous, overcrowded room, with flock wallpaper, bookcases crammed with leather bound volumes, an Adam fireplace, a grand piano, a loo table in polished walnut with a game of chess set out on top, in play. Ruth glanced up at the great engraved glass globes in the wall niches, then down, at the deep feather-filled cushions in the chairs and sofas. Almost lost in one of these was Eluned Drago. She rose slowly and turned toward them in welcome.

"I'm so pleased you could accompany your daughters, Ruth Owen – if I may call you that? It is how my husband always refers to you . . . Now, I believe you are Daisy, my dear? And this must be Clementina?" She sank back on to her dented cushions. "Here, come and sit one on either side of me! And you, Ruth, will you take the chair opposite?"

Eluned Drago was surprisingly tall, matching Daisy for height, plump and fair haired, her face carefully rouged. Her blond locks were elaborately plaited into the latest coronet. But it was her clothes which provided the biggest surprise. She wore loose silk trousers, a baggy matching tunic with sleeves which fell away from her elbows revealing many bangles, dazzling drop earrings, a choker embroidered with pearls – their hostess obviously had a passion for jewellery. Even her soft felt slippers were beaded.

"I hope you don't mind the breeze" – Mrs Drago indicated the open windows – "but in my youth I was consumptive and fresh air was imperative at all times of the year. I never feel the cold. You will observe, Ruth Owen, that I like loose light clothing, most of which my husband brought back for me from India which he visited – lucky fellow! – before we were married. His parents indulged him in his travelling, said he should visit the world before settling down with a frail invalid like me. They had brought me up from a baby, being my aunt and uncle, for my father was in the Indian army and my mother, naturally, wished to be with him . . . I was so cherished by Raoul's family it was always understood that we would marry . . . So you see, my garb is very old and as far as fashion goes I am a loser." She touched her hair, with the same vain gesture which Bay employed, Ruth saw; then Mrs Drago laughed, "My maid insists on this and if it keeps her happy . . . She will be bringing tea shortly, lots of cakes, which I am sure you girls will enjoy – the cook panders to my sweet tooth. Now, Misses Barley, I wish to know all about you – your way of life sounds so intriguing."

Ruth knew instinctively that it was only Clemmie she was interested in.

Clemmie naturally responded in her artless way. "We're im—, er, impecunious! Is that right, Daisy? She's in charge of my schooling, Mrs Drago! We're here just for a summer season on *Pili Pala* but we've already had several invitations, including yours of course!" Clemmie was in full flow, much to Eluned Drago's amusement and to her mother and sister's embarrassment. "I like your clothes; Ruth is like you, she thinks tight lacing is abom— awful, so she and Daisy don't go in for that; anyway she's so skinny she doesn't need corsets but Daisy has got bosoms so she has to wear a bust bodice for decency—"

"Don't worry, my dear," Mrs Drago smiled at Ruth and gave Daisy's arm a reassuring squeeze, "I never go out, so I've no reason to tell a soul! I think you have a lovely figure, Daisy! Your little girl is a delight, Ruth; she is very like you. My husband tells me you were the brightest pupil he ever taught. He was devastated when you did not carry on under his tutelage. Do you play piano, Clemmie? If so, would you like to try ours?"

"I haven't had much chance to practise, but when we rented a house in Bristol once, when things were going well – remember Ruth? – you gave me a few lessons . . . I'd *love* to play your piano, Mrs Drago!" She bounced out of the sofa, rushed over to the grand piano and eagerly raised the lid.

Clemmie had certainly inherited her mother's musical ear. As she began to experiment with little harmonies, Eluned Drago turned to Daisy. She delicately touched the black eye but did not mention it.

"Such a lovely face too," she said warmly, "if such a grave expression. I can see that you are a good listener. We chatterboxes need you quiet ones to keep things in balance. I would have loved to have had daughters like you, but it was not to be."

She paused and Ruth thought that she might be addressing Daisy but that the words were meant for *her*.

Eluned sighed then continued, "A *proper* married life, if you understand me, was not possible after my long illness. He kept his word, did not break our engagement, although I would not have blamed him . . . There *was* someone . . . once . . . she had a baby but refused to let us help . . . Perhaps you will think it impossible that I could accept my husband's straying, but – he *is* a man – and despite this we are fond of each other still and are now growing into a comfortable old age together.

You see, Daisy, I said you are a good listener!" But her challenging gaze was fixed on Ruth Owen.

Before Daisy could assemble a suitable response the maid arrived with the tea. There was a silver service and a cakestand piled high with madeleines dredged with coconut flakes, shortbread and chocolate truffles in little fluted waxed-paper cases.

"I'm not quite ready for mine yet – anyway, I can't drink hot tea, so I'll entertain you a little longer, shall I?" Clemmie called over her shoulder.

Mrs Drago smiled indulgently. "You haven't forgotten what your mother taught you, Clemmie! I know my husband will be most delighted to hear you play. Carry on for five minutes, my dear."

Ruth Owen had the strange feeling that someone else was listening in to this conversation. "I must apologise, she's rather headstrong," she said evenly.

Mrs Drago passed her a delicate cup and saucer, then another to Daisy.

"Bluebirds!" Daisy exclaimed. "That's strange: we saw just such a pretty set only recently – 'for happiness' our hostess then informed us, didn't she, Ruth?" She looked beseechingly at Ruth who was so quiet today.

"A good choice then by Polly!" Mrs Drago smiled. "Now tell me, surely you have a young man, Daisy? Don't be offended for I am an incurable romantic—"

"Allow her to keep her secrets, eh?" Ruth forced a lightness to her voice she certainly did not feel. "You know how it is – when you are seventeen . . ." Immediately, she regretted saying that.

"I can tell that *you* certainly recall being that age," Mrs Drago returned.

Daisy, puzzled, looked from one to the other.

Clemmie abandoned the piano to drink her tea and to select a plateful of cakes. Both Ruth and Daisy found the offerings a little too sweet, like Mrs Drago; they had to avert their eyes from the chocolate smears on her face as she ate four truffles greedily, in swift succession.

Drago appeared suddenly via the French doors, expressing his pleasure at their presence. "Why did you not call me in from the garden before, Eluned? I am surprised, but most happy to see you, Ruth Owen, with your daughters. Shall I ring for another cup, my dear?"

He sat alongside Ruth Owen in a large armchair, which was obviously kept for his exclusive use, and joined them at their tea.

"I would have had a new dress on today," Clemmie babbled on. "Ruth bought the material but Daisy had a headache – you've been too polite to mention her black eye, haven't you? She usually does all our sewing, you see, but she was injured doing an act of *bravery*, that's what Alun said—"

"Ah, *Alun*," Mr Drago observed, listening with obvious interest.

"Anyway," Clemmie continued, "she's promised to make my dress before we come for your party."

"So you enjoy sewing, Daisy, do you?" asked Eluned. "Then you might like to have some material I have had put by for many years: gauzy, fine stuff, again from my husband's stay in India."

"Thank you, that is very kind of you . . ."

Mrs Drago pulled the bell rope. "Mari, my dear, take the ladies up to the Painted Room and show them that material in the chest of drawers. You may select whatever you like for I shall never use it now. All those years ago, when Raoul talked of you, I rather fancied I might parcel it up and send it to *you*, Ruth, to make up and wear on the concert platform. I have already far exceeded the years the specialists decreed to be my lot!" The girlish laugh dispelled the solemnity of this.

The Painted Room was up two flights of stairs at the very end of the house. Mari unlocked the door with the key attached to her belt. "We don't use this room – please don't look at the dust!" She crossed to the windows and pulled the curtains by their twisted cords.

Ruth did not notice the dust. She drew in her breath sharply at the beauty of the elegant furniture, painted ivory with pictures on the panels, circled in gilt. Cherubs they were, she discovered on closer inspection, round dimpled and rosy, seated on snowy clouds in azure skies, their naked skin painted so realistically she felt sure they must be warm to the touch. There was the great bed, clothed in matching satin with tassels sweeping the ground; vast wardrobes with ornate brass handles; a toilette set on the washstand decorated with cherub heads haloed in fluffy yellow curls; a dressing-table laid out with mother-of-pearl backed brushes and combs, silver scent bottles – but it was a companion chest of drawers to which their attention was directed.

Drawer after drawer was pulled open for their inspection. Layers of brittle tissue were carefully unfolded to reveal lengths of diaphanous material in rainbow colours, often threaded through with silver or gold. The stuff was light to examine, so Ruth and Daisy carried it to the window to admire the colours by daylight.

"Take her at her word, ladies. 'Tis such a shame all this is just shut away: it's no weight so have all you fancy." Mari's voice was wistful.

"Wouldn't you like a length too, Mari?" Daisy asked impulsively.

"Oh, she wouldn't let *me* have it, miss: she must have her reasons for giving it to *you*!" Mari replied enigmatically.

Ruth Owen thought, Oh, she has. *I* know. And I intend to take what was meant for *me*, all those years ago.

Daisy was excited by all the possibilities. "I'll be able to sew you a really dazzling dress for the celebration, Ruth!"

Mari was thrilled at their reaction. She piled the chosen material on the bed to rewrap in tissue. "This room, all this furniture," she confided, "it was a wedding present from Mr Drago's parents when they took over the house. But I hear they never slept in here, never used this bed." She gave a daring little bounce on it, for she was quite young still and full of suppressed liveliness. "They've always had separate rooms because of m'lady's health." She gave a saucy wink.

They carried their bounty downstairs. Clemmie was back at the piano with Drago seated beside her on the long stool, guiding her hands gently over the keys. They were totally absorbed. Ruth bit her lip at the sight.

"Your young daughter should be encouraged and my husband is the finest teacher she could have," Mrs Drago told Ruth. "Oh good, you both have a nice armful, I can see. Mari, go and wrap it all up in brown paper and tie it nicely for carrying, if you please."

"Thank you," Ruth said evenly. "We appreciate your generosity. I'm afraid however that we will not be staying anywhere long enough for the next few months for Clemmie to have regular piano lessons."

"We shall see," Eluned Drago said firmly. Then, "Yes, what is it, Mari?" she asked as the maid returned quickly.

"Mr Barley is here, Mrs Drago. He says he won't come in if you don't mind, for he has Miss Barley's little dog with him. He would be grateful, he says, if the ladies could be ready to leave soon."

Clemmie was disgruntled but mollified by the gift of a book of music for beginners from her new tutor.

"I'm afraid I cannot tell your husband to join us, regardless," Mrs Drago said, apparently regretfully. "The least trace of animal hair" – she sighed dramatically – "would cause severe problems with my breathing . . . Now, shall we see you all again before our great celebration? I meant it, you know: Clemmie must have regular tuition."

"She has music in her blood," Drago stated quietly. "Not surprising, given her parentage."

Ruth challenged Drago with a little flash of her eyes. He raised his hand slightly in mock submission. He knows how I feel about him, she thought, that nothing has changed between us.

"Come on, Clemmie, say goodbye and thank you, for we are keeping your father waiting."

"Thank you for the tea – and the cakes!" Clemmie said. "And don't worry, I'll wheedle round Ruth to let me come and practise on your piano again soon!"

"I'm sure you will." Drago smiled at her. "You are as determined as I remember your mother was when she was young."

They walked back to *Pili Pala* across the lush meadows, encouraging Clemmie to run ahead with the dog. They had not moored up outside the house on this occasion, but on the other side, on the way to Ivor's.

"I was thankful you came when you did," Ruth said to Bay when the girls had walked the plank but she and Bay were still on the towpath.

"I guessed that you might be . . . Any problems, Ruth?"

"No . . . except, well, they both made rather a fuss of Clemmie – she doesn't need much encouragement as you know. She wants to visit there again soon; Drago wants to teach her piano – he says she has a definite talent—"

"How do you feel about that?"

"I'm not sure. It would be such an opportunity . . . he . . . is an inspired teacher. When I realised it was he who had paid for all those extra lessons when I was at school I was bitter. I told Rachel that I didn't know how she could have accepted such charity. She said he had insisted. Should I deny Clemmie her chance? I really want to put the past behind me, but it's so much harder than I imagined." Her eyes suddenly blurred with tears. "We went into a special room there today. They call it 'the Painted Room' – it was so beautiful, but like a mausoleum, full of buried hopes and desires . . ." She shivered violently. "Fetch Old William, will you? High time we moved on, I think."

Sixteen

"Bacon sandwiches seemed the easiest thing to do," Daisy said, coming up on deck with a plateful for the workers. She saw that Bay was distancing himself from his family this morning, walking silently ahead with the horse.

"Bay!" Ruth Owen called. "Shall I aim your breakfast at you or shall we tie up for ten minutes?" He slackened his stride. They were approaching the place where Daisy had taken her bathe the first morning, when she had met Alun. She had only managed strip-washes since, she thought ruefully.

"Ruth, can't we stop here for half an hour?" she asked on impulse. "I'm longing to take another dip and I won't forget the towel this time! I've left the tea brewing. I just want to clear my head as much as anything."

"I can do with another cup of tea and I'm sure Bay could too. Mind you, it looks like rain at any moment so you'd better hurry, or you won't need to plunge into the river to get wet."

"You always understand – thanks!"

"I wanted an egg," Clemmie grumbled, picking out the fat from her sandwich and throwing it down for Pompom. She seemed out of sorts this morning. Too many sickly cakes at the Dragos' was the likely explanation.

"We forgot to ask Alun for eggs," Daisy told her.

"Then I'm going back to bed!" Clemmie decided.

"Oh, I thought you might like to come down to the river with me?"

"No!"

"Then go back to bed!" Daisy and Ruth Owen said simultaneously; then they looked at each other and grinned.

Bay duly halted the horse and Daisy and Pompom went down to the rim of the river.

To her disappointment she found that someone else had had the same idea. There was an untidy pile of clothes, concealing other things – for instance Daisy could glimpse the corner of a drum.

"The One Man Band, I reckon," she told Pompom. She was wondering whether to venture in further along when she remembered Alun's warning. Then she spotted the boy swimming towards her from the far side.

"Hey!" he shouted. "I didn't get a chance to thank you for sticking up for me the other day!" He had a powerful stroke, thrusting his lean brown arms over and under the water.

Daisy, in consternation, went to back away, for it was obvious that The One Man Band was as naked as the day he was born. As he heaved himself up on to the bank, she seemed to be frozen to the spot. Her grandmother's strictures on modesty were still deep-rooted.

"Ain't you comin' in?" he asked cheerfully. "Bit of a shock at first but it's real good to get clean."

Daisy, closing her eyes, threw the towel at him.

"I don't mind you lookin'," he said, standing there, towel in hand and making no attempt to cover up, "for ain't we the same? Open your eyes, miss, an' you'll see."

"You're a *girl*!" Daisy accused The One Man Band. "Fancy alarming me like that!" The slim, dark-honey-coloured body displayed before her unashamedly had definite budding breasts and rounded hips.

"'Course I am. Jem – Jemima, you see. It's a bit safer to be a boy when you're on your own like, though I don't know how much longer I can keep it up now I've turned fourteen, miss."

"Just you dry yourself and get dressed at once!" Daisy ordered, as if the girl was Clemmie. "I must just wash my feet; then you can come back with me to our boat. Are you hungry? There's a bacon sandwich waiting and there's bound to be tea still in the pot. D'you really wander round the country all on your own, Jem?" she asked.

"I do. I can usually wriggle me way out of trouble, like the day you saw me in town; I'm real sorry you got hit, you know. I hoped we'd meet up again – that feller, well, it wasn't wise I found out soon enough to be a *boy* like, the night he took me in so I come clean about bein' a girl . . . He told me to get out but he was so drunk he slept all night and I curled up by the front door – 'course I had nowhere else to go – and then I pinched his boots, to show him." Daisy saw that Jem was bare-footed once more. "He hadn't found out then, when he come roaring out, that I'd rifled his pockets too!"

Daisy couldn't bring herself to reproach the girl for that.

"Born in dockland," she told them as she wolfed down the sandwich and slurped the hot tea noisily from her saucer. "Me mam was a white girl; my pa, if you can call him that, for I never saw him, not once, was a seaman from the Gold Coast. Handsome devil, Mam said, even gave her his gold earrings, more'n she got from the rest of 'em."

Clemmie, naturally, had surfaced once more, hearing the interesting stranger. "Is that why you're that lovely colour?" she asked Jem.

As usual, the rest of the family sighed over Clemmie's frankness but The One Man Band was not offended in the least.

"'Course! All the colours of the rainbow our family, so my mam says – just like your sister's eye what she got in my defence like."

"How'd you come to be a One Man Band?" Clemmie wanted to know next. Well, the rest of them were dying to hear the answer to that one too.

"Any more grub? I'm starvin'! Thanks – wait 'til I've swallowed me mouthful. Well, I got a good mam, you know – we never went short in our house we didn't, three brothers younger'n me and not a pa between us. Alf my next brother is the lightest; well, his pa was a Chinese cook, Mam said. So Alf got to cook our supper at nights – use your gifts, Mam says. But when I was eleven, Mam brought a new man home and, unlike them others, he stayed. Said he'd shape us lot up, he did, and he took off his belt to the boys to prove it. Mam wouldn't let him touch me . . . Time I went out to work, he said when I was twelve: Mam could show me the ropes. She didn't want none of that for me, bless her soul, for her life ain't been no bed of roses. So she slipped me some money and told me to go and make something of meself and to steer clear of what she'd had to do, to look after us."

Daisy looked apprehensively at Ruth Owen and Bay cleared his throat warningly.

"Oh, don't worry, I won't go into no details, I was young and innercent myself once," Jem assured them, knowing they meant she must not be too explicit in front of Clemmie. "Well, my luck was good, I met up with some buskers outside the music hall and I started collecting the pennies for The One Man Band. He was a kind little old man and his chest rattled like a money box. He taught me all I know about busking, he kept the wolves from the door, if you get me, and when he died I inherited his gear like. I started along the canal here a year or so ago and I must say I like it."

"Nice in the summer," Ruth agreed, "but however d'you manage in the winter? Surely you don't sleep out in the open then?"

"You know the lime kilns? Well, I join up with all the old tramps in sleeping near 'em; the warmth is quite blissful and if it rains or snows we covers ourselves with sacks and old coats and that – you won't find *us* frozen and stiff, while the kilns are still firin'."

Clemmie was quite enchanted. "I love your hair, Jem – can I feel it?"

"'Course you can!" Jem's wide grin was reminiscent of Eli's, Daisy thought, only *she* displayed a marvellous set of strong white teeth, likely inherited from her generous Pa. She bent her head to Clemmie's touch as the girl gently pulled the springy, tight short curls. "Have to keep it short – s'easier, specially when I'm s'posed to be a lad; anyway I like to avoid any visitors."

"Lice, d'you mean?" Clemmie asked. "We all caught them in a boarding house once – remember, Ruth and Daisy? Daisy treated us all with paraffin and a horrid steely comb, only

Bay said he wasn't having his head done, because nothing would dare crawl on *him* . . ."

Jem looked boldly at Bay, seeing the look of horror on his face at the memory.

"I reckon your Pa's right," she observed. "He's far too lordly-like!"

"Clemmie," Daisy put in quickly, "you're making me itch. I'm sure I shall start scratching in a moment."

"So will I," agreed Ruth Owen. "Look, Jem, would you like a ride along with us – are you going our way?"

"If I wasn't, well, I am now! I can earn my passage, you know. I can steer or walk the horse, and I'll help the gentleman cast off when you're ready like."

As Bay beat a hasty retreat, Jem promptly followed him up the steps.

"We'll make her a bunk up under ours, shall we?" Daisy asked Ruth when they went on deck. "And there's those boots in the trunk which I had when I first came to you, the ones we were saving for Clem – she's got such small feet, I'm sure they'd fit. Oh, I *do* like her, don't you, Ruth? She's so young and vulnerable to be all on her own like that. D'you think Bay'll object?"

"I don't think he will, Daisy darling," Ruth surmised, waving blithely at her husband to start walking as Jem jumped aboard. "Haven't you noticed the difference in him since he stopped drinking? He hasn't said so, but I do feel he means to stick to it, if he can."

The soft rain began to fall as they moved easily down the canal.

"That ring round the moon last night," Daisy mused, "it must have meant rain was on the way."

"Oh, we have a lot of rain in Wales," Ruth told her, "that's why the land in the valleys is so green and fertile."

They bought a rabbit from a furtive poacher which the versatile Jem skinned and jointed at their next stop along the bank.

"She's going to be an asset," Bay actually remarked, watching her at this task. "I gather she's been immersed this morning but, well, can't you do something about her *clothes*? They . . . *smell*, Ruth."

"I'll root through the trunk," Daisy offered. "I want to start on the sewing soon. I've had an idea for that material from the Painted Room."

Jem had too-keen hearing. "I'll keep my trousers on," she called cheerfully, " 'til I've legged it through the tunnel!"

When they were safely through and in sight of the wharf, looking forward to seeing Ivor and Annie again, Daisy duly delved for the kid boots, the last pair her grandmother had bought her, grumbling over the expense but buying the best, as always, which were still in their linen draw-string bag. They were as soft and supple as ever, she thought, pleased.

"Try these, Jem," she said to their new friend.

Ruth Owen shook out her second-best blue cotton dress, the one with the pin-tucks on the bodice and tiny pearl buttons on the tight cuffs. "Here," she offered generously, "anything of Daisy's would be too long for you – you being a little pippin like me, eh?"

Clean drawers and a shift they provided for Jem, even though they were desperately short in the under-garment department themselves. The lean years had certainly taken their toll.

"Don't none of you throw away me One Man Band clothes, mind," Jem instructed. She smoothed the skirt down. "I'm a *girl* again!"

"You look so pretty – blue is your colour," Daisy said warmly. "We'll hang your old things out for a good airing, but not today, even though it's stopped raining, for folk won't approve of that on the Sabbath."

Jem did a little jig in the boots. They hadn't any stockings to spare but she didn't care. "Don't feel like boots at all – so soft and comfy!"

Her voice was attractively husky which prompted Daisy to ask, "Can you sing, Jem?"

" 'Course I can!" and she promptly gave them a demonstration. 'The Last Rose of Summer' she sang soulfully, if not quite as it was composed. Bay's calls for assistance went unheeded.

"The *first* rose more like," Clemmie said. "Oh, you'd better get to the steering, Ruth, for look, we're coming up to the wharf and I just heard Bay yell for someone to lead Old William." The horse had been ambling obediently on his own for the last ten minutes.

It was all hands on deck. They were contrite at neglecting their duties whilst dressing up Jem, and Bay was in a huff.

Ivor was off duty, being a pillar of the chapel, but his assistant had been warned of their imminent arrival and he hastened out to assist them to the side mooring reserved for *Pili Pala* near the wharf buildings.

"You'll have Sunday dinner with us, won't you?" Ivor beamed. "Annie always does plenty of vegetables in case we have unexpected guests and today the visiting preacher will also be with us."

"We had a rabbit pie in mind," Ruth Owen told him, "but I must admit we haven't got around to cooking it! We'd love to accept your invitation, Ivor, though you'll see we are five today for we have a friend with us—"

"Ah, The One Man Band . . . I had my suspicions about you, my dear. Yes, of course you are welcome. Mind, I shall expect some of you to come with us to the evening service. The preacher is not to be missed – he does a rousing sermon."

Being someone of importance Ivor had a big solid house, with not only a separate dining room but a scullery, complete with a pump over the sink, a copper and a fine hip bath, at which Daisy glanced longingly, hanging on the wall. Even the privy she saw was protected by a covered way.

Annie was delighted to take them on a swift tour of inspection. She showed off her latest acquisition, a sewing machine. "No sewing on a Sunday, mind – I stick to that – but I'd be glad to let you try it out, Ruth."

"Daisy'll be the one for that, Annie," Ruth said ruefully. "We've costumes to sew for an engagement; it would be such a help, thank you."

"We've had an enquiry too, by the way, for you to sing," Annie remembered as she led the way into the dining room.

"Preacher's here and something's boiling dry on the stove,

Annie . . ." Ivor called out urgently, causing Annie to come over all fluttery and to rush out to see what was what.

Ivor had wound out the table and added the extra cutlery and napkins. A roast leg of lamb sat steaming on a serving plate, 'resting' while he sharpened the carving knife.

"Coo . . ." breathed the young One Man Band at the sight of this.

Bay was already seated at the table, conversing with the preacher.

"Reverend Dick!" exclaimed Clemmie as he sprang to his feet and their polite smiles broadened into recognition.

"You've met already?" Annie asked, relieved. "Oh good, then if you'll excuse me do sit and talk for a few moments while I finish up in the kitchen – fetch the warming plates, Ivor, there's my boyo, and start to carve, will you please?"

"How did you get here?" Ruth asked Dick.

"On horseback. Still the easiest form of transport for me; my legs seem too long for a bicycle though naturally, that needs no hay or water." He pulled out chairs for the ladies and Daisy found herself seated beside him. "Daisy – Miss Barley—"

"Daisy!"

"Mother and I were distressed to hear of your mishap—"

"Mr and Mrs Pentecost, from the shop, kindly passed on your concern and good wishes," she put in quickly. "I am perfectly well now, Dick, really. Have you met Jem?"

"Ah, the one you championed? Yes, we have met. You had a larger crowd outside the mission, one day, than we had inside, Jem! And you gave the impression then of being a young lad, rather than the demure young lady I now see before me."

Dick Bucktrout, Daisy thought, had the rather endearing habit of speaking seriously while his twinkling gaze belied his gravity. She had the distinct impression that he was not surprised at all to see them and that it was no coincidence that he was here. Eli no doubt had told him where *Pili Pala* was likely to be at rest today. If only *Alun* had joined them too!

107

Seventeen

As Ivor sliced meat generously on to the Royal Doulton plates, Ruth Owen and Annie appeared from the kitchen with the covered serving dishes, the brimming gravy boat and, of course, the fresh mint sauce.

Naturally, Dick said Grace, then they tackled the meal with undisguised enthusiasm. There was water to drink, crystal clear, pumped up straight from the well. Daisy felt the constriction of her waist band when her plate was empty but then Annie brought out, in triumph, a perfect golden crusted plum pie – "fruit bottled last year from our own tree". The fresh cream poured over the generous wedges of pie was almost too much.

It was a relief to go out into the garden, to sit and drink dark coffee from tiny cups, and to relax. Bay and Ivor were soon nodding off.

"I ought to go back to the boat to let Pom stretch her legs, she's been cooped up long enough," Daisy said at last.

"I'd come for a walk with you, only I'm too full," Clemmie sighed.

"So am I," said Jem complacently.

"And I'm going to do the washing up with Annie; tired and replete as you are, you two, you can help," Ruth Owen told Clemmie and Jem. Daisy was pleased to see that Jem was already treated as one of the family.

"That leaves me, I think," Dick remarked, glancing at the snoozing older men. "I'll accompany Daisy, shall I, to see that she doesn't get into any more scrapes!"

He waited while Daisy went aboard, then brought Pom out on her leash. The little dog was more wary of this stranger than she had been of Alun, Daisy thought, and, perversely, this satisfied her. They walked along at a fair pace for his strides were so lengthy that Daisy had to hurry to keep up. They walked up to the meadows behind the wharf so that Pompom could be released when Daisy was sure that there were no other dogs lurking about, for there were quite a dozen other narrowboats moored below and judging by the noise most of them had dogs.

"I was preaching at Brynbach this morning," he told Daisy as they paused to watch Pompom rolling in ecstasy in what Daisy thought ruefully was probably something rather nasty. "I met a relative of yours," he continued, "Miss Megan Hughes. I asked after your whereabouts and she told me I should probably find you already here—"

So it was Meg who was keen to get them together, not Eli, after all. "That was kind of her," she interrupted, and her tone caused him to glance at her sharply but he did not comment on her reaction immediately.

"Miss Hughes invited me back for refreshment before I rode on; I met her brother, Alun, and her mother. I have not been on this circuit long," he went on, watching Daisy's face, "so it was the first time I had made the family's acquaintance. There is a problem, eh, Daisy, between you and Megan Hughes?"

The unexpected question took her by surprise, caused her to stumble over her reply. "Well, yes, I suppose so, Dick. You see, she doesn't approve of my friendship, even though we've only just met, with her brother."

"She is jealous, poor soul," Dick stated, showing the compassion Daisy could not feel. "I can understand that, if not condone it, for it is a very human failing." He offered his arm. "Quite a climb ahead of you, Daisy, but the view should be worth it."

She had the strange feeling that he meant something else altogether by this, even if she could not fathom what. Perhaps if she had met him before she fell so suddenly, headlong in love with Alun she might well have found herself responding to Dick's evident interest in her company, she thought, blushing so hotly that Dick asked, concerned, if she was winded and would like to rest?

Back at the house Ivor told them of a retirement party which the local school governors, of whom he was proud to be one, had planned for the village schoolmistress, who had spent her entire working life at the little school. "We would very much like The Singing Barleys to entertain the children and the parents, the old pupils, at a picnic tea next Saturday; the reward would not be much, you'll understand but I am sure you would enjoy yourselves and hopefully, if the good weather returns there will strawberries ripe enough to serve as a special treat. A wagon or two will take us all to the picnic place where there will be games for the children – the singing, I suggest, could come after the tea? I calculated that you will be down to the end of the canal and back again by then – what d'you think?"

"Splendid idea. We accept of course," Bay said for them all.

As if they hadn't eaten enough at lunchtime, Annie served up a gargantuan tea. It was drizzling with rain again so they abandoned the plan to eat this in the garden.

"Just a cup of tea for me; I am sorry to turn down such a selection," Dick apologised, "but I find it is unwise to orate on a full stomach—"

"The same applies to singing," Daisy put in. "*We* won't have to overdo the picnic!"

"It doesn't apply to The One Man Band!" Jem was eager to consume all that was on offer.

"You'd like Mrs Drago's cakes," Clemmie told her. "Do *you* know her, Uncle Ivor, Auntie Annie?"

"I can't say we have ever met. She is a recluse, due to bad health we understand," Ivor said evenly.

"She wears trousers!" Clem said. "No, not like yours, Jem! Hers are *ladies'* trousers."

"You could study some local history while we're here, Clem." Daisy had observed the fleeting agitation on Ruth's face and thought it best to turn the conversation. "Dick was telling me what he knows about the limestone quarries and how that long train road – eight miles, didn't you say Dick? – was constructed over a century ago."

"Here's a local song for you," Ivor said, "about a famous engine made by the man we call 'Crosha' Bailey – The Old Cymro, it was called, The Old Welshman to you! The engine carried the pit wood to the colleries."

He hardly needed urging to rise to his feet and to sing:

"Crosha Bailey made an engine
Which was puffing and ablowing.
Did you ever see such a thing before?

"When it stopped it wouldn't start,
When it started it wouldn't stop.
Did you ever see such a thing before?

"For according to her power
She could do four miles an hour.
Did you ever see such a thing before?"

The spontaneous applause amused and pleased Ivor. "Oh, I'll remember some more of the old ditties no doubt – maybe you could learn one or two for the party? Those that are suitable for youthful ears that is!"

"I must go," Dick said, "to the chapel to collect my thoughts for the sermon. Who will be coming, apart from Ivor and Annie?" He looked directly at Daisy.

"I will," said Ruth Owen, "and Bay, I hope? Clemmie? And Daisy?"

"Yes," they all said, even Bay.

"Jemima?" Dick asked.

The One Man Band looked doubtful. "I fancy a good long rest now I'm sure of me bed for the night. I can look after the boat and the dog for you – I won't touch nothing, I promise."

Ruth Owen hesitated for a split second only and Daisy willed her to agree. Their young protégée needed their trust; she hoped Bay wouldn't put his oar in.

111

"Thank you, Jem, that's kind of you. Can you spare another pillow, Annie dear?" Ruth Owen asked. "You've been so good already, I hesitate to ask."

"That's what family are for. Of course, and another blanket or so would be useful, eh?" Annie replied immediately.

If only Meg were as kind, Daisy thought.

The chapel was at the heart of the village. There were hooks for the men to hang their hats on inside the entrance; the usual simple rows of chairs; a railed gallery and a harmonium to the left of the altar steps. No fancy carving here but good mellow wood, lovingly polished by the faithful ladies who also made the brass lamp fittings sparkle. One whitewashed wall was illuminated with these words, painted exquisitely in blue and gold: 'His Mercy Is Everlasting'.

Daisy and Ruth were glad that Annie had tactfully lent them a Sunday bonnet apiece for they would surely have felt overdressed and conspicuous in the one town hat they each possessed.

Ivor had his duties to fulfil as an elder of the chapel, gravely handing out the books to those who did not carry their own worn bibles and prayer books. Daisy had in her hands her mother's prayerbook: she was unsure if the order of service would be the same, but she opened it anyway and was aware that Bay, on her left, was looking at the inscriptions. "Yes," she whispered, "this was your Anne's, my mother's, book," and she heard his catch of breath.

There were grand singers among the congregation, they soon discovered. Stirring hymns, ringing to the rafters. The many prayers were intoned devoutly and quietly with all, however difficult the task might be for some, attempting to kneel. For the first time she could recall, Daisy found herself in touch with her father as their hands met when they turned the flimsy pages of the shared book.

When Dick rose and came forward to preach, she looked up and she fancied that he was speaking to her directly. The theme of his sermon was Truth. By the time he finished, the hush was broken by a tiny sigh which seemed to pass from one to the other along the packed rows of people.

The final hymn was clearly a favourite, written by the popular Fanny J. Crosby. There was much clearing of throats, then again the joyful singing.

(Refrain) *"Praise The Lord, Praise The Lord*
Let The Earth Hear His Voice!
Praise The Lord, Praise The Lord
Let The People Rejoice!
O Come To The Father Thro' Jesus The Son
And Give Him The Glory
Great Things He Hath Done."

Dick was to spend the night with Ivor and Annie, would ride back first thing in the morning. He said quietly to Daisy as they walked along together, which she suspected Bay had engineered, "I will willingly deliver a letter for you, Daisy, to Alun Hughes; it is on my way home . . . I'll call in at *Pili Pala* to say farewell; I can collect any message from you then."

She looked at him, startled. Here was another one who seemed to know what she was thinking. He had such a warm, nice smile, she thought. "Thank you, Dick," she said gravely, "I would appreciate that. Your sermon was quite . . . inspiring!" she added, meaning it.

Back on the boat they discovered Jem already asleep on the bunk they had rigged up below Daisy's and Clemmie's. The blue dress, Daisy saw, had been folded carefully and placed on the coil of rope. On her curly head Jem wore her cap o' bells which would hopefully not disturb her companions during the night. On the end of her bed was piled her musical paraphernalia, just as a child might put her toys. But the thing which made Daisy's throat constrict was the sight of Jem's feet, protruding from the blankets for the girl was sleeping in the precious boots.

Something stirred, another head peeped out from the coverings. As they all tiptoed past Jem to the cabin, for it was not yet eight o'clock, more like time for another cup of tea, not bed, they saw that Pompom was clutched in Jem's arms. The dog wriggled her way free; tail wagging furiously, she followed them.

"Really, Pom . . ." Daisy reproved her mildly.

"Your strays certainly hang together," Bay told her. Daisy felt all warm inside when she realised that his usual sarcasm was absent.

She sat on the trunk to write a letter, resting the paper on a book on her knee, while the others grouped round the table.

Dear Alun, Just to say I hope to see you again soon. We are with Ivor and Annie for a day or two, as we planned. Not too far for you to come, if you can manage to get time off?

It was hard to write a letter to someone you cared for, she discovered, when you were not alone. She mused over what Dick had said regarding Meg, then she dipped her pen in the ink again and wrote firmly:

Please tell Meg that I am sorry if she feels I have upset things for her at home. I would like to try to be her friend. I would like her to know that I would never encourage you to leave home until you feel the time is right because I care about Rachel's feelings, I care about hers too and I want her to be glad that we two care for each other so much even if it has all happened so fast, and I'm sure you feel just the same . . . Dick Bucktrout is very kind and has offered to bring this note to you on his return journey. It was his suggestion. So we have made another good friend! (And he will no doubt tell you about the latest member of our little band.)

Please, oh please make up with Meg, won't you?
All my love, always. Daisy.

"You've reminded me, Daisy – pass the pen and ink and paper when you've finished, will you?" Ruth Owen asked.

114

"I must write to Miss Prince and enclose the money we owe her."

Daisy sealed the letter inside the envelope before she could have second thoughts. She said, "It's the best idea you ever had, Ruth, coming here, being on *Pili Pala*, even though it seemed like the last resort when we left poor Miss Prince in the lurch." And she and Ruth exchanged that special look as she tucked the letter in her bodice, fancifully, she thought, next to her heart.

Eighteen

R uth Owen and the girls joined Annie on her washing day.
"Bring all your linen!" she told them generously.

"Why don't you go with Bay to Ivor's office, Clemmie?"
Ruth suggested when Clemmie began to fidget. "You should be
able to write a splendid composition if you keep your eyes and
ears open – so much going on here on such a busy wharf."

"All right. I suppose so," Clemmie agreed.

"Tell your father I said so," Ruth instructed, "for otherwise
he'll just laze around on *Pili Pala*. However, remind him to
make sure that Pom is shut away, won't you?"

"I will!"

Now, they tossed their whites and fast-coloureds into the
sudsy bubbling water in the copper and chattered like magpies
as they worked. Ruth sang out, "I'm really enjoying doing
all this washing for once, aren't you girls?" And she rubbed
vigorously at Bay's collars on the dolly board.

She observed that Daisy was quiet again today. Dreaming
away, no doubt of Alun, she imagined fondly. Daisy stood
carefully washing their best silk blouses by hand. She had
seen Daisy passing that letter earlier to Dick and overheard
the softly spoken words: "I am going to try to put things right
with Meg, about me and Alun; you see, I *did* listen to what
you said yesterday."

"Good," he replied smiling. Yes, it certainly looked as if
Daisy had found a staunch ally in Dick but she hoped that he
wouldn't be hurt in future if Daisy chose Alun.

Jem sang too as she pegged out the long lines of billowing sheets, towels, voluminous nightshirts, lacy drawers and
petticoats.

116

"Cold meat and pickles, I'm afraid – that's all on washday," Annie's grin belied her apology. "Then we'll tackle that sewing and I'll show Daisy how my machine runs like magic along seans and hems; all you have to do is keep on turning with one hand, while you guide the material with the other."

It was Jem who came up with the bright idea of what to make with the rainbow material. "I used to love to see the Indian ladies what lived round our way, in their saris – one of them showed me how to arrange them, it's so simple when you know how and it will save all that cutting out – shall I show you?" And she did. At the end of the afternoon they were all gracefully attired having called Clemmie back for the grand trying-on. They formed a mutal admiration society.

"Of course" – Daisy sounded rueful – "you dark-haired ones look just right in these gorgeous colours – I just look as if I'm dressed up to match, with my sandy hair!"

"*Red* sand, Daisy!" Clemmie reflected.

"I didn't realise you were going to dress me up too," Annie said, pleased. "I must admit I feel quite – unrestrained? – without those wretched stays but, there, what can I do, with a figure like mine?" She looked at her reflection sideways on in the cheval mirror.

Her sister-in-law gave her a hug. "You look beautiful, Annie! It's our way of saying thank you for all you've done for us since we came. Wait 'til Ivor sees you, eh?"

"Those drapes hide all the fatty bits, Auntie Annie, really they do," Clemmie added helpfully and Annie, being Annie, did not take exception.

"Is this one really for *me*?" asked Jem. "I really don't mind if it isn't," she added quickly, "for where could I fasten all the things for The One Man Band?"

Ruth Owen, knowing she was on sure ground, even though she hadn't yet discussed it with the family, told her, "We are hoping you'll be a Singing Barley now and then, Jem – particularly at a special celebration—"

"A Ruby Wedding – that's forty years!" Clemmie interrupted. "At the Dragos', they live in a great big house with hundreds of steps and a huge, great *piano* . . ." She bestowed upon her mother a most reproachful glance. "You must have seen the house when you go up and down the canal, Jem."

Annie looked at Ruth. She gave a little shrug. "Bay said we should accept the invitation, Annie. At first I thought, No! but – it was all so long ago, wasn't it, and we can, of course, do with the money." Annie, being around at that time, knew all the ins and outs of the situation.

"She's a mischief maker," she stated. "Mrs Drago. But it won't hurt to entertain there, as the others will be with you, I reckon."

Jem was thinking, obviously, about being a sort of Barley for she said suddenly, "I can't promise nothing. I'm The One Man Band, you see."

Jem would hate to lose her independence, Ruth appreciated that.

Then Jem added, "Still, I guess I might be there!"

"You can keep the sari, whatever you decide, can't she?" Daisy asked.

"Of course she can! Look, we must get changed quickly then tidy up all this mess for Annie, or Ivor will have a fit when he comes up to bed, eh, Annie, and sees what we've been up to in your bedroom!"

"He might, if I'm still wearing this!" Annie sighed, but her eyes were so bright as she looked at herself again in the mirror, that Ruth knew that Annie intended to parade for Ivor, all the same.

"Please listen, Meg," Alun pleaded, when Rachel was in bed and they were tidying the living room, before retiring themselves. He withdrew Daisy's letter from his pocket.

Meg turned to face him. "Oh, you're speaking to me again then," she said, so bitterly that he winced, for he loved his sister despite her paddies. Her eyes were red-rimmed, looked small and sore as if she had done much sobbing, yet he had not seen or heard it.

"I never stopped speaking to you; you just refused to listen. Meg, this is a letter from Daisy: look, I can't tell you why it is so, but we both know that we are meant, one for the other – we just *do*, that's all." It was perhaps tactless that he chose to add: "You would understand, Meg, if that had happened to you."

"How kind you are, Alun," she said coldly.

"It's not her fault," he continued urgently, for he was determined that his sister should hear him out, accept that he was a man now, with strong feelings, not her little brother still. "This . . . *thing*, between you and Ruth Owen. I don't understand it, I really don't. You must know it upsets Mam, and you love *her* as I do – as Ruth still does! – or you wouldn't care for her so kindly. Meg, I want you to read this letter – I insist – even though you may think certain parts of it are private – please, Meg."

She took the letter from his outstretched hand. When she had finished reading, she still stood there silently, the letter clenched against her chest. Alun felt pity for her. Oh, of course it was right to say she loved their mother and until now had borne the burden of caring for her, of working a full day as well, admirably. But, he thought sadly, Meg deserved to find that special person who would love her, for he knew that she must envisage a lonely life when the time came for him to leave, as he knew he would when Rachel was gone. The doctor had given his verdict following his last visit. Rachel was weakening perceptibly, her heart was not strong, they must prepare themselves for the worst, at any time. He suspected that Rachel knew. Wasn't it fate that had brought Ruth Owen back to them at this moment?

He said suddenly, as the silence continued, "Meg, am *I* something to do with why Ruth Owen left as she did – I sometimes wonder you know?" The fancy had been so strong since her return. He could not ask Rachel.

"Don't," she said quite quietly, having regained her composure. She handed the letter back at last. "Maybe this is the truth, Alun, or perhaps Ruth put her up to it . . . But I shan't try to stop you from seeing her again in future. If you want to go down to Ivor's tomorrow, when I get in from work, you may borrow my bicycle. But just remember, Alun, how young you both are; first love can make such fools of you! And don't expect me to change the way I feel regarding Ruth Owen, for I won't."

Clemmie sat quietly over her composition all afternoon. She had cramp in her writing hand and her fingers were more ink-stained than ever. She blotted the last paragraph and closed the book. "That's enough for today – here you are, Daisy – I learned an awful lot from Uncle Ivor, you know. 'Limestone was needed as flux in making iron,' he said, but I'm not too sure what flux is though . . ."

"Look it up in the dictionary, Clem."

"I've looked up quite enough for one day," she replied with feeling. "All those spellings—"

"You're a hard task-master, Daisy," Ruth put in, smiling. "Clear the table, eh, Clem – time for supper . . ."

"The tram road mechanism is really simple," Clemmie continued, gathering up her things reluctantly, "or so Uncle Ivor says. It sounds quite amazing to me. Did you know that four full trams, weighing about five tons, going down, make enough energy (mo-mentum, Uncle Ivor said, but I looked that one up already) to pull up four empty trams? The links of the chain which connects them runs round a greasy turntable at the top. And six full trams going down can pull up four – or was it three?"

"Arithmetic too. More than just a history lesson! That's good," Daisy observed.

They had rabbit stew for supper – well, as Jem remarked, "That bunny's been hanging around quite long enough – too long by tomorrer!" so Daisy said why didn't Jem cook it, having more culinary expertise than she had.

They were crowded round the table when Daisy glanced out of the window on the towpath side and remarked rather too casually, "Oh, here's Alun. I wonder if he's eaten yet?"

Clemmie leapt up to open the door. "We've got some left for you, Alun, rabbit stew that is; Jem made it – she's The One Man Band, you know, who Daisy saved and got a black eye over – only Jem's a One Girl Band really – Jem, this is Alun."

Jem grinned. "Pleased to meet you. I know all about you,

from Clemmie. I'll squeeze up, then you can fit in next to Daisy. Clem tells me you two are walking out together."

"You gossip too much, Clementina!" Bay said quite sharply.

Daisy knew intuitively that he would rather it was Dick who had come specially to see her. Yet she did not realise that her father liked Alun well enough but could foresee future complications if the relationship flourished.

"We're moving on tomorrow, I'm so glad you could come this evening," Daisy told Alun, when at last they managed to snatch some precious time on their own on deck while the others, at Clemmie's insistence, played Old Maid with a well-worn pack of cards they had discovered in the dresser drawer. "We'll wash up," Daisy had offered.

He dried the last dish and poured the washing up water over the side of the boat. Daisy hung out the dish-rag to dry. Then they sat close, but not so close that Bay, who had been watching them all over supper, could have objected if he had come up the steps unexpectedly, which they rather suspected he might.

"I showed Meg your letter," he told her, stroking Pom's ears as she nestled in Daisy's lap.

"Good."

"She says she won't stop me from seeing you again." He brushed a tendril of hair which was clinging to her moist lips and she could tell that he longed to kiss her. But was this the time or place? "We should be young and carefree, Daisy, at our age," he told her tenderly.

"I've always had to be so sensible. Ruth Owen has always depended on me, for you can remember, no doubt, how impulsive she is, bless her, and right from the start, when I was hardly older than Clemmie is now, Bay expected me to behave like an adult. I had to look after Clem while they were on stage, in the early days – later I became her teacher. It was a great effort to stay a few learning steps ahead, I can tell you, for you can see how bright and precocious she is! Surely she takes after Ruth? Then I was one of The Singing Barleys myself, all of a sudden, it seemed."

"I missed out on being young too, caring for my Mam, much as I love her," he said simply.

Despite the proximity of the neighbouring boats, Daisy leaned towards him impulsively and their lips met in a brief kiss. Then she looked up at him, her eyes shining. "We'll wait for each other, won't we, Alun?"

"If we are ever parted, we will be together in the end," he promised.

"Why did you say that?"

"I don't really know."

"It sounded, well, prophetic," she told him, and her eyes were clouded now.

It was his turn to kiss the doubts away. The surprised dog slid from her lap as she wound her arms round his neck.

Only Jem glimpsed them as she peeped round the door, which she then firmly closed.

"I hope to see you at the school party," Alun said in parting, to them all. "For wasn't I a pupil there myself? Mind you, old Ivor was there when Miss Harrington was still quite a young teacher!"

They watched as his bicycle disappeared from view along the towpath. Ruth Owen slipped her arm through Daisy's. "You look so pretty with those flushed cheeks!"

She knows I've been well and truly kissed, Daisy thought.

"I'm looking forward to that celebration much more than the other one at Ty-Gyda-Cerded," reflected Ruth.

"Guess what, Daisy," Clem said. "Jem was the old maid."

"I don't care," Jem returned, laughing. "I enjoyed the game anyway. And if Daisy'd been playing, well, *she'd* never have drawn that card!"

Nineteen

The bottom end of the canal was even more industrial than the top end. They came to a great wharf, teeming with activity and boats of all kinds. Smoke billowed from towering chimneys and an acrid smell pervaded the atmosphere. The water in the canal really was as black as pitch here. There was *The Molly Kelly*, a welcome sight, taking on coal: but they merely received a distracted "Hello!" from Juniper and Rose.

When they had been allotted their mooring, paid their dues, seen to Old William, exercised the dog, Ruth Owen was ready to take them into town. "Not nearly as gloomy as it seems from here, but not as salubrious as the top town either," she informed her family cheerfully. "Are you coming with us, Jem?"

She shook her head. "I reckon I'll tidy up here if you don't mind. If I feel like coming out later, well, I'll lock up and put the key under the bucket like you showed me." Jem had her own plans obviously.

"When we've done the shopping," Ruth Owen said, "we might perhaps go to the park to see if the brass band is playing. We'll bring something back for supper."

"I'll see you all later then," Jem said, waving them away with a smile.

Later, Jem walked along the busy streets, familiar with the town, smiling at the gossiping women standing, arms akimbo at their open front doors, with little ones hanging on to their skirts, which reminded her of Mam, far away in Cardiff. When she observed a group of energetic lads kicking an inflated pig's bladder, which they had begged from the butcher to use as a football, memories were instantly conjured up of her own

123

young brothers. She missed them still. She hoped that Mam's man was not treating them too badly.

It was 'early doors' time at the theatre. Those who had already booked their tickets for the evening and paid for the privilege of entering before the crowd who already lined the pavement, swept past smugly. Prosperous shopkeepers and their wives, young dandies with lady friends hanging on to their arms: 'Good Family Entertainment' said the poster in the foyer. There would be no 'big names' appearing here, Jem knew, but plenty of local talent and a monopoly of singers. This was not the venue for risqué comedians, or leading ladies with a naughty gleam in their eye. Even Bay might not have thought it beneath his dignity to appear here with The Singing Barleys, Jem thought, for she'd soon got his mark, with a grin.

The buskers were part of the evening out for the crowd waiting to surge upwards to the gallery. There were two tonight, at the top end of the queue: a fiddler, solemnly drawing his bow across the strings, as his companion, a younger fellow, soulfully sang that powerful ballad 'I Dreamt That I Dwelt In Marble Halls'. The tenors in the crowd sang along loudly with this, exacting their own applause. At the stragglers' end, The One Man Band endeavoured to attract attention to herself. One or two obligingly sang along:

> *"I love new friends, but still give me*
> *The dear, dear friends of old . . ."*

They were moving along now, jostling one and another; only a few pennies lay scattered at Jem's feet.

Even as she stopped to scoop them up, a heavy hand jerked her upright again, by her shoulder. "Missed the dear, dear friends of old, did yer?" a harsh voice jeered.

Jem swung round and there was naked fear in her eyes.

"I was told you was often to be found 'ere," the stranger went on. He was a burly man, with a fleshy face, hard deepset eyes and a mouth like a rat-trap. "Yer man wants you back 'ome." His grip tightened like a vice. "You've bin on the loose for two years now – it's time you came and did yer duty by *her*.

124

Got another little 'un she has, mine this time, and she needs yer help on all counts. Yer just the age now—"

Jem struggled violently, panic stricken. She knew exactly what he meant by that. "Let me go, Albert!" she panted.

"Do as she says or I'll clobber you!" The tall woman crossed swiftly over the road and faced the bully, fists clenched, just as Daisy had done for Jem in the market.

He loosened his grasp, turned Jem to face her. "I got every right to appre'end her . . . *madam*," he said sarcastically to Juniper as Rose and Huw stood indecisively on the other side of the road still. "Tell 'er, Miss Jemima Rees, that I'm your stepfather – married your ma, din't I? Her mam wants her back, where she b'longs. She's still under age, under our 'thority. I'll be obliged if you will kindly see to yer own bus'ness."

"Is he telling the truth?" Juniper asked Jem, ignoring him.

She nodded, her dark eyes brimming with unshed tears. She wasn't going to give *him* the satisfaction of seeing her blub, she thought.

A horse and cart suddenly rounded the corner and Albert dragged his captive towards it. Her drum echoed hollowly and all the bells were protesting. He gave Jem a shove up into the cart, hauled himself smartly up after her, intent on pinning the girl down.

Juniper caught hold of the horse's bridle, ignoring the raised whip of the driver. "Who shall I tell? Know who might help you, lass?" she shouted to Jem.

The muffled reply was cut off by the rough hand clamped smartly over her mouth, but Juniper heard: "Reverend Dick—" before the whip descended on the horse's neck. The startled animal broke free from her grasp, veered round, the cart swaying wildly behind and clattering noisily down the road.

"Mam, look: she dropped this – she had it under her coat," Rose babbled, thrusting a newspaper parcel roughly tied with string at her mother. From a torn corner protruded a swatch of bright material.

"Never mind that – did you read the name on that cart?" demanded Juniper.

"I did!" Huw was glad he'd managed that, at least. His

mother-in-law would think he was a right coward but he'd been protecting his Rose. "Henry Stoop – Coal Merchant, Cardiff – Gantry Hill, I think."

"Good boy, Huw! Either of you know what she meant by that name she managed to yell?"

"Rev'rend Dick? One of them travelling preachers, Mam, seen him at our mission once or twice. Lives up the top end, I think. Mam, did you see the gal's boots – real kid, I reckon, white, didn't look right with them old clothes, eh? We seen her before too, 'member? Ain't she the one Daisy Barley tried to save from trouble – when you saw to her eye like? But I was foxed first, 'cos I thought *she* was a *he*!" Rose thought her mam was a marvel.

"So did I. Then I know by the way she bent for that money, poor thing. I see *that* was pinched while we was trying to help. Well, hurry you two, we'll go on to your Aunt Jules, as we intended, but we won't stay too long, then back to the boat to make ready to cast off real early in the mornin', we got a long haul ahead on us, if we're to find that travelling preacher at the end of it . . ."

They were naturally unaware of Jem's recent connection with their friends The Singing Barleys and because of the urgency of their mission, they would not now call in at *Pili Pala* this evening as they had planned.

"You are too trusting, Ruth," Bay told them when they realised that Jem had must have gone. "You'd better look and see what is missing."

"I can't believe she'd steal from us," Ruth said reproachfully. "Look in the trunk, Daisy – please prove me right!"

"Nothing touched by the look of it," Daisy reported, "but see, Ruth, here's your blue dress, neatly folded at the very top."

But it was Clemmie who realised that: "She's taken her sari!"

"We gave it to her," Ruth reminded them all. "The only other things she appears to have taken are her own old clothes and her musical instruments. If only you could speak," she said to Pompom, "you'd tell us if she was coming back, wouldn't you?" but Pom just nosed at her dish to remind Daisy that she wanted her dinner.

Much later they discovered Clemmie's slate, which she used for her sums, scrawled with the cryptic message: 'Gone Buskin''.

The One Man Band had made her bed. It was silly to worry about Jem, Ruth told them all, trying to believe it herself, for hadn't Jem coped on her own, against all the odds, for so long now? Young as she was, she was well aware of the dangers of her way of life.

When Clemmie said her prayers to Daisy, she held her tight as if she feared that her sister, too, might disappear. She murmured, "Please God, let Jem be safe and let us see her again soon."

The neat bunk made them think she just might be back. Bay hung out the lamp to guide her aboard.

"Goodnight, girls," Ruth said softly, after locking the door. She undressed swiftly and slid into the comfort of Bay's embrace. She dreamed, when she finally drifted into a troubled sleep, of little Jemima Rees dancing and laughing, vividly pretty in her rainbow dress.

For two days they waited at the bottom end for Jem to return. They would have been pleased and touched if they had known that Bay, who had gone up into town by himself the next morning, had made random enquiries regarding The One Man Band. However, as he described a girl, rather than a boy, he received no information at all. The one person who could have told him something was the scruffy youth who had grabbed the money poor Jem had been forced to abandon. He didn't intend to hand over what he considered a stroke of good fortune rather than a petty theft.

"We must turn around, go back, to make sure we are in good time for the school party," Ruth Owen decided. She looked at Daisy's worried face. "We'll probably meet Jem along the way, she possibly prefers to travel on her own ... I'm sure she won't let us down, Daisy, she seemed so thrilled to be a Singing Barley and to be wearing that lovely dress."

"I do hope you're right, Ruth . . ." Daisy sighed, "but I can't help having a bad feeling about all this."

"Cheer up," Ruth said softly, for her ears alone. "For won't you be seeing Alun again very soon?"

Twenty

They enjoyed the luxury, in turn, according to age – which meant that Clemmie had the privilege of being first and Bay last – of a bath in the privacy of Annie's scullery. The water was topped up generously for each bather from the bubbling copper. Annie's towels were thick and absorbent unlike the worn old ones they shared on *Pili Pala*.

It felt good, Clemmie thought, to put on the clean dress on top of the clean underwear Annie had thoughtfully provided.

"I kept these from Myfanwy, our daughter, Clemmie—"

"Where does she live, Auntie Annie? We haven't met her yet."

"Oh, she married at nineteen and went off to Canada with her husband. We've grandchildren we've never seen, more's the pity . . . You may just as well have all her petticoats and drawers!"

It was a pity, the grateful recipient considered, to hide all that frothy lace trimming under plain muslin.

"Don't you have other children, Auntie?"

"Not so blessed, my dear. But your uncle thinks a great deal of young Alun – *he's* like the son we never had."

Up in Annie's bedroom the female Singing Barleys combed out their locks, Daisy, as always, wincing over the tangles in her curls.

"Bite your lips and pinch your cheeks, girls, to add a little natural colour," Ruth Owen advised. "We don't want to look like painted ladies on this occasion, it would seem far too theatrical."

"We *are* theatrical – look, Ruth, I've drawn blood!" Clemmie moaned, having taken the advice 'to bite' rather too literally.

She dodged her mother's comb, only to be caught in a mist of scent as Annie sprayed them lavishly with something potent.

She was despatched to bang on the scullery door to remind her father that it was his turn for the bedroom and the dressing up, then they sat down to "await our chariot!" as Clemmie blithely remarked.

Ivor popped back to admire them all, to regret that he had to work that afternoon, and would be unable to join them until later.

"I just glimpsed Alun in the distance, peddling hard, Meg must be standing in for him, eh? Be ready, waiting outside for the wagonette at two-thirty sharp, mind."

Clemmie was filled with joyful anticipation. She was not disappointed. It was a covered wagon, drawn by one huge horse, with great hairy hooves, a plaited tail threaded through with scarlet ribbon, likewise his mane which patient fingers had coaxed into a myriad of tiny braids. The seating was on planks and once inside the brightness of the afternoon was obscured by the thick canvas overhead. Clemmie chose to sit by the opening so that she would not miss a thing during the ride.

"We are privileged to travel with the hierarchy," Ruth whispered when she saw who was already inside.

"What's hierarchy?" Clemmie asked, loudly of course.

There was laughter among the honoured guests already seated: the minister, the doctor and his wife and their three young children, the guest of honour, Miss Harrington, joined by Annie, naturally, as the wharfinger's spouse.

Clemmie thrust her hand possessively into Alun's – Daisy was on his other side and they were already whispering to each other. She strained her ears and heard Alun say, "I hope I'm not crushing your skirt, Daisy?"

He was, but Clemmie could tell that Daisy didn't care one little bit.

"Don't you think Clem looks pretty?" Daisy asked, well aware of her sister's disappointment at Alun's lack of attention. "Annie very kindly finished sewing her dress on the machine

130

while we were away and, I was right, that blue ribbon makes a perfect sash."

Alun turned to Clemmie, smiling. "Yes, you look very nice indeed, Clemmie – how like Ruth Owen you are!"

Clemmie beamed and squeezed his hand.

Along the village street they rumbled, past the row of shops, butcher, baker, post office and undertaker. The cottages were attached, each roof lower than its neighbour because of the gradient, with colour-washed walls, slated rooves and front doors opening directly on to the narrow pathway. The bunting which had been hung for the Old Queen's Jubilee recently had been left in place for the Empress of the School. There were cheers as the wagonette passed those crowded in the doorways.

"Little Old Queen Vic is Empress Over All," Clemmie aired her knowledge. "But she always looks so grumpy, doesn't she?"

They met up with two more conveyances outside the school: hay carts, crammed with children together with four large hampers for the feast. Joining the procession, to Clemmie's excitement – for weren't *they* leading? – were those old pupils who had come up in the world, in smart dog carts, gigs. Then more on safety bicycles and still more on foot, but all dressed up for the party.

They reached the parkland picnic area, opened to them on this special occasion by a local dignitary, a governor of the school, who seized his chance to give a long-winded speech of welcome. Miss Harrington, in rustling violet silk and a straw hat trimmed with a spray of flowers which Clemmie was tempted to touch because they looked so real, sat happily holding court under the spread of a cedar tree. She spread her bulk on a carved oak chair, "just like a real throne", as Clemmie remarked.

Children scampered everywhere, swinging from low branches, rolling on the grass, girls in white muslin like Clemmie, boys unbuttoning stiff collars and discarding stuffy jackets while their old teacher smiled and enjoyed her big day.

Clemmie, usually so confident, hovered on the periphery of the juvenile high spirits.

"*You* should be at school, making friends, rough and tumbling like that," Alun told her, and she knew he understood her longing.

Two youthful teachers were now rounding up the children, persuading them into sets of eight for the country dancing. A father stepped forward and tuned up his fiddle, a bigger lad blew a few uncertain notes on his mouth organ, then the dancing began. Clemmie sighed enviously, "Oh, I do wish I could join in!"

"I expect they've been practising for months," Ruth Owen said.

The children danced on and on, the boy with the mouth organ had to wipe his instrument on his sleeve more than once and the fiddler began to perspire profusely. Miss Harrington came to their rescue. She rose, led the clapping, thanked them all warmly, then suggested wisely, "Shall we have tea? Afterwards, I hear, we are to be entertained by some special guests!"

Sandwiches were consumed swiftly, great draughts of lemonade were gulped, sponge cakes were sliced, then came the 'oohs' and 'ahs' as the baskets of strawberries, picked by the Big House gardeners that morning, were uncovered. Jugs of cream were fetched from the cool dairy and the berries were counted out on to the plates piled on the garden tables.

Alun said, "*I* must have the biggest strawberry of all," and he lifted the monster by its green cap and dipped it deeply into the cream. "Here, Daisy, you have it!" And he put it to her lips.

Clemmie couldn't understand why they were looking at each other like that. "What about *me*?" she protested, having eaten her share in five minutes flat. Her fingers and mouth were stained with the scarlet juice.

Of course there were the speeches to be sat through, so The Singing Barleys had a chance to recover from all they had eaten, despite their avowed intention previously not to overindulge. There was respectful mention of Miss Harrington's unique service to the community, proud mention of two of her pupils who had made it to University, of the one who had become a scientist and of the other who was now headmaster of a grammar school.

"Here's Ivor," Annie whispered to Ruth Owen. "He has changed places with his assistant – Ivor knew he wanted to see his children in the dancing."

"Always kind our Ivor!" murmured Ruth in reply.

It was Ivor who referred to the rest of the past pupils here present: "Our dear Miss Harrington has, I know, taken just as much pleasure in seeing very nearly every one of her pupils turn into a good member of our community," he declared. Those who had poached a bit, not always lived up to the morals instilled by their worthy teacher, looked a trifle hot under the collar. But Miss Harrington beamed approvingly at them all.

A small girl, Clemmie's age, presented a large bunch of flowers with a curtsy, and the minister, as chairman of the governors, gravely handed over a sealed envelope.

"What's in it?" Clemmie's clear tones cut through the reverential silence as Miss Harrington opened the envelope.

"Shush!" Daisy admonished. "A cheque, I imagine."

More clapping, then at last The Singing Barleys were introduced.

With her parents, Clemmie leaned on the rail of the hay cart which had been trundled into the centre of the assembly. Daisy sat by herself on the tail board at the back, intent on fingering her guitar.

Towards the end of their repertoire, Ruth Owen sang unrehearsed the solo requests, for songs in Welsh.

"Let all the children sing too!" Clemmie shouted excitedly, and they needed no second bidding. Exuberantly, Clemmie led them in the song Ivor had taught her.

Miss Harrington wiped away happy tears. "I shall miss you all, oh so much, but I shall not be far away, you know, and I shall expect to have young hands knocking on my door most days after school . . ."

It was all over, too soon, but six o'clock was the time decreed.

"I can't stay," Alun told them regretfully, when they were

put down at the wharf. "I promised Meg and Mam I would be back for supper."

"Remember, we'll be at the Dragos' on the fifth," Ruth Owen reminded him quietly.

"Are you coming, Alun, to *that* party?" Clemmie asked.

"I haven't been invited, Clem, well I hardly expect that, but I shall see you all then, or hopefully, before."

"I wish I could go to school and make lots of friends and do that dancing . . ." Clemmie sighed, "but we never seem to stop anywhere long enough for that, do we, Daisy?"

"Wish very hard, Clem," she said solemnly. "Come September, when the new school year begins, maybe we'll be settled down, in these parts, I hope, and Ruth Owen and Bay will say, 'Oh, we'd better put that child in school, don't you think? She needs taking down a peg or two!'"

"Daisy, *you've* got a good reason for wanting to stay, haven't you? And the reason begins with 'A'!"

Daisy gave her sister a sudden hug. "Keep on about wanting to stay here then, Clem – and we'll *both* reap the benefit, eh?"

Clemmie nodded. "I will! But Alun might have given *me* that giant strawberry, you know!"

"Clemmie!" Ruth Owen called from the open doorway of Ivor and Annie's house. "Come and change out of that dress . . . Goodbye, dear Alun – are you going to see him off, Daisy? Fetch Pom from the boat – she must be dying for her run."

Ruth had engineered privacy for their farewell. They didn't waste time. In the cabin, with Pompom dancing impatiently round their legs they embraced, murmured and kissed. These were different kisses from those first tentative ones and as Alun's fingers twined convulsively in her hair, Daisy closed her eyes to the sweet urgency of it all.

She broke away at last, surprised to find that she was shaking.

"Alun . . ."

"I'm sorry – have I upset you?"

"No, of course not! It's just that—"

"It's all so soon, I know. But I mean it, Daisy: I love you. *I love you!*" he repeated.

One last kiss, then she waved him goodbye. She couldn't go back to the house, she thought, until she had cooled down. Smiling, then breaking into a laugh, she began to run with the dog, up the meadow where she had gone with Dick. It was wonderful to be in love!

Twenty-One

H ere they were, tying up *Pili Pala* under Drago's direction, for all days, dreaded or looked forward to, come round inevitably, don't they, and it was late afternoon on the celebration day.

"Eluned says you must come rather earlier than suggested, as she thinks it will be so much more convenient for you to change into your costumes in the house. A bedroom for the ladies, my changing room for you, Barley, and the bathroom are completely at your disposal," he told them. "You must also feel free to try out the piano in the drawing room before dinner. We are both so pleased you could come." He was looking directly at Ruth Owen as he said this.

There was an awkward silence for a moment or two. Then Bay said, "Go and help Daisy, Clemmie, collect up our clothes in the cabin."

Startled, Clemmie obeyed without question for once.

Bay stepped forward, so that he was between Ruth Owen and Drago. The three of them stood at the very edge of the long flight of steps up to the house.

He said, "I must tell you, Drago, that I am now aware that you were the cause of some unhappiness for my wife when she was a student of yours . . . I was unaware of this when I accepted your invitation." They stared at each other for a tense minute.

"It was all a very long time ago." Drago's voice was grave.

"It has caused *me* pain ever since." Ruth's reaction was quick. "I haven't yet been able to face telling my husband the whole of it."

Bay brought her within the circle of his arm, firm round her

136

slender waist. He was protecting her, she realised. It was a good feeling.

"We would prefer to keep this as a purely business arrangement," Bay continued. "I ask you to respect that decision. We will honour our commitment, that is all. However, we thank you for the invitation to dinner and for the amenities offered, which we accept."

Bay, you old rogue, Ruth thought gratefully, your pomposity is standing you in good stead today.

"Having made this clear," Bay went on, "I promise you we shall perform to the very best of our ability this evening. Thank you. We will come up to the house shortly."

Without another word Drago turned abruptly and went swiftly up all the steps of Ty-Gyda-Cerded.

"You were *wonderful*, Bay!" she exclaimed and she stretched up and gave him a kiss.

As they gathered up their things, Daisy counselled Pompom. "Be good, little Pom. Here's an osborne biscuit, as eaten by the Queen. I'll pop back during the evening to allow you to stretch your legs, eh?"

"It doesn't look as if Jem is coming, does it?" asked Clemmie.

"No, it doesn't," Daisy answered regretfully.

"I wish we could have some news of her," Ruth added. It was strange how responsible they felt for the girl after such a short acquaintance.

"House of Many Steps – here we are!" Ruth actually sounded cheerful as Clemmie raced ahead of them and pulled the bell so hard, it must have echoed through all the house.

Drago himself, now in immaculate evening dress, opened the door. "Do come in," he invited jovially, just as if his exchange with Bay had not occurred. "The servants all have the night off. You will discover why later. Eluned is waiting upstairs for the ladies – you come with me, Barley, will you?"

They trod noiselessly up the deep pile carpet which covered the stairs. On the wide landing above stood Eluned Drago, still wearing a voluminous silk housecoat, her hair hanging in improbable ringlets bunched behind her ears. How she must have worn it forty years ago on her wedding day, Ruth Owen imagined.

"Make yourself at home in the Painted Room please. And Clemmie, my dear child, I do hope you will manage to enjoy yourself for a while on our piano before we have dinner. Have you everything you need, ladies? I am in the room just along the corridor, if you need me. I must finish dressing myself, but don't be afraid to knock."

Without waiting for an answer from any of them she closed the door behind her and was gone.

"It's such a beautiful room, isn't it," Clemmie said, "but it makes me *shiver*, I don't know why—"

"It's cold, unused," her mother said quickly.

Clemmie, first dressed, darted over to the window and daringly drew aside the curtains. "It won't be dark for simply ages!" she said, then, as she gazed out over the sweeping drive round the back of the house she exclaimed, "Here comes Eli, and Gwennie in their donkey and trap! I wonder if they've been invited too? Mr Drago's just come out to help them carry in some big baskets and now Eli is unharnessing the donkey and leading him into the stable—"

"Come away from the window, Clem," warned Ruth. "They'll catch you staring – it's very rude!"

"It will be a relief to see such friendly faces, Ruth," Daisy said perceptively, "if Clemmie is right." She scooped her hair on to the top of her head. "D'you think it looks better like this, with the sari?" she asked.

"Sit down," Ruth suggested, "for I can't reach otherwise! Here, hand me some pins – yes, you look quite grown-up now, Daisy darling. Bay will certainly approve," she smiled.

"I'm not doing it to please *him*," Daisy said firmly, "and I grew up a long time ago only none of us realised, including me."

Ruth gave her a startled look, then squeezed her bare shoulder.

"Falling in love has that effect," she said softly. "I suppose we will lose you soon and we must let you go with a good grace . . . Well, are we all ready? I imagine we must knock on Mrs Drago's door and say so – Clem, pull that curtain across, there's a good girl."

"Do go down," Mrs Drago said. "I shan't be long."

Bay and Drago were already in the drawing room but there were no guests so far, Ruth saw with surprise.

"I offered your husband a drink, Ruth, but he declined." Drago put down his own glass. "Would you care for something, Daisy? Clemmie?"

"I'm only allowed lemonade," Clemmie said ruefully. "Can I play the piano please? Mrs Drago said I could."

"If your parents permit—" Clemmie did not wait for confirmation but opened the piano lid reverently, flexing her fingers in a fair imitation of her father.

"Nothing to drink, thank you," Ruth said forcefully, so that Drago turned his intense gaze from her daughter to herself.

"Nor me, thank you," Daisy echoed politely.

"Dinner will not be too long." Drago gestured to them to sit down. "The Pentecosts from Brynbach are in charge of the catering for this evening and even now are setting out a splendid cold collation in the dining room, most appropriate for a summer's evening. Ah, here is Eluned: I can summon our other guests now." He took hold of the bell rope by the mantel.

"So beautiful!" Eluned almost crowed at the sight of Ruth, Daisy and Clemmie in their rainbow hues. "Don't stop playing, Clemmie dear. I listened with such pleasure as I was coming downstairs."

Clemmie's toes stretched toward the loud pedal. Bay sat down quickly beside her. "A gentle touch, Clem, you're not performing yet, just a little background music, I think – like this." He demonstrated.

Mrs Drago's elaborate dress put their simple attire into the shade. She wore ruby-red silk taffeta, in honour of her anniversary: a pleated tunic, buttoned high to her white throat, with enormous sleeves and what seemed like matching pantaloons. Her collar sparkled with what looked like real gems, outshining the simple rhinestone-studded bands round the necks of The Singing Barleys. The stiff curls on her head were entwined with red silk roses. Because her skin was so smooth under its layer of powder, she looked remarkably well preserved. As if the trials and tribulations of life had passed *her* by, Ruth thought bitterly.

The door opened somewhat tentatively, and the rest of the company filed in silently, nervously. It was soon obvious why, when introductions were made, for these were all servants of the house.

On the surface, Ruth mused, it appeared that the Dragos were kind, thoughtful employers who had asked their staff to join them in their happy celebration and generously arranged for other help – hence Eli and Gwennie – in order that they might be able to do so. But where were their friends? she wondered. Perhaps there were none because Mrs Drago was so reclusive.

Daisy sat between Arthur the gardener, a silent young man with a convulsively bobbing Adam's apple, who smelt strongly of the bay rum with which he had drenched his hair, and Bridget, who did the family washing. She possessed bright red hair and sore red hands to match, poor thing, but she at least became talkative after her first glass of wine.

At the top of the table, in the place of honour, were Raoul and Eluned with Clemmie between them. Ruth sat on Drago's right and Bay on his wife's left, just as if they were family.

The long table was beautifully polished and set with cut glass, silver cutlery with mother-of-pearl handles, red linen napkins and a huge centre display of fruit and flowers. By each plate there was a gift, wrapped in tissue and tied with red ribbon. All the guests glanced speculatively at these.

Both Eli and Gwennie had really dressed for the part. Gwennie wore a tight shiny black dress, with buttons so strained that Ruth worried that they would pop off when Gwennie leaned between each diner while she was serving them. Her apron was immaculately goffered and she had secured her flowing hair with a mass of pins beneath a starched white cap. Eli's dark suit was battling against his bulk too, but his smile was as wide and blissful as ever as he poured wine, splashing only the merest drop when he whispered in Daisy's ear, "You'll be more at ease here, away from the nobs . . . You'll see a good sample of Mam's cooking tonight, it took hours to boil and bread that great ham – that's an aitch-bone of beef, that is, as tender as can be – and those mutton chops we did this morning. Wait 'til you see the great confection my Gwennie's made, and the anniversary cake. We must have earned nearly enough with all this to retire on!" he joked. He tweaked a tendril of Bridget's hair in passing.

Ruth spoke as little as possible to her host. Clemmie was as uninhibited as ever and for once Ruth was truly thankful, as she demanded Drago's attention. Eluned, she noted wryly, was not above archly flirting with Bay.

They seemed to sit on at the table for ever, as plates were whisked away, smaller dishes presented, until some of the guests, unused to such largesse, were reduced to protesting feebly, "Just a very small piece of cake please, Mrs Pentecost – and would it be possible to have another glass of water, Mr Pentecost? These little cups of coffee don't hardly slake your thirst."

It was time to open the presents, to exclaim over the contents, silver hip flasks for the men, which were unlikely to be filled, and silver bangles for the ladies. They then retired to the drawing room, uncomfortably replete.

"A time for talking, I think – then for our entertainment . . . Please will you all be seated? Some of you will, of course, remember Mrs Barley as our own Ruth Owen from Brynbach, so very proud our community was, eh, when she achieved her first triumph in Y Cymanfa, the festival, in her youth, and when she was awarded a scholarship to the college of music where I was proud to teach myself, for many years." Drago cast an almost pleading look in Ruth Owen's direction. Her expression remained stony: she was not to be disarmed by his flattery, oh no, she resolved to herself.

Bay was already seated at the piano, Clemmie beside him on the long stool, and Daisy moved closer to Ruth.

"Sit down by me, Daisy," Eluned commanded, patting the cushion beside her on the sofa which the other guests had studiously avoided. "I knew that material would suit you," she gushed. "Such a splendid figure deserves to be shown off. Make the most of it, Daisy, for the inches are soon added, particularly if you have a sweet tooth and are forced through ill-health not to have the company of your husband during his career, and to be as inactive as I am." She had spilled cream on the front of her tunic. "D'you think Ruth Owen is happy to be here, tonight, in this house?" she probed.

"I really can't say . . ." Daisy murmured unhappily.

Ruth had gone to her husband. "I shan't wear the bangle and I imagine most of the other female guests will have no occasion to do so either," she said in his ear.

"The flask would have been acceptable to me before I enforced sobriety on myself! It has not been easy you know, Ruth." There, something else was now out in the open.

"I know," she said. She was pale behind her rouge.

When The Singing Barleys were grouped round the piano, Drago summoned Eli and Gwennie to join the company.

"Not really dressed for this." Gwennie removed her cap and apron with alacrity.

"Thank goodness we have friendly faces to focus on, Ruth thought gratefully, as they sang their first song. They had chosen the medley they had sung recently at the hotel, 'Sweet Violet', of course, and 'My Love 'Tis Like A Red, Red Rose'.

"Would you allow me to accompany you for the next item, Ruth, on the piano?" Drago asked jovially. She had no option but to let him take her place and to stand beside him at the piano to turn the pages of the music.

She felt her breath come in shallow gasps and she suddenly felt faint and sick. Fortunately her ordeal was soon over and Drago relinquished his place to Bay. She gave him a little nudge, and he glanced at her, startled, as she slid beside him on the stool.

After an hour or so Eluned remarked brightly that it must be time for a short interval, for the singers must be feeling the need to rest their vocal chords. "Will you be kind enough to pour some drinks, Mr Pentecost?"

"I really ought to take this opportunity to pop down to the boat and take the dog out for a short walk," Daisy told her hosts.

"Of course. Arthur I am sure will be glad to escort you along the towpath. It is past ten o'clock and this is a lonely spot, my dear." Both Daisy and the young Arthur looked unhappily embarrassed as Drago showed them out.

Quite suddenly Ruth Owen sagged against her husband as

they rested still on the piano stool. She clutched at her midriff with one hand. "Oh Bay, I feel . . . so sick." As the clamminess overcame her, her eyes closed.

They carried her upstairs to the Painted Room, and laid her on the vast bed. She opened her eyes to see Mari holding a bowl at the ready and dear Gwennie lifting her, to place a towel under her head.

"It's all right," she managed. "I won't disgrace myself now – the feeling's passed."

From the doorway Eluned Drago said, "You are obviously very unwell, Ruth. You are to stay here, I *insist*, overnight with your husband." She could not hide her resentment at the sudden curtailment of her party.

"Daisy, Clemmie . . ." Ruth said faintly.

"Daisy insists she will look after Clemmie on the boat. I could not have the dog indoors and she will not leave it any longer."

Bay, standing awkwardly to one side, told her, "They will lock the door."

"But as Drago said, this is a lonely place."

"They will be perfectly safe. Mrs Drago is right – you must stay where you are . . . I shall be here," he assured her.

When the others had gone he helped her out of the rainbow dress and she slid under the covers wearing just her petticoat. The sheets were chill to her skin, seemed unaired, she thought, but she could hardly protest.

Downstairs, Drago appeared tired and disappointed too. He closed the lid of the piano. "Goodnight," he said dismissively to his staff, hovering uncertainly, not sure whether they were summarily returned to duty or not. His wife did not come downstairs again; she had obviously gone straight to her bedroom.

Although she had believed that sleep was unlikely, in fact Ruth soon fell into an uneasy doze, waking with a start, to find the room flooded with moonlight, for Bay had pulled back the curtains before he joined her in bed. He certainly was in a deep sleep, she thought ruefully, pulling the covers over his shoulders for no one had thought of providing them with night attire.

She looked toward the doorway, suddenly afraid, although she had not heard the door open. Eluned Drago stood there.

Ethereal she appeared, strange in one so bulky, in flesh-pink satin so that Ruth only just suppressed a scream, mindful of Bay snoring beside her.

"You ruined my happy day, my celebration!" the apparition hissed, as Ruth sat bolt upright in the painted bed. "He'll never leave me, you know, because he belongs to *me!*"

Ruth was suddenly galvanised into action: she swung her legs to the floor and propelled Mrs Drago outside the bedroom door, which she closed firmly. They stood, face to face, both breathing fast. Ruth felt her legs shaking, the weakness was coming over her again. "I'm sorry for him!" she told Eluned Drago. "Yes, despite everything. I'm sorry for you too—"

"Ruth, I must apologise for Eluned; this must seem unforgivable to you." Drago had come up silently behind them, taking them by surprise. He grasped his wife's shoulders, turned her round and held her close to him, in his arms. "*I* am the one who fully deserves your contempt, Ruth Owen. I should have realised that the whole idea of a celebration was a mistake. But it was only because I wanted to see Eluned happy. I shall make no further claims on *you*, if that is what you desire – come," he said compassionately to Eluned, so compliant in his embrace, "let me take you back to your room. Goodnight, Ruth. I do trust you will be fully recovered from your indisposition tomorrow. I am sorry, I really am." He ushered her into the Painted Room.

She returned, trembling, to the bed. She subsided limply beside Bay, thankful that he had slept all through this. She knew that she would have to mull over and over everything that had been said.

Before Ty-Gyda-Cerded stirred, Ruth and Bay crept stealthily downstairs, along the hall and through the front door. It was something they were well used to doing after all. It struck her as odd that the door was unbolted, the chain hanging loose. Almost as if their early departure had been anticipated, she thought. Or perhaps Drago lurked somewhere in the shadows . . .

Twenty-Two

S o it was breakfast once again at the lock cottage, and Alun smiling happily when he saw Daisy waving, for she was leading the horse. Bay was steering, while Ruth rested limply on her bunk and Clemmie slumbered on, having been so late to bed.

There was a guarded welcome from Meg of course, but she sent Alun to collect fresh eggs and handed Bay the toasting fork. "Tea is already made," she said briefly.

Ruth smiled at Rachel ruefully. "So silly of me, Rachel – I imagine Mrs Drago thinks I made myself ill on purpose, eh? It must have been a surfeit of rich food. Eli and Gwennie never stint the butter and cream, do they? Mind you, I enjoyed it at the time, despite having to sit next to Drago." She would not tell Rachel of the disturbance in the night; she had not even confided in Daisy, though naturally she had to explain to Bay why they were leaving Ty-Gyda-Cerded in such an underhand way. She really was still feeling quite poorly. "Just dry toast for me please, Meg, I think."

When Meg had left for work and the others were outside as Alun was so busy with the lock, Ruth sat down beside Rachel and looked closely at her drawn face. "You are not looking so well yourself," she exclaimed, concerned.

Rachel smiled, touched Ruth Owen's hand gently. "Some days – you know . . . But it has cheered me no end to see you all again, Ruth Owen. You don't know how much it means to me to know that I shall see you every few days!"

"I shan't go to that house again, I think." Ruth did not elaborate.

"The boy has really fallen for your young Daisy: he moons

about which makes Meg very cross – she has not the patience for calf-love, never having been so stricken herself, you see."

"Daisy is star-struck too," Ruth Owen smiled. "Personally, I think it is wonderful! They seem as if they are meant for each other—"

"She doesn't know?"

"Oh, no."

"The same as the boy, then. You've not felt, you know, that you could forgive Drago, after your welcome at his house, like."

"I must admit I . . . felt sorry for him. I saw for the first time clearly what a sham his marriage must have always been," Ruth said reflectively. "Well, I must dash up the hill and do a hasty shop, let Eli and Gwennie see I am in the land of the living – they really were concerned last night . . . Will you come with me, Daisy?" she called out of the door.

Gwennie did indeed enquire solicitiously after her health.

"Oh, just one of those days; we women do have them, don't we?" Ruth said airily.

"I felt quite nauseous after the party myself," Gwennie sighed, "but there, if I *will* taste my own cooking – and Eli can't rouse himself this morning . . . Eli! Where are you, man?"

Eli had news of *The Molly Kelly*, of Juniper and company, which he had not found time to impart at the party. "Came through a few days ago now, they were in a hurry, Meg saw them through the lock apparently, or surely Alun would have told you when he saw you? They had news of The One Man Band, who Daisy rescued – a *girl* they said, not a boy at all, and they were going to seek help from the travelling preacher, like: it seems the girl was dragged off by her stepfather and taken back to Cardiff—"

"She was with *us*," Ruth interrupted. "We gave her a lift down to the other end—"

"Ah, I didn't know that and nor did *they*, it seems . . . And Meg obviously didn't tell Alun or Rachel, eh? Or, maybe Juniper didn't tell *her* . . ."

Daisy and Rachel looked at each other, shocked.

"Tot it all up quickly, Eli, please – we'll have to follow

them up, as quick as we can!" Ruth exclaimed. "If *only* we'd known."

Back at the cottage Ruth Owen hugged Rachel Hughes – very gently because she felt thinner and frailer even since she had seen her last.

"We'll be back, when we've sorted this all out," she promised.

"Don't be too long away, will you?" Rachel whispered.

And Alun stole a swift kiss from Daisy as she took hold of the leading rein. If her father saw, he did not comment, for which she was thankful.

It was stifling in that dark basement room that evening. What had her poor mam come down to? Jem thought dully. They had always lived in the poor part of town, near the smells and noise of the docks but Mam had managed to rent half a house, with decent neighbours kept in ignorance of her profession, in the days before she married Albert. Only young Ted still remained reluctantly at home – the other boys, twelve and thirteen now, had run away to sea, so Mam said. They were big for their age for Mam had fed them well until *he* took all her money. Maybe their stepfather had done them one dubious favour, Jem agonised, wondering how they were faring, toughening 'em up with all those beltings.

Jem's mam was sick: she had been troubled with swollen throbbing legs since the baby was born. The tiny girl was not thriving either: she cried constantly, a thin distressed wail, like a kitten, for nourishment was lacking in her mother's scrawny breasts. Mam had lapsed into bad ways again, of a different sort, Jem soon discovered, yet she could not bring herself to blame her because Mam was so obviously in pain and could only shuffle about. She averted her eyes from the cracked cup full of gin at her mother's elbow and from the sight of Mam dipping a rag in it for the baby to suck on. The feeble cries subsided, the almost transparent eyelids drooped, tiny Elsie gave a convulsive hiccup, then drooped in her mother's arms, already asleep.

"Useless Mariah, *useless* to me you are," Albert said contemptuously, thumping his fist on the rickety table so that the gin spilled over. "Can't work, can't satisfy *my* needs, can't even feed the bleedin' baby!"

"Don't you dare say that!" Jem cried indignantly. Mam had brought her children up to speak clean, the boys had had soap stuffed in their mouths for less than that. Albert lifted his arm threateningly and the stench from his sweat was overpowering in that unventilated room. Ted flinched, expecting a blow, even though he'd learned to keep his mouth firmly shut of late.

"Leave him alone! He ain't said nothin', poor boy – it was me." Jem sprang to her feet from the stool, standing between her brother and her stepfather. He caught hold of her arm in a cruel grip for he was strong, being a coal heaver – the dust was ingrained in the seams of his face. In his hands too. He was in constant agony from his back, for Henry Stoop, Coal Merchant of Gantry Hill, was a hard master. He may have worked, about the only good thing you could say about him, Jem thought, but he drank his money, gambled it away, that was why he resented Mam not being able to walk the streets to bring in her share.

"Time you went out, Miss Jemima Rees, and chanced *your* luck," he growled menacingly.

"I ain't goin' – you'll never get me to do *that*! Mam said I'd not have to – you're not me da, you can't make me do nothin'!" She received a cut lip for this defiance from his fist. He swung her round, propelled her in front of him, throwing her into the dark cubby hole where she slept, or tried to, each unending night since he brought her back.

"Not the belt, Albert!" Mam screamed out, so that the babe in her arms shuddered and began to squeal once more. Ted seized his opportunity, fled out of the door, up the stone steps, barged out of the front door, into the street.

For some unknown reason she thought of the handsome dark sailor, with his gold earrings, and the way Mam had sighed that *he* had actually courted her and made her happy before he sailed away and forgot them both.

He was unstrapping his belt all right. The first swipe tore the thin blouse from her shoulders. Blow after blow rained down on Jem's quivering back. She wasn't going to shout out any more because she had passed out from sheer terror and the awful pain.

"Now," he said with satisfaction, "you're going to learn another lesson, Miss Rees, and you ain't about to stop me."

Even as he turned her over and pinned her down, Mariah struggled to her feet, letting the poor baby drop down in the old armchair. She picked up the half-full bottle and brought it smashing down on his head.

Blood there was everywhere, but only the plaintive wailing from the baby, and an awful stillness.

Ted, running at full tilt, smacked straight into the outstretched arms of the bobby, ponderously pounding his beat. Another belt made contact with the boy now: the bucklet caught and lacerated his chin.

"Woah! Calm down, lad, where's the fire?" came the deep yet mild tones of one who was the scourge of the local villains but a good friend to those in distress.

"Albert, Mam's husband, he's murderin' me sister!" Ted babbled.

The bobby had heard that one before too but he always looked into things – domestic violence was common but thankfully not always as dreadful as it seemed to the children, who were, all too often, caught in between warring parents.

"Let's go back to your place then, lad. Don't you worry, you won't get hit for telling – I'll see to that." Despite the bulk, mostly due to the heavy uniform, he was a swift mover when necessary and he had his truncheon at the ready.

He kept the boy behind him, as he burst into the basement room. He took in the dazed woman, still swaying, with the shard of glass clenched in her fist; his gaze swept beyond her to the crumpled figure lying motionless and to the thin limp arm protruding from beneath the man, the defenceless limb of a child.

Half-turning, he gave the boy a robust shove. "Get down to the station. Tell 'em as I need help *urgently* – a stretcher – *three* stretchers – and to warn the hospital. Get going, lad – you can't help *here!*"

And Ted ran again, for his life.

Twenty-Three

"Will you steer, Bay?" Ruth asked after a while. He studied her closely. Her pallor alarmed him. Being so much more attuned to his wife nowadays he assumed it was delayed shock. Not surprising after recent traumatic events, he surmised. And he knew she hadn't wished to leave Rachel again so soon after their arrival.

He nodded. They were making good progress, Daisy leading Old William still and Clemmie perched up high, enjoying the ride. Pompom skittered to and fro. There were no other boats, or dogs, in sight.

They were aiming to reach the top end before dusk.

"Pull the bed out, lie down for a while," he advised her.

"I think I will . . ." She surprised them both. She was glad they would all be occupied for she hated fuss. Tired, and sick to her stomach still she felt. She slipped off her shoes, pulled off her skirt and stretched out on to the bunk. It was sticky weather. She was glad the stove had gone out through lack of attention and that the windows were open. She mustn't allow herself to cry again, she told herself sternly. But as she closed her eyes, to surprisingly fall almost immediately asleep, a single tear rolled down her cheek and like a child, she caught it with the tip of her tongue. She didn't feel like a mature woman of thirty-four years old today, more like the girl who had run away from home so long ago. "Rachel, I didn't mean to stay away so long," she murmured. Was it almost *too* late?

Over the aqueduct, through the last lock to pay their dues, to stable the horse, and Ruth slept on and on.

Dick was there to meet them, guessing they would come,

insisting that they come to his mother's for dinner, so that they could discuss a plan of action for rescuing Jem. They did not need much persuading.

They saw *The Molly Kelly*, berthed ahead. "Unfortunately they were somewhat delayed," Dick said, "for their horse fell, not injured but shaken up, and they couldn't move forward until the animal had recovered and been well-rested overnight. They came straight to find me, but I was away for several days and they had to await my return. They are loading now, so will see you later . . . My mother always has an overflowing larder, she welcomes all my friends as well as my waifs and strays and seems to thrive on it! I'll bring the carriage down to the wharf in about an hour; it's not far to walk but, as you say, Ruth is under the weather."

"Many thanks," Bay said warmly. He was rightly feeling smug for, as Clemmie cheerfully informed Dick, "He steered us all the way without a single hit-or-miss!"

Ruth roused herself at last and smiled her reassurance at their solemn faces as they crowded round her in the cabin. "A nice wash," she yawned, "a clean frock and I'm looking forward to my supper as we didn't have a decent lunch!"

When he returned Dick said, "Mother insists you all stay overnight – well, until this business is settled, if you'd like to?"

"Pompom . . ." Daisy reminded him.

"Your dog is welcome too – our garden is securely walled in and Mother says she would so enjoy your company. I'm sure it won't take too long to pack a few things, will it?"

They looked at each other. Clemmie spoke for them all. "It certainly won't Dick!"

Ruth Owen thought ruefully that they could do with a break from their floating home, the hard, hard bunks and the lack of leg-stretching space. "First, can we just say hello to Juniper and company and hear the ins-and-outs from her lips?"

Although Mrs B lived in a smart town house, it was well set back from the street with a gravelled drive leading to the stables at the rear. There was a fair sized garden with a wrought-iron table and chairs grouped under an old mulberry tree, a small fishpond and roses scrambling the high stone walls. The bustle and business of the town seemed strangely remote.

The only servants appeared to be an elderly groom who cared for a pair of horses and who drove Mrs B in the carriage when she ventured further afield. Dick's horse was stabled there too. There was also: "Nanny Broadbent, who has been with us since Dick was born!" Mrs B smiled. "We work together most happily nowadays and I find I enjoy cooking and shopping, Nanny taught me how to tuck in the beds and mend the linen, we put our washing out and we have a gas stove so Mr Hardes only has to light the fires in winter. If being a lady means being useless, then I am glad I am no lady!"

Dick added cheerfully, "When she needs extra help, I always know someone in need of a job. She is a most popular employer, my mother, for she feeds her staff so well!"

Ruth was amused to see Bay's bemused expression.

They sat round the dining table, tackling with enthusiasm the raised pork pie, the fried potato and relish. They served themselves from the sideboard.

"Dick," Daisy ventured, "let *me* come with you to Cardiff to bring Jem back. Please!"

He didn't say that this was not a good idea but told her gravely, "It could be unpleasant, Daisy – maybe even dangerous. However" – he glanced at her parents for their reaction – "I hope to take Mother's carriage – I'm sure she'll agree? – and if you would promise to remain in that while *I* go inside the house, I am positive that Jem would be so happy to be reunited with you when I bring her out, as I shall do."

"I want to come too." Clemmie knew what the answer would be, but it was worth a try.

Bay said instantly, "No! And Daisy, I don't think *you* should go either—"

"I promise to see that she comes to no harm," Dick put in quickly, seeing the flush rise on her cheeks and the light of battle in her eyes, which reminded him instantly of his mother when *she* was roused over the plight of members of this flock. This was not the first time he had been called on a rescue mission. Mrs B had quashed many a tyrannical landlord or employer in her time. Daisy was of the same mettle, even if she was only just discovering herself, Dick had realised that the moment they met.

"You can't stop me, Bay; you said the other day I must learn to make my own decisions and I intend to!"

Clemmie gleefully anticipated the sparks about to fly, but her father said gruffly, "Be it on your own head then. Ruth, why aren't you backing me up?"

Ruth put down her knife and fork. She leaned her head in her hands. "I'm so sorry . . ." she managed, faintly.

Mrs B was on her feet immediately. "Daisy, my dear, shall we take Ruth up to her room? You must forgive all this cogitating, my dear, when you are feeling unwell. Dick, see that Clemmie and Bay continue to enjoy their meal – Nanny dear, will you put the coffee pot on? There's apple tart and cream for dessert . . ."

"Ruth" – Bay was contrite – "do you need the doctor?"

Ruth laughed despite herself. "Oh Bay," she said affectionately, "the last time I saw a doctor was seven years ago, when Clemmie was born, remember? I'm not ill, just – feeling things – that's all. I'll see you later, but don't hurry up and spoil your meal, will you? Daisy will chase you to bed, Clem, in a short while."

Daisy and Mrs B waited while Ruth Owen was in the bathroom. They busied themselves with laying out her night things and finding books for the bedside table. Mrs B pulled the blind down. "There's a connecting door – see, Daisy? That's the room you and Clemmie will share. Ah, Ruth, here you are – feeling better? We'll leave you to it now shall we?" She crossed to the wardrobe and riffled through the garments. "Here you are: a housecoat, should you need to wander in the night."

Ruth rolled down her stockings as she sat in the chair. Daisy passed her the hairbrush. As she unpinned her hair, while they moved toward the door, Daisy heard Mrs B say softly to Ruth, "Men are so unobservant, my dear. Why don't you tell him tonight?"

"I might . . ." Ruth answered. "Thank you, for everything.

Daisy dear, *I* shan't worry about you tomorrow, you know, not with Dick to look after you."

On the landing outside the door, Daisy touched Mrs B's arm. "What did you mean – what's *wrong* with Ruth Owen?" she asked urgently. Ruth was never ill!

"Nothing wrong, though something totally unexpected, I imagine. My dear girl, your lovely Ruth Owen is expecting a baby! It may be that your *father* will need a day in bed tomorrow, to recover from the shock!"

"*Oh!*" Daisy exclaimed. Then she added, "If he upsets her over this, I'll . . . I'll *throttle* him!" Then she smiled and whispered to the closed door, "Good luck!"

Ruth Owen didn't feel glowing as pregnant women are supposed to do. She just felt horribly sick.

"Where have you been, Ruth?" Bay muttered sleepily as Ruth climbed back into bed after another nocturnal trip to the bathroom. "Surely it's not time to get up yet? After all those early mornings on *Pili Pala*, can't we make the most of a soft bed—"

"Bay, listen! I've something important to tell you." She spoke to the back of his neck as he rearranged his pillow with a thump. "I'm not sure if you'll be pleased or not . . ."

She had his attention now. He sat up, looked at her, in the early light of day. His gaze was wary.

"Bay, I believe I'm expecting a baby," she stated baldly.

He shook his head in disbelief. "When, how?" he asked foolishly.

"*How?* Remember the moonlight – the storm – the honeymoon night? It must have been then. Remember how mocking you were, saying that no doubt there would be a baby for Rose and Huw next March – well, *we* may have beaten them to it!"

"I'm forty-four years old," he reminded her passionately, "too old to go through all that again. Daisy, seventeen; Clemmie, seven – the gaps are too much . . . Just when things seemed to be looking up for us at last – *this!* Oh, Ruth—"

"Don't blame me, *please* don't blame me, Bay." Her voice was wavering, pleading. "Can't you see that I feel afraid too, for I'll be thirty-five before the baby is born . . . It wasn't easy for me, being so small-made, to have Clemmie and I was still in my twenties then! Not that you stayed around to see how things were going, you went out and drank too much and came back when it was all over! But I was thinking, before you came up to bed, that it would be wonderful if it is a girl and I can share her birth with my family here, especially Rachel . . ." The tears were flowing fast now.

He pulled her close, roughly. "If we must have another baby, and I suppose I'll have to get used to the idea, then it had better be a boy and named for me!" He mopped her face with his handkerchief.

Ruth Owen clung to him. She repeated what she often said when she was emotional, "You're an old fool, Bay Barley, but – I *do* love you, you see!"

After a long pause he said, "I don't deserve you. I'm frightened, Ruth. Losing Anne, so soon after Daisy was born – it brings it all back. That's why I stayed away when I heard your cries and the nurse told me it was a difficult labour. I'm not sure if I can go through that again. You see, I really do love *you*." It was the first time he had ever admitted this, in all the time they had been together, almost twelve years.

She whispered teasingly, "Then you must take good care of me, Bay – as I shall continue to do, of you."

Twenty-Four

"I'll keep an eye on Pompom for you," Mrs B said, joining Daisy and Dick at their early breakfast, as they ate their scrambled eggs. "I'll look after Clemmie too," she added, "if she comes downstairs before Ruth and Bay put in an appearance. I know you always refuse me, Dick, so I am giving this money to *you*, Daisy, just in case you have need of it. That son of mine goes around with empty pockets most of the time. Take the rest of last night's pie from the larder and a bottle of cordial, for it will seem a long day, I've no doubt, and hunger will strike! Still, it promises to be overcast, which means you will not be exhausted by the heat, eh? Will you keep this letter in your bag too, please, Daisy? I've written a few lines on what Dick calls 'bossy' notepaper; the engraved kind seems to prompt action, I find. This is to Jem's mother, offering her daughter accommodation and a job with me here, stressing that her daughter's welfare and care is of the prime importance – this is, of course, assuming that Jem has been taken home, which *seems* to be the case, from what Juniper heard . . . I have also said that, if she accepts, I shall certainly ensure that Jem sends money home on a regular basis. What d'you think?"

"I think you are being exceedingly kind," Daisy replied warmly, "showing such concern for a young girl you haven't even met." She hesitated, then said, "Jem is a most independent person though and I can't be sure she will say yes, Mrs B." Would Jem be prepared to give up her nomadic life for a while, she wondered? "I will certainly tell her she would be silly to refuse," she ended.

"I wouldn't force anything on her," Mrs B observed, reading

Daisy's thoughts accurately, "not religion, not submission nor piety: we should all accept others as they are, only to endeavour if we can, in a way acceptable to them, to put more joy, if they need it, in their lives."

"Thank you," Daisy said simply. Dick, who had been sitting there quietly, looking reflectively from one to the other, rose and took their empty plates out into the kitchen.

"He likes you very much, my Dick," Mrs B told Daisy. "Still, I understand from him that you are, as they say, spoken for?"

"I have made so many new friends, since we began our summer season on *Pili Pala*." Daisy replied softly, in case Dick suddenly appeared, "and *Dick*, I think, will be my good friend for ever! I'm so glad we met you both!"

She sat out front with him as they drove along the dusty road, past the cottages just stirring with early morning activity, and only another soul or two about. She felt the surging excitement of embarking on a real adventure.

"It is a fair distance," Dick told her, "and we will need to put up somewhere overnight, as the horses must have their rest. I see Mother advised you to bring a bag! The road is more winding than the canal, of course. I have got to know of some good stopping places in my mission travels, so don't worry." He admired her pink cheeks, the sparkle about her. She shared his sense of purpose. *Together* they would rescue the young One Man Band!

They talked and talked, each intent on discovering more about the other. He told her how he had lost his father when he was in his teens, that he had no notion of going into the mission field when he first studied theology. "I have to admit, Daisy, and I haven't even confided this to Mother, that sometimes I feel this particular outlook on life can be narrow, I am irked by the moralising of the zealots, their condemnation of others when sheer poverty and the harshness of life leads to temptation and degradation. Temperance, I do believe, is desirable, but to *me* this should be moderation. Being 'saved' should be such a joyful experience, a release, not another burden to bear through the years. One day, I hope I can work abroad, perhaps in Africa, that is, if I marry, for I believe a man needs a partner, an equal to sustain him in such a life."

"We all need someone to love," Daisy said very quietly. "Someone to live for. I can hardly believe that I have fallen in love so quickly, so unexpectedly with Alun. But I know he must see more of the world beyond Brynbach, the lock, the cottage, that he must fulfil himself, with his painting, before he really makes up his mind about marrying me. And I couldn't settle for anything less than that."

"If he feels the same way about you, how could he leave you behind? *I* could not." Then, as Daisy looked at him, startled, Dick added, "But there, the question would not arise, would it, between you and me? Daisy, shall we stop before we reach the next town, for that refreshment Mother pressed upon us? If we can reach the half-way mark by lunchtime we could eat again with my friends Eric and Margaret and rest and water the horses there."

The manse was a square and plain house next door to the chapel. Eric, another tall man, had been at college with Dick. His wife was a small woman with bright red hair, holding a baby in her arms crowned with the same. "You come with me, Daisy," she said brightly, "while I put this rascal down for his rest, then you can wash and tidy up in our room while these two reminisce, eh?" As Daisy followed her obediently upstairs, Margaret continued cheerfully, "I'm so glad to see that Dick has a young lady at last!"

"Well—" began poor Daisy, then she thought she would leave any explanations to Dick.

"See," said Margaret, "most of our furniture has one leg sawn shorter than the rest – all these sloping Welsh floors! I come from England too and even if I get homesick for Surrey sometimes, I really do love living here. Travelling the canal, I understand? Met Dick at one of the missions, I expect?" Daisy found it was enough just to nod and smile as Margaret chattered breathlessly on and on.

It was a good two hours before they hitched up the horses once more and waved their hosts goodbye, promising to call in on their way back.

They reached the outskirts of Cardiff just before four o'clock. "I shall have to enquire our way from here," Dick said, checking the address. The next hour was tiring while they searched the dock area, ruefully accepting that most information given them was deliberately misleading, particularly from one Henry Stoop, Coal Merchant, who had blustered belligerently at them.

"Perhaps it's my clerical garb," Dick mused. "I should have thought of that."

But then they struck lucky. The same bobby who had gone to Mariah's rooms with young Ted came alongside when they were asking yet another passer-by for directions and receiving yet another shake of the head.

"Jemima Rees, is it? You are friends of hers? I think it would be best if you give me a lift back to the station, just up the road see, and we talk there."

Maybe, Daisy thought, feeling hopeful at last, Dick's sober attire had been the answer on this occasion.

Jem was sitting beside her hospital bed, for it was too agonising still for her to lie on her back, and she felt too vulnerable resting on her front, for the busy nurses would tuck her in absent-mindedly as they twitched past and the weight of the bedclothes was intolerable. She looked so young, Daisy thought, a lump constricting her throat as they approached her, seeing her dressed in that coarse, unbleached hospital gown, with that downcast expression.

"Jem . . ." she said cautiously, as Dick stood back. Jem looked up, uncomprehending at first, then the relief showed on her face and she even managed a brave smile.

"I was comin' back that day, honest, Daisy," she said.

"I know," Daisy replied tenderly. She sat on the edge of the bed. "Here's Reverend Dick too, Jem. We've come to take you back with us, if that's what you'd like, and if your mother agrees. Dick's mother has written to her, offering you a home and a job—"

"I'd rather come back to you, to *Pili Pala!*" Jem interrupted.

159

"You'd really like Mrs B as we call her, she knows all about you, doesn't she, Dick?"

"She does indeed," he said, coming forward to shake Jem's hand solemnly. His expression was so kind and concerned. "We've spoken to the matron and she says that, although you still need rest and care, which we will be only too glad to give you, there is always someone waiting on an empty bed here."

"They . . . they haven't told me, what's going to happen, did you hear?" Jem asked anxiously. "About Mam, and Albert like."

"Your stepfather has a very sore head, quite a few stitches, but has received no sympathy, quite the reverse," Dick told her. "He isn't pressing charges against your mother for assault as he blustered to the police that he would, because of the seriousness of his attack on *you*. Now, you could have him charged and the police feel you should; however, we understand that your mother doesn't want you to go to court, for your sake, certainly not his, or even hers – is that your wish, too, Jem?"

"I don't want no more trouble," she said smartly. "Quick, Daisy, get off me bed, that nurse comin' along is a real Tartar, she'll have your guts for garters she will!"

"Then, while you get your things together," Daisy was smiling now, "we'll go and see your Mam, give her the letter, for you *are* coming back with us, aren't you?"

"Try and stop me!" said The One Man Band.

Mariah was isolated in a tiny cubicle off the Mother-and-Baby ward, lying on her iron-framed bed with swollen legs resting in a cradle. She looked old and grey though Daisy guessed that she was probably younger than Ruth Owen. The nurse who had accompanied them introduced them then said briskly, "Just a few moments now; the patient must be kept very quiet, Matron says. You shall see your baby tomorrow, Mariah, she's not doing at all badly."

"I can't read very well," Mariah said uncertainly, as Dick proffered his mother's letter. "Could you read it for me?"

Instinctively, Daisy took Jem's mam's hand in both of hers and gave her a reassuring smile.

160

When Dick re-folded the letter and looked questioningly at her, Mariah said at once, "Yes, my poor Jem will be safe with you. See she keeps in touch this time, mind, for I worried dreadful, you know, when she was away before. Ted, my Ted – d'you know what's to happen to *him*?" she asked anxiously. "The bobby took him home—"

"And he's going to continue looking after him for he says his wife has taken to the lad, she misses their sons now they're grown and left home. He can stay with them until you are fit to have him home with you," Dick told her.

"It may be the workhouse for a bit, like," Mariah faced facts. "But even that'd be better'n livin' with *him*. I'm not taking him back . . ." – with a wry smile – ". . . he might be too scared to try, anyway, for there's fierce I was, when I hit him."

"You're very brave; I can see where Jem gets her spirit," Daisy said admiringly. She loosened her clasp, straightened up, glanced at Dick. He nodded.

"We must go," he said, "but we'll make sure Jem calls in to say goodbye tomorrow morning, we'll be staying near here, overnight."

"Mother was right as usual," Dick remarked ruefully later. "I shall have to call on you, Daisy, to pay for our night's board and lodging. We were fortunate that our friendly policeman knew of this place! Why don't you sit down, Jem, it may be a while before our supper is ready."

Jem sat gingerly on the button-backed chair Dick had pulled out for her. "Silly, when I only just left my bed, feelin' I'll be thankful to get back in it!" she sighed.

It was a stuffy little room, mostly taken up by the table, hastily laid up by the obliging landlady. Daisy wrinkled her nose, instantly reminded of Miss Prince and the moonlight flit to Wales. Cabbage, boiling furiously in the pot, it must be! "At least we didn't have to put up at the police station, like Mrs B's horses!"

A rather moth-eaten tabby cat eyed them sternly from the windowsill, where it observed all the comings and goings of that busy street, for the house abutted on to the pavement.

161

They heard the knock on the front door, then voices. Jem struggled to her feet: "Our Ted – it must be!"

Ted came in sheepishly. He had not visited his mam, or Jem, in the hospital. Having got as far as the forbidding front entrance, he had inhaled a powerful whiff of carbolic and caught a glimpse of a nurse wheeling a patient, all wound up in bandages and blankets, in a wheelchair. That was enough for Ted: the sign might say 'Infirmary' but it spelled out 'Workhouse' and 'Incarceration' to him.

"You orl right, Jem?" He glanced out of the corners of his eyes at her companions. "Mr Benson told me you was goin' off with friends see, so I thought I'd come—"

"Oh, Ted, you saved me life!" Jem cried dramatically. Then, "You'll get back with Mam, and look after her, and Elsie, when she's better, won't you, promise?"

"'Course I will," he said stoutly. "Don't worry about me, Jem, I like it where I am, even if I'm livin' with the Law like. I'd better get back, me supper's about to be served up, and the lady here said yours is too." He gave his sister an awkward peck on the cheek. "See you in the diddy lights," he added. "Goodbye all!"

Daisy wondered what the diddy lights were, but it didn't really matter because Jem obviously took it to mean: 'I will see you again soon!'

Later, in their bedroom, she gently anointed Jem's back with the ointment from the round cardboard container which the hospital had supplied. The weals were horrific and Daisy wondered, with a catch of her breath, if Jem would be scarred for life. "There, you've been very good," she said softly when the job was done.

Jem remained on her stomach, where she had lain stoically without a murmur. She turned her face toward Daisy revealing glistening eyes, tears trembling on her lashes, but the cheeky grin was in evidence too. "Thanks, Daisy," she said. "I know I'm safe with you and Reverend Dick; he's so tall and strong ain't he, and he don't preach at you, he just wants to help you see."

"I know," Daisy said. She felt in her bag, drew out pencil

and paper. "D'you mind the lamp burning for a bit, Jem? I just want to write to Alun, to let him know what's happening." She thought with a start, I haven't had him in my mind since this morning.

Jem said sleepily, "I might be saucy like, but I reckon he's in love with you."

Daisy, startled, said, "Does it show?" Ruth Owen knew of her feelings for Alun, of course, but she had not really intended to confide in Dick this morning. It had just happened. She was not really ready to tell the world, not even Jem.

"Show?" Jem winked. "'Course it does. I can read Reverend Dick like the Good Book."

Mariah was nursing the baby when they called as promised to see her before leaving town.

Jem, wearing the blue dress which Ruth had thoughtfully sent for her, bent to kiss her mam. "Mixed blessing our Elsie, I reckon, Mam, but you got something to keep going, to get better for. Don't worry 'bout me, Reverend Dick's mam is going to send you part of my wages, reg'lar like. Mind, I'm goin' to hang on to my One Man Band stuff, what the Law's got in safe keeping, cause I don't know yet what this Mrs B has in mind for me to do." She took the tiny baby from her mother, cuddling it carefully. "You be good for Mam, our Elsie, and don't you grow up to be trouble like your Da." She kissed her and returned her to Mariah. "Bye Mam!" She wheeled round abruptly and went without a backward glance.

"Goodbye, Mariah, get well soon," Daisy said.

"Thank you for letting Jem come to us," Dick added.

"She'll get her chance now, she deserves some luck," Marish answered. Though Jem obviously took after her sailor father for looks, Daisy thought, she had inherited her mam's pluck. Mariah had made some had mistakes in her own life, but she was obviously determined that her elder daughter should not go the same way.

Twenty-Five

J em would not have dreamed of complaining, as the carriage jolted on mile after mile, and her back, despite the
comfortable seating, began to smart and ache, but she was
grateful when they arrived at the Manse. The carriage might
be well-sprung, she thought with a suppressed groan, but the
state of the roads made for plenty of jarring.

"Coo!" she said, looking at young Eric. "That's what you
call a baby that is, not a yeller scrap like our Elsie."

"So they found you safe and sound and brought you with
them all in one piece, eh, Jem?" Eric, the baby's father
observed jocularly, unaware of what had happened to her.

"Not 'zactly, eh, Daisy, Reverend Dick?"

Margaret came to the rescue. "Well, in your honour, Jem,
I've made an attempt at a Welsh dish, Cawl; lamb stew to
you, Daisy! With Bara Brith to follow – I'm on safer ground
there for Eric's grandmother is a Welshwoman and she gave
me the recipe when we were first married."

"I've made Cawl meself," Jem said, "with lamb bones
and leeks and things, but I reckon yours'll have *meat* in it,
won't it?"

It was a happy meal. After Jem's candid assessment of
Dick's feelings, he seemed content to treat Daisy as a friend,
like Margaret, Eric and Jem herself.

She looked slyly at them, once or twice. She hoped he
wouldn't be too long in telling Daisy how he felt, now *she'd*
given Daisy an inkling. Of course, there was Alun, and that
first shy kiss she'd seen *them* stealing, on *Pili Pala*, but nice
as he was, wasn't he a sort-of cousin of Daisy's? Anyway,
he was still a boy and everyone knew girls needed someone

a bit older, to take care of them like, and provide for them
. . . Reverend Dick was her hero! Despite him being holy and
all. At least you could be sure *he* wouldn't take his belt to the
woman he married.

Nightfall, and both Jem and Daisy were dozing as the weary
horses plodded up the street to Mrs B's house.

What a welcome there, too, Jem discovered, which nearly
made her blub again, only what would they think of her?
"Can I sleep with Clem and Daisy?" Jem asked Mrs B. "And
Pom?" Pompom was already curled up in her lap, in the most
comfortable chair, where the nice lady they called Nanny had
surrounded her by plump feather pillows. Mrs B and Nanny
intended to spoil Jem – a lot.

"There's room," Clemmie put in quickly. "I like sharing
Daisy's bed; I usually do!"

"You shall sleep wherever you wish, Jem, and if you like the
room, well it's yours from now on." Mrs B smiled at her.

"Guess what, Jem," Clemmie couldn't keep the good news
to herself of course, "it won't be for ages and simply ages, but
we're going to have a *baby*. Isn't that exciting?"

Bay cleared his throat, put up his newspaper. Ruth Owen
shook her head at her daughter, but it was obvious she
didn't mind.

"Well, I knowed I had to 'see' three babies in a row, what
with Elsie, Mam's baby and Eric what I met today!"

"You can't keep secrets from Clemmie – anyway when
I'd told Bay and he was happy about it, we might as well
let Clemmie tell the world, we thought!" Ruth poked at the
newspaper.

"Ruth, Bay, wonderful news!" Daisy said innocently, as if
Mrs B hadn't guessed and let her in on the secret earlier.

"Supper in bed, on a tray, Jemima?" asked Nanny.

"What lux'ry! Only if Clem comes up at the same time,
then we can have a good old gossip and she can let me know
what The Singing Barleys have been up to, see?"

"There's lots to tell, and we're going to raise the roof in The
Mission tomorrow – d'you think you'll come, too?" Clemmie
asked breathlessly.

"I'll try to," Jem replied.

Daisy took the girls upstairs and showed Jem the bathroom. "I'll come up again later and do your back for you, Jem. Look, Mrs B has provided you with a nice nightgown; it'll probably swamp you, but you'll be more comfortable with something loose, I'm sure." There were things which she must tell Mrs B which were better said when Jem was not around.

Dick tapped lightly on the door, which was slightly ajar.

"Come in!" Jem called. "I ain't disrobed yet, but Clem's already in bed!"

He had changed into an embroidered waistcoat over a fine white shirt. "Birthday present from Mother." He smiled quizzically at Clemmie, who rolled her eyes in amazement. "I have to wear it now and again, or she thinks me most ungrateful. She asked me to tell you, Daisy, to forage freely in the airing cupboard in the corner. And do you need the pillows brought up from downstairs, Jem?"

"If you would," Jem replied. Then, as Clem suddenly leapt from one single bed to the other, she cried, "Oi! If that's *my* bed, Clem, stop bouncin' on it!"

"She's over-excited." Daisy reproved her sister. "You're supposed to be nice and quiet, Clemmie; look after Jem – calm down, there's a good girl."

As Dick disappeared to fetch the pillows, Jem said candidly to Daisy, "For *your* benefit I reckon – him dressin' up like that."

"*You're* over-excited too!" Daisy said. "I'm going, before you two say anything more to embarrass me!"

Another fine evening and the sunlight set the dust motes dancing in the mission, haloing the heads of The Singing Barleys. They were five again tonight, the ladies demurely dressed in white blouses with black velvet bows at their threats, long black skirts just skimming the tops of their shoes. Sadly, Jem's little kid boots had been pawned by Albert, but they had found her a pair of shoes, stuffed with tow at the toes. Mrs B hadn't said a word about not sewing on the Sabbath, like Annie. She had shortened the length of one of her own skirts and tightened the waistband to fit Jem.

Bay, as always, looked very handsome in his frock coat, elegantly cut trousers and matching bow tie. He stood centre, with Ruth Owen on his left, Daisy on his right, flanked by the two smaller girls.

"Don't worry, Jem," Ruth whispered, "Dick will give us the song sheets and tell us the numbers to sing."

The mission seats filled rapidly. In the second row, to their delight, they spotted Juniper with Rose and Huw, wearing their best clothes. They were joined, just before the service began, by Eli and Gwennie, as usual breathless from all the hurrying, brought to the door by the moon-donkey.

Another preacher led the service, introducing the Barleys after the introductory prayers. "Please be seated, you are all most welcome to this service of praise and blessings. Our friends Bayly, Ruth, Daisy, Clementina and Jemima will now sing for us. Miss Eliza Pemble will accompany them on the harmonium."

'All Things Bright and Beautiful': they sang that favourite hymn which had been composed in this part of Wales with its 'purple headed mountains'.

Bay invited the congregation to join them in the last verse and chorus. The words swelled forth richly.

Prayers were invited, someone would rise and speak out, completely spontaneously: a James Amos Lewis witnessed to the fact that to his great shame he had been a drunkard, a wife beater but now was saved. This elicited enthusiastic applause.

Another hymn, led by The Singing Barleys, then Dick came forward to preach. The singers were ushered to seats in the front row next to his mother. Dick told the old, familiar story of the Prodigal Son, just as if, Jem whispered to Daisy, he had *her* particularly in mind.

The crowd of people, the vast majority poor, hardworking, ill-educated through no fault of their own, men and women who had learned to expect more knocks than upliftings from life, listened raptly. Even the youngest chewed on their bonnet strings or twisted their caps in hand, in concentration.

"Is there anyone here who would be saved tonight?" the older preacher exhorted the congregation. A moment's indecision, then a young mother walked up the steps, baby in arms, to be blessed.

Jem rose slowly to her feet. "*I will!*" she called out, as her friends gazed at her, startled.

The preacher came smiling down to lead her by the hand.

When she returned at last to her seat, The Singing Barleys stood once more and turned to face their fellows. They were all wondering exactly what had prompted Jem to speak out. Daisy held her hand tightly as they stood side by side.

Jem was scarcely aware what she was singing until the final verse of the hymn:

> *"Revive Thy Work O Lord*
> *Give Pentecostal Showers*
> *The Glory Shall Be All Thine Own*
> *The Blessing, Lord Be Ours."*

The closing prayers, then it was outside, to blink in the bright light, to follow the crowd to the mission hut for supper.

Juniper was waiting to speak to them. "You did well," she told Jem. "I was proud, like I was when my Rose did the same. We come special tonight hoping to see you when Reverend Dick said you was back – here – we found this parcel like, when you was carried off in town that day."

Jem thanked them, still elated from her experience in the mission. "It's my rainbow dress – I thought I'd lost it for ever!" She peeped in the torn corner, stroked the glowing colours showing. They sat at the long tables with Juniper and her family, with Eli and Gwennie.

"Got some good news," Juniper told Ruth Owen as they tucked into the sandwiches. "I believe my Rose is to be blessed with a baby."

"Oh, Mam . . ." Rose said weakly. Huw, with his arm round her, cuddled her close, grinning.

"And I don't reckon she's the on'y one, eh?" Juniper continued with a knowing smile at Ruth.

"I give in," said Ruth, hoping that Bay would not take exception to all this telling of secrets; after all it was very early days yet. "You all seemed to know before I did. Yes, all right, *me*, too!"

"Ah, but here's a real surprise for you all, I imagine," Eli put in with one of his huge smiles, "Gwennie – well *she* thinks she's expecting—"

"After all these years," Gwennie said, with mock reproach at the incredulity. "I really don't know why *you* are so surprised, Ruth Owen, for we're the same age, or why *you* didn't know already, Juniper Kelly! I never imagined myself with a baby really, I admit, for isn't my Eli child enough at times, due to having lived under his mam's thumb 'til he was almost forty? There's over the moon we are I can tell you."

"Gwennie, my dear, this is just wonderful," Ruth Owen told her. She felt choked, for didn't she know just what Gwennie meant, having a husband who required coddling like a child at times too?

He, who had sat back at all this baby talk, as if it was nothing to do with him, unlike the other proud fathers-to-be, leaned forward and actually patted Ruth's hand gently.

Clemmie said, "There you are, Jem is right, babies always do come in threes. I'm very glad about ours, 'cos Ruth says I mustn't be surprised if Daisy gets married and all, seeing as she'll soon be eighteen – but now she won't be able to, because we'll need her to look after the new baby, like she did me and teach it to read and write when it's old enough."

Poor Daisy didn't know what to say. Ruth came to the rescue, telling Clemmie, "Clem, Daisy is not a nursemaid you know, even though I'm afraid we all took it very much for granted that she enjoyed seeing to you when you were small. So, when the summer season is over, I shall gracefully retire from The Singing Barleys and look after you all myself – and don't you dare say I haven't warned you."

"I hope you intend to settle near us, for then our little ones can be friends as we are, and we can tell each other how to bring them up proper like!" Gwennie smiled.

Ruth turned to Bay, but his face was inscrutable. She

knew that he hadn't really recovered from the shock of her announcement, and that he would need time to adjust. He certainly had where Clemmie was concerned and, of course, he had literally given up Daisy to her grandmother in *her* young days, she thought ruefully.

"I don't intend to leave here again," she said to Gwennie. "But will you all leave it please to *me* to tell Rachel Hughes? She will be upset if she doesn't hear it from my lips."

They promised readily. When they had gone – to *The Molly Kelly* and to the donkey and trap, Mrs B and Dick escorted them back to the house.

"We didn't really know what to expect," Ruth said for them all, "but it was a lovely, happy service, Dick. You must have been really pleased when Jem went unexpectedly to the altar like that."

"You all sang so beautifully, thank you," he said. "But are you worrying whether Jem was just carried away, that she hadn't time to think whether she was doing the right thing? Well, I believe our young friend really does have joy and peace in her soul tonight. Am I correct, Jem?" He held out his arm to her. "You have so much to give, but right now you need more to receive, until you are fit again. There will be no pressures on you, ever. I promise." He added, "Will you all come to her baptism, in good time?"

"You know we will," Daisy said softly.

Clemmie remembered suddenly: "Alun didn't come – he said he would . . ."

Ruth linked arms with Daisy. "I'm sure he would have come, if he could."

They were unaware, of course, that at this very moment, Alun was pedalling like a mad thing along the towpath, bringing bad news. Rachel Hughes had asked for Ruth Owen . . .

Twenty-Six

It was fortunate that Eli and Gwennie were in the mood for gossiping and had lingered by *The Molly Kelly*, for they immediately turned around when Alun, alarmed at not finding anyone on *Pili Pala*, came there to gasp out his mission. They took him into town, to Mrs B's house. Gwennie tried to tell him why the family were staying there and about the rescuing of Jem, but she lapsed into silence when she saw how distraught he was.

Eli, because the boy hardly made sense, took it upon himself to tell Ruth that Rachel was very ill indeed – "failing fast . . ."

She stood with Bay and Daisy in the hall, Mrs B and Dick having tactfully whisked the girls away.

"We will take you to Rachel Hughes's. Can you come now?" Eli asked.

"One of us must come with you," Daisy said.

"You can't have got over that journey to Cardiff yet – but, it would be good to have you, Daisy." Ruth looked at her stepdaughter gratefully.

Bay said stiffly, "You do not want me then, Ruth. Very well, we will wait here, for your return."

She caught his arm as he turned. "Bay, my old darling – I know how you hate illness. Please – look after Clemmie – don't tell her tonight about Rachel, or alarm her. I hope and pray that Alun is wrong, that it is one of Rachel's bad turns; she may well be better tomorrow." In her heart she felt this was false optimism. She had tried to put the thought from her mind, several times since they last left the lock cottage in such haste, that she might not see Rachel

171

Hughes again. She was being given the chance to do so: they must hurry.

The appeal on her face prompted Bay to bend to kiss her. "Take care of yourself, especially *now*," he said gruffly.

Alun was waiting with Gwennie in the trap. When he saw Daisy he became even more upset. "Daisy, Meg doesn't want *you* to come – only Ruth – because she can't deny Mam *that* – I'm sorry."

Ruth said strongly as Eli helped them into the trap. "I want Daisy with *me* Alun. I will answer for that to Meg."

She leaned against Gwennie's comforting bulk.

Then the carriage came out behind them and Dick called out, "All of you will be too much for the donkey – Daisy will you and Alun come with me? It makes sense, for I can bring you back here."

"He's right," Eli said, as Dick assisted Daisy in her descent and then into the carriage, followed by Alun. "But we shall get there first of course, for the donkey can take the little lanes where the carriage cannot pass."

Ruth Owen looked through the window of the carriage, for they were now abreast, although Eli was about to take the lead. She saw Daisy cradling Alun in her arms, as she so often did her young sister. She thought that Daisy was acknowledging his fear, his sorrow at the thought of losing his beloved Mam. Alun would be, she realised, a man like Bay, one who would always need the support of a woman. Daisy had been born, perhaps, to fulfil such a role. But she knew that love and desire were not always enough. Like Ruth, in her turn Daisy might yearn sometimes for support herself . . . She felt so sad.

Meg met them at the door. Eli made his excuses: "Remember, you may call on us at any time – day or night; we will be there for you," he said. Gwennie had remained in the trap. She gave a little wave.

The carriage was left at the corner of the road. Dick had to see to the horses. Alun and Daisy rushed round to the cottage. The door was open.

"Go straight up Ruth Owen," Meg said.

"Meg . . ." Daisy called, still standing outside.

Her face was ravaged by much crying and she appeared near collapse. Impulsively Daisy entered, crossed the room and with a strong arm round Meg's shaking shoulders gently eased her down on to the coach. Keeping that close contact she told her, "Don't be cross that I have come too. Ruth Owen wished it."

"The boy too, no doubt," Meg replied dully, as Alun followed Ruth upstairs to his mother's room.

Ruth heard the laboured breathing from outside the door. The doctor was there. He turned from the bed, looking compassionately on them. "Good, you are in time, Ruth Owen. She can't speak to you, but I am sure she can hear you. She will be glad to know you are with her. I will go down to Meg. I can do no more, I'm afraid. Call me, when you need me . . ."

She knelt by Rachel, so close that her breath must have warmed the dying woman's face. "Rachel, darling Rachel, such news I have to tell you. There is new life growing within me – we shall have a baby next spring. I wanted you to see it – to be happy for us – to hold the new little one in your arms. It is part of us, part of our family, you see. It is as if I came back here, to you, for this. Now you are leaving me and all I can do is weep, because I cannot help you! Rachel, Rachel, I love you – thank you for waiting until I could be with you . . ." She muttered on and on, while Alun stood motionless at the foot of the bed.

In less than an hour, it was time to call Meg and the doctor to come up. They brought Dick with them.

"It was a peaceful passing," the doctor said, preparing to take his leave, after expressing his condolences. "She could never have recovered; in the end, it was a stroke, I believe. A massive one."

It helped having Dick there. His calm presence, his thought for them all.

Ruth Owen asked Meg, "Shall I see to things in here?" It was something she wanted to do. Rachel looked so peaceful, she was not afraid.

Meg nodded. "I couldn't . . . Alun, will you take the bicycle, go for Ivor – tell him and Annie?"

"Let *me* go," Dick offered, seeing Alun's face. He was exhausted.

When he had gone, Meg moved her hands helplessly. "I was going to make tea . . ."

"I will do it," Daisy said in her turn.

Some time later, before Dick returned with Ivor, Daisy and Alun slipped outside, ostensibly to see to the animals. Ruth Owen and Meg sat talking, there was obviously a truce.

"I shan't go into work until after – the funeral," Meg said suddenly. "Ivor will tell the company for me. Alun, of course, must carry on with his duties as normal, tomorrow. The boats will keep on coming."

"It will help him to keep busy," Ruth said wisely. Alun had obviously heard what she said to Rachel, about the baby, but she could not bring herself to talk about this to Meg just yet.

There was passion in their kissing, embracing. Daisy struggled, for she knew this was wrong at such a time. Alun was seeking solace for his terrible loss; she might be young and inexperienced as he was too, but she knew that was so.

"Mam," he sobbed, refusing to let her go, pressing her back against the tree which shielded them from view, from the cottage and the towpath. "She was too young to die! Both of them gone, Mam *and* Dad! What shall I do, Daisy? Help me!"

She gathered her strength, pushed him aside at last. "Alun darling, we must go back. They will wonder where we are."

"*You* won't leave me – ever?" he entreated.

"If I can help it – *no*!" But would *he* leave her, when he realised, despite the shock, the sadness, that he was free to go away if he desired now?

Dick came slowly up the meadow to meet them. They moved apart so that he could walk back between them.

It was the day of Rachel's funeral. Arranged by Ivor, who had been a tower of strength, like his Annie.

Bay and Dick, with help from Clemmie, had brought *Pili Pala* up here, to the mooring beyond the lock. Ruth and Daisy had decided to stay, for Meg had wished it, at the cottage to make things ready. Dick had returned home, of course, but would be with them today.

When Alun was otherwise engaged, Bay helped with the lock gates. They slept on the boat but spent their days at the cottage.

Yesterday, an official from the company had come to talk to both Meg and Alun about the future. Nothing had yet been said to the family on *Pili Pala*, who had tactfully made themselves scarce, about the decisions they had come to. Ruth Owen felt she had no right to ask although she sensed that Meg appreciated all she was trying to do to help.

They walked behind the coffin, as was traditional, to the chapel in Brynbach. Just the womenfolk, for the men bore the burden on their shoulders. Meg with Annie, Ruth Owen between Daisy and Clemmie, Gwennie, Juniper and Rose, who had arrived just in time for the ceremony. Other friends would be waiting for them at the chapel.

It was a moving service, short and simple, and it was not long before Rachel Hughes was laid to rest by her beloved Davey. When the farewells had been made, the family turned to walk back to the cottage where dear Gwennie would serve the food she had prepared.

Daisy found Alun by her side, and she tentatively linked her arm with his. Surely Meg would not mind? she thought. Dick, who had assisted at the service at their request, headed the little procession, supporting Meg, who had broken down at the very end, with Ivor.

"It was a lovely service, Alun," she told him. He was dry-eyed now.

"It was. Mam, bless her, is at peace now, I can see that . . . Daisy, you saw the chap who came yesterday? From the company? He said it would be difficult for them to offer me the post for myself like, me being so young, unless, of course, I was to be married." He looked at her.

She saw the anguish, the uncertainty in his eyes. They were in love, no doubt about it, but it *was* such a short time since they had met. What had they talked about that special occasion, about missing out on their youth, having had to accept responsibilities at an early age? Both of them.

She knew instinctively what she must say. "Alun" – she was glad they were bringing up the rear now – "perhaps you need to go away, try for a place at art school, if that is what you really want, and I believe you do – oh, I am sure you will always be drawn back to this place, like Ruth Owen, because of all your memories, because of your Mam – oh, Alun, I did like her so very much, you know! You are too young to be married, I know that, but what about Meg? If you leave, will she lose her home?" she asked anxiously.

"Meg has already made up her mind. She has never liked her job. She felt she was trapped here, because of Mam and me . . . She is going to stay with a cousin, who moved away; he wrote to offer her a place in his house. He is newly widowed and has young children to care for, which is why he could not come today. She told me that if I wanted to marry you, I could, even though she doesn't approve: like you, Daisy, she said I of was of no age to marry."

"You see, Alun, even Meg knows for once what is best for us." She managed a smile. "We love each other – we can wait, Alun. Look, we must hurry – they are all out of sight!"

"Kiss me first," he urged. "You are so sweet, Daisy, so kind and understanding. How lucky it is that we found each other!" They clung together as if they were to part that very minute.

Back in the deserted churchyard, Drago walked slowly toward the freshly-turned earth. Beside the bunches of garden flowers, he placed the sheaf of hothouse blooms. He remembered Rachel as he had first known her, when they met on the steps of Ty-Gyda-Cerded. She coming up, bobbing up and down on her knees, with her whitening stone and he, hastening down to the canal for he was expecting some goods on a barge. Laughing dark eyes she had. The same age as Ruth had been, when he spoke to her in the college grounds that day.

He went back into the chapel, walked over to the harmonium. The minister, tidying up, saw him there, but did not comment, in his wisdom. Music swelled loud – there was release in his sure fingering. As Rachel had said, so plainly, so coldly, he had no rights at all.

And Drago wept.

The guests were taking their leave. Beyond the lock, there was a line of boats, silently waiting for the lock keeper to return to his duties. The boat people were showing their usual respect for the loss of one of their own.

"I will collect the crockery, take it all home to wash," Gwennie said, loading her basket.

"Don't forget," Eli said warmly to Meg and Alun, "just call us if you need us."

"Thank you both, for all your kindness." Meg was quite composed now.

This promise was repeated by Juniper, on behalf of herself and her family.

When it was just family, Ivor cleared his throat, looked round at them. "I have the task now of imparting Rachel's last wishes, for she entrusted this to me, following her last attack." He looked directly at Ruth Owen. "She did not allow us to tell you of this, so soon after your return, which made her so very happy . . ."

She slipped her hand into her husband's.

"It is written down: what each of us is to have, as a special memento," Ivor said. "I am to have her wedding clock, and must have it mended, for it was a good clock in its day, when it was going like . . . You, Annie, are to have her best bedspread, the one she made herself for her marriage bed, and I am also to take care of the family bible and Father's chair.

Meg, you are to choose whatever you wish, from her personal possessions and from her china cupboard, Alun, her big bed is for you, for when you shall marry, for Rachel felt it a shame that you never had a proper bed of your own . . . If you choose to stay on here, she said, but she doubted that either of you would, the rest of her chattels were to remain for you both – if not, she wished me to sell them and to divide the money between you. She asked me to find out about a college of art in Swansea, Alun, for it was her secret dream

177

that one day you would be a student there. This I shall do, if you so wish.

Ruth, you are not forgotten my dear for" – he withdrew from his inside pocket a slender golden chain with a cross – "she wished . . ." – he paused and looked round the circle of solemn faces – ". . . her *eldest daughter* to have this precious thing, given to her by Davey on their wedding day. It was always a sadness with Rachel that she could not acknowledge you thus: it was imposed upon her by our parents, because she was so young, and unmarried when you were born. She could not sully their memory, when they died and she and Davey took you into their family, as they had always wished, for they had fostered the belief that you were Rachel's little sister."

The pressure of Bay's clasp made Ruth aware that he understood. She choked back the relieved tears: after all these years, her secret was in the open at last. She did not realise that Alun and Daisy had put a different interpretation on this puzzling relationship, that both had wondered, but not said, if Alun was *her* son.

Meg drew a deep, sighing breath. "There is more to tell, eh, Ruth Owen—" She broke off as she saw the pleading on her sister's face. "But this revelation is enough, on *this* day . . ."

Clemmie was quiet, not like herself at all. Daisy suddenly rose. "Clemmie, shall we take Pom for her walk – she's been shut up for far too long."

When they were gone, Ruth blessing Daisy's tactfulness, she spoke at last. "Do you understand a little now, Meg? I should always have been proud to call Rachel my mother. Ivor has explained how it was in those days. It was Drago who told me the truth. It hurt me more than I can say. But I never blamed Rachel for any of it, *never*! I wish you well in your new life – both you and Alun. Of course I was hot-headed when I was young, unknowingly I was curtailing your own youth when I left home . . . How could I know that Rachel would be so ill, that Davey would die, even before she did? Wouldn't Ruth have wanted us to be friends, as well as sisters?"

Ivor prompted gently, "Meg?"

Her lips were working. "I've resented you so long, how can I—"

"How can *we*, Meg – we must both try to heal the rift . . ."

She sobbed her heart out in Bay's arms that night. He waited awkwardly until she was quiet at last.

"Ruth?"

"Yes?"

"It is Drago, isn't it? He is your father. He must be. It all fits."

She reflected on the words Rachel had spoken to the young, impulsive Ruth Owen. 'He did not force me, Ruth, oh no, it was not like that. I thought I was so much in love, and he was a man married to a woman who would not – could not – love him in that way . . . I knew he would never leave her – that was never said, but I knew it. We made our loving in the Painted Room. It was wrong and I have never ceased to regret it. When she found out about the baby – you! – she tried to make me agree to give you up to them. Like you, I fled home . . . It seemed the best solution, for my parents to have you – then I met Davey. Tragic it was, to lose them like that, but then you were able to be with us here at last. It's just that I never seemed to find the right time to tell you the truth.'

"Yes," she said now, "Drago is my father." She had seen him in the chapel. She had not acknowledged him, but she had recognised the sadness in him and was aware at last that he must have loved her mother.

179

Twenty-Seven

"This is for you, Ruth Owen," Alun said. "Mam asked me to do a little drawing for you, on one of her good days because, you see, the only photograph she ever had taken was the one after her wedding, and Meg has that."

She looked at the pencil sketch of her mother. "I mustn't cry and spoil it with my tears," she said, with a break in her voice. "You have caught her likeness so well, her lovely smile and the darkness of those Owen eyes. Thank you, oh thank you for this, my darling boyo."

Meg held out her hand to Ruth. The new lock keeper was already busy at his duties, their furniture was being put in place, for Rachel's household goods had gone earlier to Ivor's to be stored for the time being. She and Alun were to leave later in the day. He would escort her on the train to her new home, and return in a couple of days to Ivor and Annie's.

"Goodbye, Ruth," Still wary, Meg.

"We can do better than that Meg, can't we?" cried Ruth Owen as she flung her arms around her.

There was no private farewell between Daisy and Alun, but he kissed her cheek, as he had for Ruth and Clemmie, and whispered, "Write to me, when I have an address in Swansea, won't you? I must take a job of some sort until the new year begins at the art college – always providing I am offered a place there, of course."

"You will, Alun," she promised. "Send your letters to Ivor and Annie. I'm not sure where we will be, but we must try the towns again for our entertaining, for we shall soon be penniless again if *we* don't work either."

"Through the lock now, is it?" he asked, as Daisy took hold

of the horse and Ruth Owen and Clemmie stepped aboard *Pili Pala*. They went below, out of sight, as Bay steered.

It was a quiet journeying to Ty-Gyda-Cerded. They tied up at the mooring below the steps and Clemmie grumbled that she wanted to go up to the house too and try that wonderful piano again but Daisy insisted, being now in Ruth's confidence, "Lessons, Clemmie – get your slate out!"

"You are sure you want to go through with this, Ruth?" Bay asked when the girls had retreated to the cabin.

"I am sure."

Drago must have observed their arrival for he came round the side of the house and met Ruth at the top of the steps.

His gaze was wary. "Have you come to quarrel with me, Ruth Owen?" he asked quietly, not attempting to usher her into the house.

"No," she said simply. "I just want to talk with you."

He led the way into the garden, into an open-fronted chalet hut which had bench seating round the walls. The smell of honeysuckle was almost overpowering. "I often sit here when I want to be alone, away from Eluned. She never ventures inside for she says it smells of my pipe, and there are too many cobwebs and spiders. I read out here, or sometimes I make notes on my music scores for I hear the music in my head. We will not be overheard here, I promise you."

"Tell me," she began, "how it was for you and Rachel. I shut my ears to your confession that day, at the college."

"You must forgive me for that. It was wrong – Rachel should have spoken to you first . . . How was it between us? She was everything my young wife was not. She was so small, so slight – like you! – so warm, so laughing. I had only been married a few years then, when she came to work at our house. I could tell she was a bright girl, she deserved better than that. Always on her knees it seemed, cleaning those infernal steps. I soon made it my business to be coming down, when she was coming up, to say I was sorry to be treading on and spoiling all her good work. She would look up, all smiles and say, 'Don't worry, Mr Drago. I will be whitening them again tomorrow!'" He paused and Ruth saw that he was smiling now too, at the memory.

181

"How did it begin, how did it go on?"

"I never intended it," he said. "Nor did she, I'm sure. She was a good, well-brought up girl, a Chapel girl. I was upstairs one morning and I saw that the door of the Painted Room was partly open. I looked in, to see her dusting off the furniture and humming happily as she worked. 'Such a shame this lovely room is never used,' she observed, when she caught my eye. Then she added artlessly, 'It is a real bridal chamber.' That was the first time we really spoke to each other, but I watched, and learned that she always cleaned that room on the same day each week. This was in the early days when I was home all day, busy with my composing – it was later that I took my post in the college. I told Eluned that I wished to earn my own living, not to live idly on the money provided by our fathers. You see, I had begun to lose my self-respect – after . . . But *then* I was there and Rachel was there and my feelings grew strong, and one day I realised that she felt the same. It was a summer season of loving, Ruth Owen, and there was the inevitable conclusion. In return for my wife's forgiveness, I had to give Rachel up."

"And when I was born?"

"I was not allowed to see you. I sent money, but it was returned. However, when Rachel took you to her own home and I learned of your gift for music, which made me both proud and regretful, I wrote to her and her husband and asked that they allow me to pay for your special tutoring, for *your* sake, not ours. I believe Davey Hughes persuaded her, he was a kind man and I knew she genuinely loved him as I knew she now despised me . . . There was the proviso, that I must never reveal my connection to you."

"You broke that promise."

"I always loved Rachel, Ruth Owen. You must believe that. I was *burning* with jealousy when she made a happy marriage and I was still trapped in mine. But she set her face against me on the rare occasions we met. Her love for me was just a youthful consuming passion, one that passed."

Ruth Owen put out her hand, but let it drop back in her lap before she actually touched him. "I know what you want. You want me to be your daughter, you want me to let you pamper and spoil Clemmie because *she* is your grandaughter – it can't be, because of your wife. You can't hurt her all over again. You must realise that."

"You are not leaving here again?" She recognised the appeal in his voice.

"I – we are not leaving, no," she answered quietly. "But it doesn't make any difference. If from time to time we meet, I would like us to be on friendly terms. Look how upset your wife was, the night of the celebration – it is no wonder she is as she is, for however you look at it, she *was* betrayed when you made love to Rachel, all those years ago."

"You are right, of course," he said.

She had not intended to tell him but, as she rose to leave, she said suddenly, "If it is any comfort, I am expecting another child. You will, no doubt, observe the growing up of your grandchildren from a distance, as you did with me . . . You have passed on to me, and now Clemmie – perhaps to the new baby, given that Bay is also musical – a precious legacy of music. I do thank you for that."

Drago shook her hand. "It will be a consolation, but I shall never cease regretting what might have been."

"We must let Rachel Hughes rest in peace," Ruth murmured.

He did not accompany her as she walked round to the steps. As she passed near the open French windows she felt that Eluned Drago watched her, but she would not look to confirm it. She just hoped that Drago would tell his wife what had passed between them, that it was all over at last.

A brief stop at Ivor and Annie's, then they travelled on to the bottom end.

"It is good you came back, Ruth Owen. It made Rachel so very happy," Ivor said. "There is a vacant cottage in the village: I shall make enquiries for you, if you really mean to stay. Come September, the summer season will be over: you will need a proper place like."

"I don't know how we can afford anything at all," Ruth said ruefully.

Bay was reading a letter which had been forwarded to him by Miss Prince, their last landlady. When Ruth Owen wrote to her to apologise for their underhand way of leaving and to return the rent they owed, she had given Ivor and Annie's address. There was a look of sheer incredulity on his face.

"This is unbelievable!" he exclaimed.

"What is?"

"This is a solicitor's letter, sent to our last known address . . . My adoptive mother passed on, six months ago. We parted on acrimonious terms when I chose the stage over an academic career, and then married Anne. She said I needn't expect another penny . . . I believed her, for she was a hard woman, obdurate when she was thwarted. In fact, she has left a considerable sum to me – 'for the benefit of any family my adopted son may have'."

"I imagine that the interest would cover the rent of the cottage I mention very nicely, eh?" Ivor said, pleased and relieved for the family who might well have become another responsibility to him, although he would never have said so.

"Oh, I should so like to be near Annie when the baby comes!" Ruth Owen cried in excitement.

"And I can go to the school!" Clemmie shouted in joy.

"Bay will take a job, and I will too," Daisy said firmly. "It will all work out, you'll see. You'll need to save some of that money for your old age!"

"You have a good girl in Daisy," Ivor observed.

"I know!" Ruth Owen smiled through the ever-ready tears. "Whatever would we do without you? But one day—"

"You always say it – *one day*, I'll want to leave you and go away . . . I suppose I will, but not just yet, not while you all need me."

"And there's Alun of course – he will go to Swansea, but this is now his home, he'll always come back," Annie put in.

"Then you must make sure *you're* here, Daisy, when he does," Ruth Owen told her.

184

Twenty-Eight

"I am going away, Eluned, just for a while. I feel the need," Drago told her. He had his back to her, standing by the open French windows. He didn't want her to recognise the despair he felt, how old memories continued to torment him. He hadn't slept at nights since Rachel died. When, in the day, he sometimes felt the irresistible urge to doze off in his chair after lunch, his dreaming was disturbing. Such sensual thoughts he had been glad to put aside long ago.

She could move swiftly when she chose. He felt her plump hand on his arm, tugging him round to face her. She was more than upset: she was in one of her rages. He was thankful that the servants had already retired to their quarters. In the early days after Rachel she had been suspicious. Very young girls were not employed. He could not blame her for her lack of trust. But he had wanted to say, '*She* was different. I loved her. I think I always will!'

They often stayed up late, he usually amusing her by playing light music on the piano, while she lay on the sofa. She hardly moved all day, which was why she was never willing to go to bed before midnight, he thought wearily.

"I did all I could, putting myself out for you, entertaining your progeny," she shouted, "then when things don't go according to plan, as *always*, you run away! You took yourself off to the college, when Rachel Hughes spurned you, you left me here to a lonely existence – you didn't care . . ." Tears streamed down her powdered cheeks.

"She is gone now, you know that," he reminded her. He was weary of it all; the wasted years; he knew that he had treated Eluned badly, that, although she might have been devastated

185

for a while, he should never have married her. Yet he believed then it was his duty; it was said to be so by both sets of parents, because of their youthful romance – before her illnesses, both physical and later mental, had eroded love on his side, and left only pity.

"I am sorry, but I *must* have a break from all this," he told her, removing her restraining hands.

The hysteria began in earnest then, and he guessed the servants were cowering in their beds. They never interfered when he was at home, unless he called for aid. Loyal they were, he appreciated that. They would take good care of Eluned while he was away.

"I am going to bed," he said firmly. "I will speak to you about it in the morning. You should come up yourself, when you have calmed down. Goodnight, Eluned."

She was lying face down on the sofa, drumming her heels in fury.

It seemed an eternity, but was in fact forty minutes, before Drago, lying tensely in his bed, heard his wife treading heavily, reproachfully up the stairs, past his door to her own room.

He called out, "Sleep well, my dear!" but expected and received no reply.

For once, perhaps because he had stood up to her at last and stated his intention, despite the dreaded tantrums, he fell into a deep sleep.

In the early hours, Eluned, dressed in the red silk tunic and trousers she had worn at her Ruby Wedding celebration, came, quietly this time, downstairs. She hesitated by the front door, which Drago had forgotten to bolt, then she cautiously turned the key in the lock. The heavy door swung open. Before her, stretching down to the canal bank were the many steps of Ty-Gyda-Cerded. Whitened, as Rachel Hughes had done in her day, according to ancient folklore, to prevent the devil from entering the house.

The moon was waning, but the steps were so white, due to all her exhortations, that she could discern each one.

It was more than forty years since she had descended that stone staircase when she ran eagerly down to meet her fiancé on his return from his studies at college. She wasn't ill then; life seemed to stretch ever upwards like the steps when they walked back together to the house.

The statues crouching at the top seemed to watch her inscrutably, as she moved forward. With her hands pressed against her wildly beating heart, she stumbled ever downwards.

"There's always a first time to try laver bread," Ruth Owen said cheerfully, determined to be bright when Clemmie was around. "I fancied it, you know. You do yearn for unexpected things when you're having a baby."

"Smells like seaweed to me!" Clemmie sniffed it on the plate. She made a disgusted face at Daisy.

"I actually cooked it myself," Ruth informed Bay, who had just been up to town to buy a newspaper. They had filled in gratefully for an absent singer at the theatre, they had been asked to go along tonight just in case, and the manager had promised to recommend them elsewhere. Things were definitely looking up and a paper no longer seemed a luxury.

"I cooked it the Welsh way, of course," she continued, shovelling some of the black mass free of the bubbling fat in the pan, on to Bay's plate. "Rolled it in oatmeal, lucky we had some in the cupboard, but I know you can use seasoned flour. It's absolutely delicious girls – believe me!"

"You're looking much more your old self, Ruth," Daisy told her approvingly. Ruth's colour was back, the tenseness of recent days seemed to have evaporated.

"It must be an acquired taste," Bay remarked, after his first mouthful. "But where's the bacon?"

"We're not *that* well off yet, even if *you* have 'expectations', as they say – eat it up, all of you, it's very good for you!"

"Why is it," Clemmie complained, "that things that are good for you always taste not nice?"

"A letter for you, Daisy," Bay remembered belatedly, feeling in his pocket. "One of the boatmen said Ivor had asked him to deliver it to *Pili Pala*. He spotted me, as I passed his boat earlier – he remembered me from the school party apparently."

Daisy read most of the letter aloud for they were all eager

for news of Alun – naturally there private pieces for her eyes alone.

He wrote, in jubilation, to say that he had been accepted by the art college, that Madeleine, a fellow student whom he met at his interview, had taken him to her home and that her parents, struggling artists themselves, had agreed that a lodger would be very welcome. He had even found an early morning job, helping with the collection of fruit and vegetables for a local shopkeeper, and the arrangement of same for sale. There was no point in him returning home before his course commenced, now things were settled. He would be living in a poorer part of town, would have to supply and cook his own food, but 'the company promises to be most stimulating', he enthused.

"I'm so glad he has found friends so quickly," Ruth Owen said. She guessed that in the weeks to come Daisy would re-read Alun's letters so often they would split along the folds.

They had already heard from Dick. Jem, he said, had decided to carry on busking in 'her spare time'. While she was still recuperating, his mother was encouraging her to carry on with her education. Dick was travelling to Cardiff again next week to see Mariah and Ted as he had promised. Jem intended to play outside the mission, for if she played some stirring hymn tunes she reckoned she could soon drum up a great congregation. Hadn't she made up her mind to use her gifts in the service of the Lord? Daisy hadn't objected to reading out the last lines of *that* letter, Ruth thought, with a smile. He had concluded: 'Dear Daisy, we miss you all. Come back soon. God bless you. Dick.'

Bay was riffling through his paper. "No *Times*," he complained mildly. "This is all local news." He gave a sudden exclamation.

"What is it?" Ruth took the laver bread from his plate and ate it herself.

Bay said, "Clemmie, Daisy, Pompom looks as if she needs urgently to go out. Hurry up about it, will you?"

They looked at him curiously, but obeyed. When they had gone, he folded the paper, indicated where Ruth should read, handed the sheets to her, silently.

Mrs Eluned Drago was discovered, drowned in the canal near her home yesterday evening. The police believe it is a case of misadventure. However, it is well-known locally that Mrs Drago had not been outside the house since suffering from tuberculosis in her youth, before her marriage to Mr Raoul Drago, recently retired Professor of Music. Mr Drago is said to be distraught. He is unable to throw any light on the mystery. An inquest is to be held.

"Shocking business," Bay said at last, looking anxiously at his wife.

"Ivor will come, I'm sure of it, he must have heard of this by now."

"A tragic accident; sure to be. We won't tell the girls until we have to, eh?"

Daisy came breezing back in. "Clemmie's just had a marvellous idea! Why don't I have my photograph taken in my rainbow dress – to send to Alun – well, I expect," she amended hastily, "he'd like one of us *all* together."

"No, Daisy," Clemmie butted in, "just *you*, so he can make moon eyes at it each night before he goes to sleep!"

"Clemmie is right for once. You can go with Daisy to the photographers," Ruth said, "while Bay and I are posting those bills in town this afternoon." She hoped that the girls couldn't see the trembling of her lips. Had this terrible thing something to do with her visit to Drago? Should she go to him? What difference would it make if she did? Tongues would begin wagging over their relationship; he was going to suffer enough without that . . . She must wait for Ivor: he would have sound advice to impart.

Ivor said, "Today a piano was delivered from Ty-Gyda-Cerded. There was no message, just a label, 'For Miss Clementina Barley'. We have it in our dining room for safe keeping. Stay away from Brynbach, down here, Ruth, until all is settled, the funeral over. It is rumoured that Drago intends to close the house, pension off the servants and may live abroad."

"Should I write to him, do you think?"

Ivor had arrived just as they were about to leave for town, and Bay had taken the girls off, despite their curiosity, so that Ruth might talk to Ivor on her own.

"Just a brief condolence, I suggest. They have laid her in the Painted Room, Mari Evans says. She will go from there."

They were sitting side by side in the cabin of *Pili Pala*. Ruth pressed her face against Ivor's broad shoulder. Her voice was muffled. "It is right she should be in there at last."

"It is over, Ruth Owen, thank God." Ivor held her in his comforting arms.

Twenty-Nine

"A parcel for you, Alun," Madeleine said, coming into the long attic room which the family used as a studio. Canvases were stacked against the walls, there were jars of turpentine, oily rags streaked with paint littering the floor, but the light was good, streaming from the skylight in the roof. Her father, who had arrived in Swansea as an Italian immigrant in the seventies, had married a Welsh girl, her mother, Victoria, known as Toria. She was a talented artist herself and doubled as his model. Today, she posed pensively, elbows on the table, as if smelling a bunch of sweet peas in a chipped lustre jug. She was as dark as her Latin husband and they made a striking pair. After many hard years they had recently had the good fortune to find a patron which meant that they were at last able to paint full-time. Madeleine, their only daughter, had, from a child, always determined to be an artist too.

Alun, sitting to one side, making a charcoal sketch of Toria while Roberto painted straight on to the canvas stretched on his easel, was grateful for the generous tuition in return for his meagre rent, which his landlord, taking to him immediately, had suggested. It would be another month before he could begin his studies with Madeleine, at the college of art.

Madeleine, voluptuous even in a calico smock, always disturbed his concentration. She leaned close to him now, deliberately allowing her oiled thick braid to brush his face. "Wipe your hands, Alun, for it looks a special parcel – so beautifully wrapped, with sealing wax and all! Open it up, we should all like to see!"

"Such a beautiful girl!" Toria exclaimed. She arched her back, easing the stiffness caused by her prolonged posing.

191

He slipped the accompanying note quickly into his pocket.

"Who is she?" Madeleine asked sharply. Her mother was right: this was a beautiful girl, with a mass of curling hair, wearing a filmy, revealing dress she would have loved to wear herself. Even in sepia, without colour, the sweetness of the girl's expression was evident. "Your lover?" she added.

From his reaction, it was evident that he was shocked by such a question. "No! She is a special friend. Her name is Daisy."

"Very special?" Madeleine probed. He was very conscious of her flashing gaze. There was nothing cool or ladylike about Madeleine, he thought uneasily: she was completely uninhibited. She could not be compared to Daisy.

"We have an understanding," he said at last, reluctantly. He re-wrapped the picture carefully.

"Shall I take it to your room for you?" Madeleine asked. She paused, looking closely at his sketch. "Oh, how you are improving, eh? You may yet get a chance for that scholarship, Alun. Your eyes will really be opened when you start your art classes proper; I know my way around already, having been a model in the life class on several occasions – I shall continue, I think, to help pay my fees. But I would let *you* draw me, like *that*, for free, you know."

Country boy he might be, but Alun took her meaning immediately. His obvious embarrassment led Toria to rebuke her daughter. "Don't tease him, Madeleine! Or no more exotic, overripe fruit will come *your* way! We are very grateful for your thoughtfulness in that respect, Alun, you know – it was just the right job for you to take!"

He snapped his charcoal in two. "I'm glad. Excuse me, I will take the parcel downstairs myself, thank you, Madeleine." He wanted to read the message from Daisy. In private.

Madeleine made a mocking *moue* at his retreating back. As the spoiled daughter of adoring parents she repeated cheerfully the words familiar to Toria and Roberto: "Whatever Madeleine wants, she shall have!" Exotic, overripe fruit might have described Madeleine herself, exactly.

The summer season on *Pili Pala* was over. Dear Ivor and

Annie had set to, as they had with the boat, and cleaned and whitewashed the cottage ready for the family to move into. Stout-walled the cottage was, cosy indoors, with roaring fires in every grate as the weather deteriorated, for Ivor kept them supplied with coal.

The piano stood in pride of place in the square living room. Ruth planned to teach pupils on this splendid instrument. The income from Bay's legacy would ensure the rent could always be met, and food always on their table, but she had always worked and did not want to stop now, even with the baby coming. Bay, she hoped, would be encouraged to coach aspiring singers and to teach elocution. It would do him no good to think he had retired!

There were some pieces of Rachel's furniture, which they had seized the chance to buy for Alun and Meg's benefit, as Rachel had wanted. The old couch had been newly covered by Annie; there were the good table and chairs. Upstairs, Ruth Owen was proud of the brass bedsteads which Bay had ordered; she had chided him for his extravagance, of course. Beside their bed was the family cradle, but there would be a long wait before that was filled, she thought.

Like Ivor and Annie, they now had a good bath hanging on the kitchen wall, and bathing by the fire was a real treat, with plenty of hot water from the copper.

Daisy had been quiet all day. Clemmie, of course, was excited about the prospect of going to school shortly.

There were sticky buns for tea, as a special treat, for Eli had delivered the groceries earlier.

"Is there something you want to tell us?" Ruth asked Daisy.

She nodded. "I – I want you three to enjoy life as a family. Oh, I know I am your daughter too, but I am eighteen years old, I am an adult, and I think it's time I made my own way in life. I want to find a post somewhere – in a private school if I can, for my lack of formal qualifications would not be a drawback in such a school . . . I will come home at Christmas, I promise, and when the baby comes, for I couldn't miss *that*! I know I can think of the cottage as my home too, that's what matters – and I want to be here whenever Alun returns!

Our summer season on *Pili Pala* was the happiest time I have known – but I *must* learn to be independent – for Clemmie will soon be at school and loving every minute, I'm sure, and *you* will have the baby and Ivor and Annie close by, and all the canal friends . . . I won't even have to burden you with my darling Pom for Jem loves her so; it seems right she should go to *her*. Those two little waifs and strays as Bay called them, remember? were meant for each other, I think . . . D'you understand?" she appealed.

"Dear Daisy, of course we do – but how we'll miss you!" Ruth had tears in her eyes, but she managed a smile. She gave Bay a nudge under the table. Oh, let him say the right thing for once . . .

"*I'll* miss you," Clemmie said dolefully.

Bay looked at Daisy for what seemed a very long time. Then, "Ruth's right," he said, not sounding at all like himself. "We have a wonderful, caring daughter – Ruth, who is so much wiser than me, as you know from bitter experience, has told me *that* often enough . . . You must keep your promise to return home to us – and often – thank you for everything you've done for this family, Daisy. I can't tell you how much I'll miss you too."

Daisy said softly, "I never thought I'd ever say I love you, Bay, but to my surprise – well, you see, I *do!*"

It was hugs all round then and Ruth Owen was crying, "I'm *so* happy!" when she felt the first flutterings of the unborn baby. She put her hands to her abodomen in wonder.

"What is it? Are you all right?" Daisy asked anxiously.

"It's the baby – just letting me know that *he* didn't want to be left out of all the excitement!"

Daisy was on the train, travelling to Swansea. She smiled at the little boy opposite who was kneeling up on his seat to watch out of the window. "Don't you dare poke your head out, Tommy," the child's mother warned him. "A smut in your eye can be sheer agony!"

She instantly recalled the pain and smarting from doing just that when she, Bay, Ruth and baby Clemmie travelled by train from her grandmother's home to London, leaving that dull, safe life behind for ever. Bay had exclaimed, exasperated, "Don't fuss, Daisy!" Ruth Owen, however, had comforted her, saying to her father, "It'll do her good to cry, Bay: not only will it ease her eye, but she needs to shed tears for her loss, too, you know."

Daisy knew she would miss Ruth Owen even more than she had imagined that she would. Since she had learned the full story from Ruth of her family background she had felt that they had even more in common. Both had suffered the deprivation of a father when they were young. Thank goodness she was closer to Bay now than she had ever been. For it was not too late for her, if it was for Ruth, for Drago had gone away.

She was on God's Wonderful Railway, the G.W.R. – Great Western Railway, of course. She glanced at the family opposite, but they were now engrossed in their magazines. The little boy was noisily sucking a barley sugar cane, dribbling stickiness down his new jacket. Daisy smiled to herself: just like Clemmie, she thought. The lady next to her sniffed at her bottle of sal volatile, choked a little, then closed her eyes as if she had a headache.

Daisy felt sufficiently unobserved. She took Alun's latest letter from her bag.

Dear Daisy, How wonderful that you are coming to see me! My landlady says you can stay the two days with us. Her daughter is willing to share her room with you. It is not a smart house but I know that will not worry you in the least. I have the scholarship! But I must still work to pay for my lodging and food. However, I am able to take this time off to be with you this weekend. All this excitement, this new life, has really helped me not to dwell on the loss of my dear Mam. I love you cariad, I always will. Believe me! I will meet you from the train. Alun.

She tucked the letter tenderly back into the depths of her bag. There was another shorter note which she now glanced at, from Dick.

My dear Daisy, I am sorry to miss seeing you to say goodbye, please convey my good wishes to Alun for his success. We will look after Jem and little Pompom, I promise – it seems unlikely too that I will be able to come to see you off to your school in Kent next week – I have commitments to meet. May I presume to write, when you are settled? God bless you. Mother and Jem send their love. Dick.

She leaned back now and relaxed. If she couldn't doze off, at least she could let her imagination explore how it would be when she saw Alun again. Two months they'd been apart!

There was the usual scramble to lift luggage down from the rack, to gather up her gloves and bags, to straighten her hat.

She searched anxiously for her ticket, standing well back on the platform to avoid the hustle and bustle, the billowing clouds of steam from the chocolate coloured engine.

He stood just beyond the barrier, scanning the travellers.

"Daisy! I thought the train would never arrive, but they tell me it is always on time . . ."

Then she was enveloped in his arms and his lips were joyously pressing hers and she felt such a surge of love for him that she thought she would burst.

A cool, amused voice remarked, "Won't you introduce me, Alun? Even though I realise this must be Daisy, of course."

She had not expected him to be accompanied. Certainly not by a lovely, black-haired girl with a proprietoral air, for Madeleine took Alun's other arm while they followed the porter with the trolley.

The family made Daisy welcome and she blushed at Roberto's twinkling suggestion: "You shall let me make the quick sketch of you, Daisy? You need to be seen in colour! Your photograph tells some of it, but now I see you in the flesh, I itch to make a *real* picture!"

There were paintings all over the walls in the small room she shared with Madeleine. "Alun is just next door, we often sit together at night with our hot chocolate, when he gets in weary from work," Madeleine said. "It is good for me to have

196

someone my own age to talk to. He understands the way I paint. We think alike."

The precious days were not spent at all as Daisy had hoped: she was never alone with Alun for Madeleine was only too delighted, determined, to show them the sights.

"Perhaps," she suggested, "you would like to visit one of the smaller, less busy bays, the weather is so good, we could take a picnic tea, eh? Or would you rather we climbed Kilvey Hill, such magnificent views all around, or we could, with less effort, take the train from Swansea to Mumbles for an equally scenic delight?"

"The Mumbles railway was the world's very first passenger rail service, Daisy – Madeleine keeps me well-informed!" Alun said. "And she tells me that some of the most famous singers and poets live in these parts – not that I've met any yet – except for Roberto and Toria, of course!" They decided on the beach.

They rested their backs against a convenient dune, shading their eyes to watch the sailboats in the bay, sleepily aware of the wheeling seagulls quarrelling over the picnic leftovers. When, at last, Madeleine shed her stockings and shoes, running across the damp sand to the sea, lifting her skirts and petticoats deliberately high, no doubt in the hope that Alun would join her, Daisy and Alun snatched a few moments together at last.

This was a different Alun, she soon discovered, both bolder and older. His hands slid deliciously round her and his kisses were so passionate that she wanted it to go on for ever, but Madeleine too soon returned and afterwards, she thought ruefully, perhaps it was just as well. They parted abruptly and she brushed the sand from her skirt and knew that there was sand in her hair too. How much had Madeleine seen?

"Come on," Madeleine said sarcastically, "you really must cool off with a paddle in the sea, Daisy."

There was just one more kiss, a parting one, as Daisy boarded the train again. As she waved from the window, Madeleine linked her arm in Alun's and she saw her mocking smile.

197

Thirty

The ice-boats, pulled by teams of strong horses, were out on the canal. Picks were wielded to break and disperse the glassy sheets which imprisoned the dark water and had brought traffic to a standstill. "Rocking the boat!" the boatmen said as they sweated, despite the raw cold, at their vital task. For goods must be carried, defying the weather.

Daisy, standing on the canal bank with Clemmie, watching all this activity, put her arm round her sister. They wore warm tweed capes, tam o'shanters and stout boots.

"I love having you home, Daisy. I do wish you didn't have to go back to that school after Christmas," Clemmie sighed. Their breath curled like dragons' smoke.

"I was fortunate to be offered another term; the teacher whose place I have been filling is not so lucky, she is not yet fit enough to return. Anyway, you'll be back at school yourself before you know it – you don't need me to tutor you any more."

"School is not *quite* what I expected."

"Oh, why not? You couldn't wait to go there – remember?"

"They say I show off – that I'm *too* clever."

Daisy hugged her sister close. "You have to learn very fast how to fit in, Clem – as *I* know now! You have to adapt, to listen to other people, not always come up with the answer so fast so that the other children don't get a chance to show what *they* know, you see. Perhaps I taught you too much, concentrated on books, when I should have been teaching you to give and take, how to play . . . But, Clem, it was hard for me, too, because I never was childish when I was young . . .

198

I only passed on to you what I was familiar with. Still, I think *you* have had a great deal more laughter in your life with Ruth Owen for your mother!"

"I think I know what you mean," Clemmie said earnestly.

"You have one great advantage," Daisy said wisely, "in your musical ability, for, as Ruth so often says, don't the Welsh have music in their souls? It will take time, but you will wonder in a year or so why you ever worried about it."

"D'you fit in then, at your school?"

"It's not been easy for me either," Daisy confessed. "One or two of the teachers, I feel, disapprove of me just because I'm young. They are qualified too, which I am not. I am still a pupil-teacher, learning myself. Some of the girls are really snobbish, and some don't want to learn, or intend to, for they say they'll only get married, to a rich husband hopefully, then they'll only need to look decorative and arrange the flowers or embroider a thing or two. I felt so out of place there, those first weeks, I felt I would be much happier teaching at a board school, where the pupils have a thirst for knowledge, where they have to cram as much as they can into the few years they are able to be at school."

"My school sounds much nicer than yours, Daisy." Clemmie had cheered up.

"Well," Daisy said, as they walked away from the canal towards home, "I did get to go to the end-of-term dance, arranged by the school governors; there were even gentlemen to dance with! I felt just like Cinderella, it was most enjoyable. Only it was well past midnight when I slipped into my bed! I was so thankful that Ruth taught me to dance. I don't think I trod on a single toe!"

"What did you wear – your rainbow dress?"

"I spent most of my salary on something a little more, well, conventional. Bearing in mind the advice I just gave to you about fitting in . . . But it is a *lovely* dress, I know you'll think so, too."

She wished she could have worn the dress for Alun, danced with him . . . Creamy voile it was, softly draped round her bare shoulders, impossibly tight at the waist but billowing out into a full skirt, sprigged with embroidered rosebuds. She wore pink gloves and matching satin dancing slippers. She had gazed at her reflection in a long mirror, shy to see herself so grand, young, slender, smooth-skinned with her hair tied back with rose coloured ribbon, even though she possessed no pearls like her fellow teachers.

They met dear Ruth Owen at the coal shed in the yard. She was twice as large, very heavy and obviously weary. Daisy took the coal scuttle from her, scolding, "Bay should do this! Don't forget the baby is due in less than three months!"

"How could I forget?" Ruth asked wryly. "Anyway, Bay is out, giving a singing lesson – then he is going on to the choir in the chapel to coach them."

She sank down awkwardly on the sofa.

"I wanted to buy you a nursing chair," Daisy told her. "I had my eye on one, second-hand, but good as new. I put something down on it – I thought there was plenty of time before you needed it. Now I can see that the nice straight back would be a comfort to you. I'll have it sent straightaway when I get back to Kent."

"Thank you, I shall look forward to that! We ought to start on the Christmas baking, it being Christmas Eve tomorrow; Annie has already made her mince pies, she says."

"Annie is always well organised!" Daisy looked at Ruth. "Did she call in today as usual?"

"Yes she did. No letter for you from Alun, I'm sorry – but *they* have heard that he cannot afford to come home for Christmas. I'm sure *you* will hear from him tomorrow!" Ruth knew exactly how disappointed Daisy must feel.

"I hope so . . ." At first the letters had come frequently, addressed to Daisy at her school and she had written by return post. The letters were in affectionate terms but lately there had been no mention of when they could be together again. Alun, it seemed, was all-consumed by his art. Her face clouded, for it was hard to believe that he would not be home with Ivor and Annie for Christmas. It seemed an age away since he had kissed her until she was breathless, among the sand dunes in that little bay. She couldn't help remembering Madeleine's possessiveness; yet he had hardly mentioned Madeleine in his letters. Surely she was worrying about nothing?

She sighed. "I'll make the fire up, get the stove nice and hot then Clemmie and I will get out the rolling pin and make that pastry!"

They were to spend Christmas Day with Ivor and Annie to make things easier for Ruth Owen, but there was the midnight service at the chapel first and to Daisy's pleasure, Dick was there, assisting with the service. They sang the joyful carols and greeted Christmas morn together.

He had brought presents for them all, which he presented after he had walked them home, receiving theirs in return for himself, Mrs B and Jem. "I'm so excited at the thought of seeing them again," she told him, "and tell Jem to give Pom a special cuddle from me!"

"You are to expect us *en masse*," he answered, smiling, "on New Year's Day, for Ivor and Annie have invited us to spend that with you all. I understand that Ruth does not feel up to the journey to our house."

"Won't you come in, Dick?" Bay asked. "Instead of shivering on the doorstep? Ruth, take that child up to bed, she is yawning her head off."

"No, I'm not," Clemmie protested, blinking hard to prove she was wide awake.

"Happy Christmas, Clemmie! And to you, Ruth and Bay. I must decline a warming by your fire, tempting though that is, but it's a long ride home – I daresay Jem will be up and at her stocking by the time I arrive. You go in, don't get cold on my account, and Clemmie must get to her bed before *her* stocking is filled, eh?"

Then it was just Daisy and Dick by themselves, for a few minutes.

"I have missed you," he stated and to her complete surprise, he bent from his great height and kissed her. Just a brief warm kiss, unexpectedly on her lips. "Your face is cold . . ." he added, and he couldn't conceal the tenderness in his words.

Perhaps because she was lonely and Alun appeared to have let her down but probably because she was genuinely very fond of Dick even though they were not romantically involved, she stretched up her arms impulsively and entwined them round his neck. This was a longer, more serious kissing.

He straightened up. He composed himself quickly. "A happy blessed Christmas to you, Daisy . . ."

"And to you," she answered. "Thank you for all your letters, Dick, they keep me so in touch with life here in Wales. Ruth Owen and Bay are not ones much for writing – anyway I'm glad they are so busy with their teaching!"

"Did he – Alun – did he write too? How is he?" he asked.

"I heard today," she said. There had been a shock announcement in the letter, but the tone had been as affectionate as ever. She could tell Dick, it would help to explain that embrace . . . "He isn't going to continue with his studies at the college, such a pity for he seemed to be doing so well. Poor Ivor and Annie will be so disappointed! The family of artists he has been lodging with – did I tell you that their daughter is a fellow student? – have decided to go to Cornwall to join a colony of artists and he has decided to go with them . . . Of course" – she had to believe this – "he *will* come home, he promised! To see the family – *me!* – as soon as he can." It seemed to Daisy that Alun was going to the ends of the earth.

He said nothing, just looked at her searchingly under the light of the lamp.

"He sent presents for us all, Annie brought them to us today; he couldn't afford much, we appreciated that, it was enough that he thought of us. But Dick – I saw him in Swansea, you know, when he was first there, and I thought of going again in the New Year before he leaves for Cornwall."

"But he didn't ask you to," he stated.

"No!" A small word, hanging in the cold still night air.

The door opened behind her. "Good gracious, are you still out there in the cold?" Bay asked. "You might just as well have come inside, Dick."

"I must apologise for keeping Daisy – I'll fetch the horse now. Happy Christmas, once again! I will see you next week. Sleep well!"

*   *   *

Two hours later Dick warmed himself by the stove in the kitchen at home. All was quiet. Then his mother appeared. "You'd like a hot drink I'm sure, my dear – well, it's Christmas morning! We thought of you, Nanny, Jem and I at our service. What a long ride home! You met up with our friends, did you? How was Ruth Owen – and Daisy?"

"Ruth Owen was in good spirits and Daisy—"

"Yes?" She passed him the cup of coffee and poured one for herself.

"She was sad because she would not be seeing Alun Hughes."

"Does she realise how *you* feel, Dick, about her?"

"After tonight," he answered wryly, "I rather think she does. But she is so young, Mother."

"Not too young to fall in love, I gather."

"In love, yes, she really believes she is – the last thing I want is for her to be let down badly: we have to remember that he is no age, too. I can only wait and see what happens. Be there for her, if she wants me to be."

"She's the right girl for you, Dick, I feel it in my old bones!"

"The only chance *I* have, is if he gives her up. Well, I must get some sleep, and so must you – it won't be long to the early morning service! Happy Christmas, Mother!"

Sleep was actually a long time in coming. He guessed that it was the same for Daisy and he wished he could comfort her and wipe away her tears because Alun had not come home.

Christmas dinner at the house on the wharf: a great goose nicely browned but oozing succulent juices; floury potatoes, sprouts, picked with the frost on them, root vegetables from the clamp, bread sauce, redolent with cloves and onion, lean pink ham and crispy bacon – all the trimmings of a feast. While they tucked into all this, the pudding steamed briskly in its pot, tied round with a snowy cloth turban.

Round her throat Daisy had fastened Alun's precious gift, a flimsy sliver chain with a tiny pearl pendant. He had painted a card specially for her: Pili Pala, the butterfly. When she at last

203

had money of her own in the purse from her teaching, Daisy had taken that first picture he had given her to be framed. She intended to do the same for this beautiful card. The inscription would then be concealed but the words were as if engraved on her heart: 'To My Darling Daisy, I'll Love You Always, Alun.'

Ruth Owen was not able to do the meal justice for she was suffering from heartburn of late, but she looked as bonny as ever in the dress Annie had kindly adapted from one of her own generously sized frocks.

There was after-dinner entertainment from Clemmie. "I have to say it, Auntie Annie, your piano is not as tuneful as mine! I wonder if poor Mr Drago misses it, eh? I wonder if he's spending Christmas on his own – wasn't it *awful* his wife had that accident? Oh well, I'll do my best!"

She played with aplomb while the others reflected on the fact that they had probably eaten far too much and might well suffer for it later.

They were not late in leaving, for Ruth Owen's sake, for she looked weary. As she heaved herself to her feet Annie said, "Don't forget we are having another party on New Year's Day, will you? But I can't face another goose, can you? A nice round of beef then, eh?"

Daisy slipped her hands into her soft muff, Dick's gift. Ruth Owen and Clemmie had been similarly blessed, so she did not question his extravagance but was grateful, for it was raw cold outside. "Oh, Alun, *why* didn't you come?" she thought aloud and Ruth Owen nodded sympathetically. To herself she said, I miss you so much . . .

Thirty-One

N ew Year's Eve and snow threatened.

"I hope Mrs B, Dick and Jem will be able to come tomorrow," Clemmie fretted.

"The roads are still clear, Clem," Ruth murmured, putting her feet up on the sofa with difficulty. She rubbed her swollen abdomen with small, circular motions of her palm. She added, "All being well, they'll come, don't worry."

"Time for your piano practice, Clemmie," Bay reminded her. "Are you sure you're all right, Ruth?" He had seen a certain expression cross her face and vague memories stirred, although he had not been so concerned when Ruth Owen was pregnant with Clemmie, he thought with real remorse.

"Please stop fussing, Bay – see she does a full hour – you will have to teach her when I'm busy with her baby sister." She sounded really tetchy.

"I've decided to become a concert pianist," Clemmie told them cheerfully, raising the piano lid. "Bay says it's the perfect occupation for *me*, 'cos I can't talk if I'm concentrating on the keys."

"I haven't noticed that." Daisy was busy at the table with scissors and material.

"I don't know why you keep insisting the baby will be a girl," Bay put in, for he was hoping for a son – they all knew that.

"It'll be one or the other and the sooner the better," Ruth muttered grimly.

There was a knock at the door. "Juniper – come in!" Daisy invited. "How's Rose?"

"She's very well. You can hardly see *she's* expecting – and how are you, dear Ruth Owen? We're stopping off here for a few days, seeing the weather. Thought you might be glad to see me?"

"You don't know how glad," Ruth gasped as she felt another twinge. "Dear God, the baby isn't due for another eight weeks."

Juniper took charge in her calm way. "Daisy, my dear, you come upstairs with us, you should know a thing or two in case."

Seeing Bay's alarm, Ruth Owen struggled to her feet, one hand supporting the small of her back. "Bay, my old darling, there's nothing wrong, nothing at all . . . Why, you are one ahead of me: your third child and only my second. The first is always the worst, not knowing what's what; I expect the baby is only changing position. Don't you *dare* come upstairs, unless you're called for!"

Clemmie was sitting very still, quiet now on the piano stool. She looked very solemn as Juniper and Daisy supported Ruth, one in front, one behind, as they climbed the stairs which led off the living room. The door closed firmly behind them.

Juniper's sure fingers probed gently as Ruth lay on the coverlet of her comfortable bed. "Get that fire lit, Daisy – good, it's ready laid. Got a match? Ruth must stay up here. I'm going to take a little cottage myself soon," she said, making conversation to help her friend through the next spasm. "The young couple are doing well on *The Molly Kelly* and I reckon I can be more use, looking after the children in a settled place, so that they can go to school reg'lar."

"Times are certainly changing . . ." Ruth Owen gasped.

Daisy obediently put a match to the sticks and paper in the grate.

Ruth said quite calmly, "It's on the way isn't it, Juniper? I'm so big with this baby compared to your Rose, with that little bump you can hardly see when she wears her apron – and Gwennie, so round already that *her* baby is accommodated in the folds . . ."

"You are carrying a lot of water, the baby itself is small I believe," Juniper stated. "Yes, it's coming, and there's nothin'

I can do to stop it, I'm afraid. Daisy, will you be very brave and help me? For a baby when it's early comes all in a rush – the danger will be after, for it will struggle to survive in this bitter cold weather. Let me help you undress now, little Ruth Owen; Daisy, tell your father he must keep the fires going, the water boiling in the copper, he must keep Clem busy and out of our way . . . You have the towels ready? The pieces for the bed? Tear this rag in three – plait as tight as you can, for a pull on the bed rail. Then put them napkins I saw you hemmin' the other day to warm with a baby's nightgown, should you have one ready."

"I have the flannel ready cut out – I was doing that when you came, but it's not sewn yet," lamented Daisy. "I was going to bag the use of Annie's machine – you want me to tell Bay what's happening, is that it?"

"*That's* it . . ." Ruth Owen exhaled the words in a deep sigh.

Bay looked up sharply as Daisy came into the living room. Clemmie's fingers faltered on the piano keys.

"Yes, the baby is coming," she said huskily, as if her throat had dried up. "Juniper says we – you – are not to worry and that you can best help, Bay, by staying down here, getting in plenty of coal and boiling lots of water in the copper and in pans, on the stove. I am going to help upstairs if I can, and we will call you if we need you. Clemmie" – inspiration struck – "*you* must keep playing, soft soothing music mind, Bay will advise; that will be *your* part in helping Ruth relax until the baby is born."

"I'm not sure," Clemmie said, her lips trembling, "where babies actually come from – how it will be born, Daisy – d'you know?"

"I am about to find out, I think!" Daisy managed a wry smile at Bay. "I am not your teacher now, Clem: this is something for Ruth to tell you and I'm sure she will if you ask – but not for a few days, there's a good girl."

As she returned swiftly upstairs, Clemmie struck up *Au Clair de la Lune* and there was the sound of Bay shovelling coal in the yard.

207

"Should Bay call the doctor?" Daisy asked Juniper, as she saw Ruth pulling desperately on the improvised rope.

"No – no!" Ruth cried, "Juniper – is better – than – any – trained nurse!"

The music was loud and clear, as Clemmie had neglected to take her foot off the loud pedal. Ruth was groaning in agonised gasps.

"Fetch the basin, Daisy," Juniper said calmly. "We will need that to catch the afterbirth. A needle and strong thread, too, dear girl. You c'n shout down to Bay: tell him to bring the water, but put it down outside the door."

"I don't – want – *him* – to see me – like this!" Ruth managed through clenched teeth.

"Shock might be too much for him." Juniper caught sight of Daisy's widened eyes, the shock on *her* face as she saw what Juniper was at. "*And* for you!"

Ruth Owen gave a convulsive heave, then the baby was born, caught in Juniper's sure hands. "There, my darling, just an hour from start to finish – what a brave little Ruth Owen you are . . . Lie back, rest a moment, 'tis a very little baby, see? I have to rub its tiny chest to get it breathin' safe like – Daisy, are you *struck*? The towel, dear, and the cotton for clearin' its nose – don't be afraid, that's on'y the cord; you must hold your little sister now, whilst I cuts and ties it – good cap'ble hands your Daisy has, Ruth Owen, she'll cradle this little scrap to her, keep it warm, whilst I sees to the rest on it . . ."

The afterbirth was duly delivered, examined to ensure it was complete, then well disguised in newspaper. "A job for your father, Daisy, to burn all this. Tell him not to set the chimney 'light as fathers tend to do."

Ruth felt the kind strong hands lift her, turn her, remove the soiled linen. Then the gentle sponging, the clean nightgown eased over her head. She slipped back gratefully into the hollow in the mattress, weary beyond words but immensely content. A thought drifted dreamily in her head: I must let Drago know, somehow.

"There, my darlin'," she heard Juniper say, as if she was far away, "I daren't bath the baby today, just pat her dry with a soft towel for she *is* so tiny, not ready for this world. No finger nails, see and such fine skin. Let me tuck this napkin carefully into place . . . Now, don't fret, Ruth Owen – the crib is to hand, but you won't have need of it, for a while. You must lay the baby against your breast, against your bare skin, let her take the warmth of your body, so she's still close to you in that *special* way; pull your nightgown round her, cuddle her and sleep, both of you. She will take no harm; you will not overlay her, I promise. She will take her time to learn to suckle, even though she is near to her supply, for she is not a lusty hungry baby – she only need your mother-love for now."

"Did you say – a little girl?" Ruth asked faintly, her lips caressing that minute, downy head, still smeared with lanolin. "It was to be a boy – named for Bay . . ." But she was not disappointed.

The baby's body moved in a fluttering, feeble way against her, but she was sure this was a heartening, hopeful sign. So fragile, so tiny, so *wonderful*, Ruth thought with joy and ready love.

"Fetch your father and sister – just to peep," Juniper told Daisy.

As she ran happily downstairs to impart the good news, Juniper advised, "You must rest and rest, Ruth Owen. Do not move the baby from its nestlin' place for a few hours . . . Bay *should* go for the doctor now, I think, to make sure that all is well with both of you."

"Thank you, Juniper, for everything." Ruth murmured.

Bay knelt emotionally by the bed, placed his arms so carefully round the two of them. "Ah Ruth, another daughter! Thank you, Juniper, for all your care and strength."

Clemmie, clutching at Daisy in the doorway, said solemnly, "She is so small, not as big as my dolly even. Ruth, can I stop playing the piano now? I've run out of all the pieces I know!"

"Darling, of course you can!" Ruth Owen smiled.

"The doctor . . ." Juniper gently reminded Bay.

"Tell Ivor and Annie at the same time; say I'm sorry you and I won't be at the party tomorrow, but that Daisy and Clemmie will be there!"

"Oh, I can't leave you," Daisy said quickly.

"Nonsense! You must go. They will be so disappointed if you don't. Bay can take care of me, and I promise I won't lift a finger except to change the baby, or to slide myself on to the bedpan!"

Bay rose reluctantly, still gazing wonderingly at Ruth and the baby.

"Rachel," Ruth said dreamily, as her eyelids fluttered. "That's her name, of course." For Rachel, with love.

Thirty-Two

Pompom leapt straight up into Daisy's arms the minute she saw her, her whole body wriggling in delight, her warm, wet tongue doing overtime. "I didn't need my neck washed, you know, Pom!" Daisy said in mock reproof.

Then they were surrounded, being hugged by Mrs B, a strangely grown-up Jem, so much taller in her smart new clothes, and by Ivor and Annie. Dick stood a little apart but she knew that he was looking at her. She was glad that she was wearing her special Christmas dress, which she had made specially in her spare time at school, in fine scarlet needlecord.

"Happy New Year!" came the cries; and a new baby too, they all marvelled. What an auspicious start!

"Did you see the New Year in, Daisy?" Jem asked, and she recognised the hint of shyness in her friend's voice: she, too, had changed, after all, and looked very different in her fashionable dress with her hair swept up.

"We went to the Watch Night service at the chapel," Jem added.

"I was sitting up until almost two," Daisy said ruefully, "finishing off a nightie for baby Rachel." She thought her eyes probably matched her dress, for they felt so sore and red-rimmed after she had plied her needle by lamplight.

"I write to my mam every week, Mrs B helps me with what to say," Jem chattered over lunch. "She's back with Ted and little Elsie now; my money coming in means she can afford a room, and Ted's friends, the bobby and his wife, help out with food and that. She ain't had to go to the work'us like she feared. I'm Mrs B's gen'l fac-totum, that's what she says, it

211

means I help out anywhere, do anything I'm asked to, at the mission and all, as well."

"You look so happy and well, Jem," Daisy approved.

"Oh, I am, Daisy, I *am*! I do lessons with Mrs B too, and if I work very hard maybe I'll be able to train as a nurse one day, for she says I'm good with children and old folks in partic'lar – but I'd *really* like to be a missionary you know."

"And why not?" Dick put in, settling himself down next to Daisy. He had been called out in the middle of his meal to speak to someone at the door.

They played parlour games in the afternoon, spinning the plate for forfeits, hunt the thimble, when Jem and Clemmie nearly turned the house upside down, while Annie smiled indulgently, and then they settled down to memory games with pencils and paper.

Mrs B said to Daisy, "Your hair is coming down, dear – all those energetic games. You look so lovely in that dress – the colour really suits you."

"Thank you," Daisy said, fumbling with the pins in her hair.

"Leave it loose," Dick said, putting out a restraining hand. "You look more like our old Daisy now."

"We mustn't be late back," she said regretfully, just after tea. "I rather thought that Bay would be pounding on the door in a panic by now."

"Wavin' the white flag?" Jem grinned.

"I'll walk you both home," Dick said, "unless you want to go in the carriage? We will soon have to be making a reluctant move ourselves, unless we want to see midnight in again."

"It's not far. Let's walk," Daisy decided. They made their fond farewells, and Pompom in Jem's arms hid her head reproachfully when Daisy tickled her behind her ears. "She'll get over it, Jem; she loves you, I know," she said wisely, but she felt a twinge of sadness. Yet another change in her life, she thought, giving up Pom.

"We'll be up to see the baby in a day or two – Juniper advised no visitors just yet," Annie said. "Here, I made this jelly for Ruth."

"And will you give her the basket of fruit from us?" Mrs B asked, giving it to Dick to carry. When she kissed Daisy she whispered in her ear, "He is so happy you are not going away immediately, you know."

Clemmie skipped ahead, kicking a pebble, while Daisy and Dick followed, not talking much but comfortable together. When she stumbled slightly, he tucked her arm in his and it felt nice: there was not that throbbing awareness, the intensity of being close as there had been between herself and Alun; there had been an element of pain in that pleasure, she recalled, wondering belatedly what Alun was doing at this moment.

She lifted her face for Dick's farewell kiss – it felt right and good, the gentle pressure of his lips and the warmth of his big hands on her shoulders.

"When do you go back?" he asked.

"Not for another ten days, and if I feel that Ruth Owen still needs me, well, I will let the school know I must take a longer leave, my family must always come first," she said earnestly.

"I will come again soon to see you then," he said. "It may be that Ruth and Bay will want the baby baptised as she is so premature. But don't worry, you are all in my prayers, particularly baby Rachel just now."

There was such longing in his eyes that Daisy thought, He *loves* me! He is a strong character, such a good person, if only I felt free to return his feelings . . .

But her dreams that night were, as always, of Alun.

He was walking slowly along the deserted beach. The house on the cliff-top, with lights burning in every room, illuminated the rocks he had scrambled down hours earlier. He knew he should go back; they would be wondering where he was.

It was a rambling old house, cold and draughty, owned by Roberto and Toria's patron. Five other artists, sponsored by him, shared the premises, cleaning was disregarded, but they took turns with the cooking, mainly great pots of thick vegetable soup.

He had a room at the top of the house, with a bed, a chest of drawers, a shabby mat which slipped about on the bare floor-boards. He shivered at nights, glad to add the good overcoat which Ivor had sent him, to supplement the meagre blankets. This was such a different way of living, he thought, from the simplicity and stability of the lock cottage just a few months ago: dear Mam on her couch, smiling and wise; Meg busy with delicious concoctions on the stove; the heat from the fires he stoked constantly – he missed it all. He yearned to see Daisy again: had he been foolish to come here with Madeleine and her family, to give up all he had strived for, gained at the college? He wouldn't be given a second chance there, he realised that. Yet, now he was free to paint, to express himself, not forced to conform as his tutors thought desirable.

Drink had flowed freely at the New Year's Eve party. In the cottage, under Meg's regime, strong liquor had been taboo, for she had signed the Pledge at the Chapel. Mam had enjoyed a little of Gwennie's 'medicinal' wine of course. He remembered, with a faint quirk of his lips, that his da had been led astray, as Meg so righteously put it, by old Eli, the Midnight Grocer, regularly once a week on pay day. Mam had not objected, she was more tolerant than Meg.

There had been surprising news of Meg, though, at Christmas. She was 'walking out' with her cousin, so Ivor said, for *she* would not write to him since he had let her down leaving the college like that. He was glad for her, for wasn't that what she had always wanted: a home, a husband and a family of her own? Their cousin, as he recalled, was as strait-laced as Meg herself, and indeed, she would have considered no other kind of man.

He had gone to bed before midnight struck, feeling fuddled and very sick, for no one had bothered with food, just drunk much wine. He was drifting off to sleep, when the door opened and Madeleine came creeping in. He felt her hand stroking his brow, tousling his hair. It was such a familiar caressing, just as he remembered Mam doing when he was poorly as a child.

"Poor boy, do you feel ill?" she whispered. "It is midnight, Alun, a new year for *us*." The shouts went up downstairs, there was much noise and laughter. The party was going on.

"Daisy . . ." he murmured.

"Not Daisy, *me!*" Thick-headed as he was, he heard the jealous sharpness of her tone. "She is not here, but *I* am."

Had he imagined what happened next? he hoped now unhappily. But the awakening this morning had been real enough. Madeleine lay beside him, unclothed, in that narrow bed, her arms still fast around him, content in her sleeping.

On the chest, he saw that Daisy's portrait had been lain face down. His head seemed to be splitting in two, he could smell the almond oil with which she dressed her hair, which was loosened from the heavy single braid, spread, crimped from the plaiting, all over his pillow. There was the warm odour of Madeleine herself; her bare arms were like plump smooth olive satin, her breath came softly from her parted full lips.

He felt a dangerous desire, but he jerked free from her embrace. Her eyes opened instantly, she smiled at him triumphantly.

Alun could say nothing, he just snatched his coat, his clothes and rushed from the room.

The partygoers had slumped in action some time before dawn. He skirted the sleepers, noticed abstractedly in passing the clock in the hall that it was almost midday. Out into the swirling cold air he stepped, breathing deeply, cleansing his lungs. Self-disgust, shame were paramount.

He ran down the grassy slope from the house to the cliff edge.

Now he saw that the tide had receded; then, it had been almost in. He had moved from the hollow where he had been sitting for so long and began the aimless walking. Here, in the spring, he imagined setting up his easel, painting the craggy beauty around him, or further along at the quay, trying to capture the local fishermen with strokes of the fine brushes Daisy had given him, or the boats, dipping on the swell of the green sea, in full sail.

Madeleine came up to him, demurely attired now in a flowing cape, her face framed by the hood, calling out in her throaty voice, "I thought you had run away from me! Come back up now to the house, Alun, for it will be really dark within ten minutes and the climb will be dangerous. Mama has made such a delicious meal for us all."

She took his arm and he went with her, unresisting. Madeleine talked to him, just as if nothing had happened at all. He had betrayed Daisy; he dared not think of *her* now.

Thirty-Three

Ruth Owen was crying silently; she didn't really know why, except she was so tired and the baby had been fretful all night. She had tried to nurse tiny Rachel but although her milk was in, her breasts felt painful and unyielding. The baby's feeble sucking was not strong enough to ease her.

By the flickering of the nightlight on the bedside table, she lay Rachel on a towel on her side of the bed, and began the careful cleansing with soft cotton and olive oil, the gentle wrapping of the little bottom in the flimsy muslin squares; the terry-towelling napkins had proved far too big and bulky.

Bay was stirring reluctantly; he lumbered out of bed obediently though when she asked, "Stir the fire will you, Bay – we must keep her warm."

She heard the muttering: "I told you I was too old to go through all *this* again . . ."

Then Ruth was really sobbing out loud at the sheer unfairness of it and Bay, thoroughly alarmed, was out of the room like a shot and knocking on Daisy's door.

"Shush!" she warned, reaching for her gown and slippers. "Don't wake Clemmie. You go down and make us some tea, then fetch up some nice, warm water for Ruth to wash. She must feel so hot and sticky holding the baby to her like that, all night."

"You don't think I should fetch Juniper, do you?" he asked as he went obediently downstairs.

"We'll see. I'll see what I can do first," she said soothingly, as if she was the one so much older and wiser.

Ruth was now sobbing intermittently and Rachel was emitting a thin wail. "I feel so sore, headachey with the milk coming in; it's always an emotional time – I remember it from Clemmie."

"I wasn't involved then, of course," said Daisy, taking the baby carefully into her arms, "and you were two weeks in the nursing home, weren't you?"

"Bay pawned his dress suit that time," Ruth said ruefully, mopping her eyes with the sheet. "I really don't know how we could cope without you, Daisy – you are always so dependable."

"Bay's bringing up some warm water in a minute; you'd appreciate a refreshing wash, I know?" Ruth nodded. "I hope he's made tea as well! I know Juniper said keep Rachel warm against you, but it won't hurt, I think, if I lay her beside you for a short while, in Bay's cosy place." However, as she did this she exclaimed, "Ruth!"

"What is it?" She was thoroughly alarmed.

"Look, she's all *yellow* – whatever does it mean?"

"Jaundice, it must be! Some new babies get it, particularly if they are premature. Daisy – Bay will have to run and rouse Juniper on *The Molly Kelly* – *I* really don't know what to do!"

The tea and the washing were forgotten; Bay had to bundle his nightshirt inside his trousers, while Daisy fetched his boots, coat and hat and lit the lantern.

In less than half an hour Juniper was holding little Rachel Barley in her arms and looking her over. "'Tis worryin' I know, Ruth Owen, my dear. The doctor might say, 'Just leave it alone, keep her close and warm', just as I advised, and hope your milk, when she can take it, will strengthen her. I have my own tried remedy but I will not do it if you don't wish. Don't fret, it won't do no harm, even should it do no good."

Bay looked doubtful, but Ruth Owen said at once, "If it is safe, of course try it, Juniper. I trust your judgement, you know that."

"Fetch me a 'postle spoon." Juniper roused Bay to further action. "Daisy, while I holds the baby steady, you are to spoon in the castor oil drop by drop. She won't like it, but she has to take it. Is that the bottle on the table over there?"

"Yes, I had it ready, to take a large dose myself, in case the baby was late like and needed a reminder to come!"

"That's right, smile my dear, that'll help. Ah, the spoon . . . You go downstairs again, there's a good fellow, for didn't Daisy tell me you left a pot of tea brewing on the stove? This'll be done afore you get back, eh?" She shut the door after him. "You close your eyes, Ruth Owen, don't you watch and distress yourself, there's nothing to hurt little Rachel, on'y the taste o' it."

Drop by steady drop, Daisy dripped into her sister's mouth every time she opened it to cry in protest. That tiny spoon seemed to hold an endless supply of the foul oil. The baby grimaced, drawing up her puny legs in distress but Juniper urged Daisy to keep at it, slowly but surely. When she had completed her task, her hand suddenly shook and she dropped the spoon with a clatter on the floor.

Ruth Owen's eyes opened immediately. "Now, soothe the poor little soul with a feed," Juniper advised, knowing just how to coax the baby to nurse with a gentle pinch of her nostrils so that she was forced to open her mouth and then to seek comfort.

"Now I'll walk her up and down a while, 'til the oil passes through her like," Juniper said after a minute or two.

Bay brought the tea and Ruth and Daisy drank it in great gulps, hot though it was.

"Strange," Juniper remarked. "This on'y happens with a second baby, never the first, and the baby is always early – that's a sign. Often a mother can have no further children, or if she should fall, she is likely to miscarry."

They watched as up and down, up and down, Juniper walked the room, then, quite suddenly, the baby began to retch. "Quick, Ruth, lay her across your knees," Juniper ordered, "face to one side. Here, let me slip this towel under her cheek." She knelt by the bed, on a level with little Rachel. "That's right, my little darling, bring it all up."

More retching, then Rachel began to cry. Juniper wiped her

damp face tenderly with the muslin Daisy silently handed to her. "Look, Rachel's mam – just look at what we have here!" Juniper displayed the napkin to Ruth Owen.

She stared, fascinated, at the yellow, glistening ball the baby had vomited. Oily, like a butter pat it was. And to Ruth's joy here was Rachel, already turning pink again, and nestling content once more, inside her cosy hideaway, in her mother's tender embrace.

"We're having no more babies!" Bay said forcefully, stroking Ruth's forehead.

"Just you hug Juniper for me!" Ruth Owen said gratefully.

Daisy hugged her too. "I hope you're around, Juniper, when I have babies!"

"Oh, you won't have no trouble, Daisy, none at all," she replied confidently. "And you'll be far away, over the sea, you know, when you have *your* first!"

"She's usually right!" Ruth reminded Daisy, smiling widely now. The baby knew how to nurse now, the pain would diminish, all would be well.

When they were alone once more, settling down, hopefully to sleep for it was not yet four o'clock, Bay put his arm very carefully round Ruth's waist and held them both close. "I wasn't much good, was I, Ruth? I'm sorry I said – you know! – and upset you earlier."

"You are as you are, Bay – I can't change you – and yet," Ruth said softly, "I love you very much. I have to admit I'm far from perfect too. We are so lucky, to have been given a second chance together, with little Rachel, aren't we?"

He gave a contented sigh. "You're wonderful, Ruth Owen, you really are." He paused. "Anne would have liked you – more than that, she would have loved you for bringing up *her* daughter so well too . . ."

Ruth was up and about again, with the baby still close to her, tied securely with a shawl, when the postman brought a letter from Alun. Clemmie was back at school again. The weather was not too bad; the expected snow had thankfully not materialised. Daisy had written to her school and resigned her post. "They say there may be an opening there again in the summer term, but we'll have to see how things go here," she told Ruth Owen.

She was pleased to have Daisy around for moral support, naturally, but she suspected the girl was missing her short-lived independence. She was glad Alun had written at last, for this was the first letter since Christmas. Much as she loved the boy, she had begun to wonder regretfully if he really was the one for Daisy.

She mused that she was so fortunate that her ailing marriage had revived after that desperate moonlight flit back to her country. There was the miracle of Bay discovering that he really loved her, the reconciliation with Rachel and the acknowledgement now that she was her daughter. She had even reached a sort of understanding with Drago – she supposed she had acknowledged *him* in her own way, at last. She had rediscovered old friends and made some new ones. Clemmie had a proper home at last and a promising future. She must not dwell on the sadness of losing Rachel Hughes, or how she felt for Drago with his tragedy. Daisy had been so much a part of all this. Please God, she would find the happiness and fulfilment *she* deserved.

She looked down at the little face peeping from the shawl. Dark hair and the Owen eyes.

"You will look like your grandmother, I think," she murmured with pride. "And if your nature is as sweet and loving, well, can I ask for more?"

Thirty-Four

D ick had called for Daisy earlier for he was passing on his way to the far end of the canal and had an hour or two to spare.

They walked and talked as was their wont, about Jem's latest doings, Pompom's current mischief, stealing and eating half a fruit cake, and events on the mission trail.

"When are you off again?" he asked, as they rested on a stile before climbing to the top of the hill. "*I* may be going to Africa soon, if it can be arranged. There is much unrest in South Africa of course, but the mission is growing in Rhodesia."

"I don't think I'll be going, Dick," she said simply. "I didn't tell Ruth Owen of course, but the school was not too pleased I let them down, though there may be an opportunity there later on. Oh, Dick, do you have to go so far away? I'll miss you if you do!"

His arm lay easily round her shoulders. "You could always come to Africa with me." Lightly said, but those very blue eyes revealed so much more.

"I'm not nearly good enough to be a missionary," she replied softly. She felt his hold tighten as he turned her to face him.

"You are one of the most unselfish people I know, Daisy. You are simply – good. You are a born teacher and Ruth says a most caring nurse; you helped so much when Rachel was born, and since. But they would learn to cope on their own . . . I am asking you to come with me as my wife."

She thought that she shouldn't really feel so surprised. She had recognised long ago that Dick loved her dearly, because of the way she felt for Alun. She knew, to her sadness, that she must be prepared for the fact that *he* would not be returning to marry her one day. She had not heard from him for weeks. He had not even written to Ruth and Bay to congratulate them on the baby.

She must be honest with Dick. "I do love you, you know – not perhaps in the way you want me to, but I'm always happy when I'm with you. It would not be fair though to marry you – this might not be enough . . ." she faltered.

"You don't have to give me your answer yet – you see me as a patient person, and I really hope I am! – but I can be tenacious too – I won't give up easily! Time to go on, I think – for I must soon make tracks." He offered his hand to help her over the stile. She would have been surprised, and perhaps a little disconcerted if she had known of the passion within him, for he controlled his feelings well.

They slipped back into their easy conversation as they walked back to the cottage, hand in hand, like the very good friends they were.

"Can't you stay for lunch?" Ruth Owen was disappointed. "Clemmie will be dismayed when she finds you have been and gone without her seeing you, due to her being at school!"

"I'm sorry, I would dearly love to accept your offer but I really must reach my destination before dark," he said. "Don't worry, you can't keep me away – I'll call if I may, on my way back!"

It was very natural for Daisy to kiss him goodbye nowadays. Ruth vanished to the kitchen unobtrusively. Today he held her just a fraction longer than usual as they stood on the step.

"Daisy, I don't really have the right to say this, I know, but I have assumed from what you said earlier that you are aware of the depth of my feelings for you. I would not ask you to marry me if I did not love you dearly."

"I know that, Dick," she said. She watched as he mounted his horse and rode off.

Indoors, Ruth said, "Oh, a letter came by the second post for you. It looks as if it is from Alun, well, I certainly hope so, for your sake. He had been so lax in writing of late, busy painting I suppose, but I do feel he might reply to all the letters we have sent."

She took it upstairs when she went to put her cloak in the closet. She sat on the edge of the bed, and opened the envelope slowly, reluctantly, as if she already knew what it contained.

My dearest Daisy, I can be cowardly no longer. I must tell you that I have to marry Madeleine very soon. I know how much this will hurt you, but there is no alternative. I have behaved abominably towards both of you.

I should not say this, but I want you to know that I still adore you and that I am positive that I always will . . . I have to make the best of things here, you see. I wish I had never left Brynbach, that I had married you, while I had the chance, but it is all too late now.

One promise I mean to keep. I really will come back one day when the hurting is over for both of us, when I can say to you how sorry I am, in person. But I don't expect you to forgive me, my darling.

When you can put my betrayal behind you, try to remember how happy we were together, for that time you were on *Pili Pala*, the Butterfly Boat.

I shall not write again. Please explain, however you think fit, to the family. Tell them I was glad about the baby. Maybe I am like Ruth Owen, as Meg always said, having to leave those I love so much – yet, didn't Ruth come back? Do not upset yourself by replying. Alun.

"*I have to marry* . . ." Daisy said these words aloud, then repeated them. If *she* had succumbed to Alun's demands, as she had longed to do, she thought dully, it could have been *her* he had to marry . . .

She could not cry, which was strange. She spoke aloud again, but it did not sound like her voice at all. "I am going to Africa," Daisy declared.

He took her hands in his and looked at her quizzically, with love and concern. "I will marry you, Dick," she said quietly.

"You make me feel very proud. Mother will be so pleased,

and Jem. *She* intends to come out to Africa too as soon as she is old enough!"

He knew her reasons, she thought, for Ruth Owen had waylaid him first to whisper of Alun's marriage in haste, but he did not ask her to make painful explanations. If she could bring herself to do so, in a while, she would show him Alun's letter.

She said only, "May I ask you to wait a little longer, while I prepare myself for Africa? I would like to spend a few months at one of the mission schools, here, or in England, so that I know how to *really* teach. I want to be a partner, in every way, to support you in your work, just as much as I can."

"Yes, you need some time on your own," he said intuitively. "It will be very hard to part with you, Daisy, but I do understand."

"I know you do! And I shall miss you, miss my family, especially watching little Rachel grow, very much. But – I have some more growing up to do myself, you see."

Ruth Owen had left them alone in the parlour. When Daisy and Dick joined her in the kitchen she asked, "Is everything all right?"

"Yes – Daisy has agreed to marry me."

"We are going to Africa together, not yet, but in a few months' time . . . But, dear Ruth, I want to undergo some training first – as soon as that can be arranged, well, I shall have to leave you all, you see . . ."

Ruth dabbed at her eyes. Daisy bent and took Rachel from her.

"I am happy for you both, I really am—" Ruth Owen wept.

Later, when Clemmie and Bay came in, Daisy said, "You're a big girl now, Clem. You must help Ruth Owen as much as you can. You must see that Bay toes the line" – she smiled at her father – "and *you* can give Rachel a kiss from me, every night I am away. And I promise you, when it's time for the summer season again, I'll come back for a trip on *Pili Pala* and we'll sing, we Singing Barleys, for old times' sake, eh?"

Rachel's first smile – or was it wind? – illuminated that tiny face. She was so like Ruth, so like *him*. She'd never have an Owen baby now, Daisy thought fleetingly, with shining dark eyes like this: both she and Dick were fair.

She handed the baby to her father. "You won't mind if Dick and I go out for a while before supper? We have so much to say to each other." In fact, when they were alone, she just clung tightly to him.

In a few days' time she would have a lovely ring on her engagement finger, with a sapphire as blue as the painted butterfly.

Thirty-Five

"See, Rachel Barley." Daisy hoisted her baby sister higher on her shoulder so that she could take in the stillness, the beauty all around them. "Here is the river where I bathed, exactly a year ago. Here I met Alun and here, my darling sister, is where I must say goodbye for ever to him. D'you think he knows I am thinking of him on this lovely, special June morning?"

Rachel, still replete from her early dawn feed, merely yawned widely and snuggled back down into the folds of the shawl which securely fastened her to Daisy. She was catching up fast on her early arrival, Daisy thought, but, despite her two months' headstart, she was still much smaller than Molly, Rose's baby, with flaming hair just like the first Molly Kelly, or Elijah, Eli the Second, who gurgled happily on the counter in his moses basket in the Midnight Grocer's shop, or slept placidly among the goods in the trap whenever his doting parents took the fancy to make late deliveries.

Clemmie came running down the slope to meet them. "Oh, there you are!" she cried reproachfully. "You might have woken me up and asked me to come too!" She looked at the baby with just a hint of jealousy. "Daisy was *my* sister first, you know, Rachel Barley . . . I've missed her too, all these months she's been away, and now, after just two days on *Pili Pala* she's going away again for *ever*!"

"Now, Clem, you know I'm not! Oh, I'd love to have a paddle, wouldn't you? I'd forgotten how clear, how clean – and cold! – the river water is."

"We both had a bath last night, there's no need. And *you* had the privilege of the first lot of water!"

227

"It really revived me after all my travelling," Daisy smiled, turning away from the river and the distant mountain.

They made a fuss of Old William, out of retirement yet again, for only he must draw the boat on this very special journey, Daisy stipulated. "I miss Pom around – *she* should be here. I'm so looking forward to seeing her again!" Daisy confided.

Clemmie gave her a knowing look. "I should have thought that there was someone else you would be glad to see first!" she grinned.

There was a good smell of cooking coming from the cabin, for now Bay was, amazingly, something of an expert at lighting stoves and when Ruth Owen had risen, after she had passed the baby over to Daisy early on, she had woken him with: "A long haul ahead, and fathers, ancient or not, must do their bit . . ."

So there was her father, to Daisy's delighted astonishment, frying eggs and bacon with studied casualness as if he had been domesticated all his life. "I invariably break the yolks though," he sighed.

"He *had* to learn to cook when I was so busy with the baby, after you went off to do your training for your great adventure," Ruth Owen told Daisy. "Well, as I said, one of us has to cook if we're to survive without Daisy!"

She sat down on the trunk, packed with very special things, all lovingly pressed by Annie for the morrow. "Clem," she said, before she forgot, "I would like you to have my dancing dress, you know, the one with the rosebuds. I only wore it that once; you can keep it for the future, when you are the famous Miss Clementina Barley, Concert Pianist!"

"You won't still be away *then*?" Clemmie demanded anxiously, not doubting that she really would be famous one day.

"I believe trips home are allowed!"

"I wish you hadn't had your hair cut," Ruth sighed, "not that it doesn't look pretty, curling all over your head like that."

"You could have stuffed a cushion with the clippings!" Daisy said with feeling. "The hairdresser insisted I save a curl or two for 'my loved ones' – shall I share them between

228

you and Dick? It feels so light and airy, cropped like this. I had to be practical going out into all that heat, you see. It took so long to wash and dry, my great mop. It's like a weight lifted off my head – though the clothes we have to wear will be cumbersome enough, I'm afraid. Long boots, long sleeves, high necks, hats, for so many fevers are caused by parasites biting unprotected skin." The words 'malaria' and 'snakebite' still made her shudder; she didn't want to think about that yet.

"You've learned your lessons well. Here, give me the baby while you eat your breakfast: she has enough crumbs shed on her head each day, for don't I always fancy a biscuit when I'm nursing her?"

It had taken some hasty organising for the family to have *Pili Pala* made ready for this trip by The Singing Barleys, as Daisy requested in her last letter home. '*Pili Pala* changed everything, for all of us; I can't wait to journey up the canal once more, but now I can anticipate the happy ending!'

As she had done that first time, Daisy sat up top watching the countryside slip by. They were nearing Ty-Gyda-Cerded.

The steps were no longer white, the moss was encroaching; the windows were shuttered, there were no curtains billowing in the breeze. The house looked forlorn, deserted, as indeed it was. With a shiver, she thought of poor, mentally unstable Eluned; of Drago with his melancholy face – where was he now, she wondered?

At this point, Ruth Owen relinquished the steering to Bay and went below to be alone with her own thoughts. They passed the place with no comment from any of them.

There were more memories for them to face when they waited for the new lock keeper to let them through Alun's lock. Of course, they were experienced at all this now for hadn't they manoeuvred through the tunnel last night with just the help of a passing mole catcher? Daisy had legged it, in a spare pair of Bay's trousers, alongside him. "Good practice for Africa, I presume!" she joked, but Bay looked doubtful.

Ruth Owen seemed to quietly accept that Rachel Hughes was there no more, that it was another one, also called Alun, who cheerfully told them how glad he had been when the opportunity came for the job and the cottage. Their Alun's cow gave such rich milk, he said, and his wife was delighted by all the plants in the garden, particularly Meg's special flowers.

"We could have gone to the shop to see Eli and Gwennie and their baby, of course – Clem says he has a smile just like his father's!" Daisy said, "but it won't be long before we see them anyway, will it – they *are* coming tomorrow, aren't they?"

"Of course! Didn't Gwennie do most of the baking, with young Eli tucked under her arm?"

It really was a voyage of remembrance: "Where we sang at the wedding – remember? And the midnight storm – remember?"

"How could we forget *that*," Ruth agreed, as she steered and Bay walked the horse with Clemmie astride. She even blushed as she looked at little Rachel – that storm had a lot to answer for.

They moored for the night on the wharf, where they had met Dick for the first time handing out leaflets, and Daisy and Clemmie recalled fondly the Temperance Supper.

"I thought he might be here to meet us!" Ruth was disappointed.

"I told him not to," Daisy said calmly.

"Can't we have supper at the inn?" A plaintive plea from Bay.

"With the baby?" Ruth queried doubtfully.

Daisy felt in her purse. Not much left, she thought, only a shade ruefully, for her wages had gone on her clothes for the new country.

"Here, Bay, take this, fetch us some pies and hot potatoes, eh, and a jug of ale to celebrate, for Ruth whispers you can enjoy a draught now and then – as Dick said once to me: 'everything in moderation'."

"Here's the *smaller* jug," Ruth suggested wisely.

After supper, they sang together. The Singing Barleys were back in business, for, to their amusement, quite a crowd gathered round *Pili Pala*, as they sat on deck, and coins spun towards them in appreciation. They would give these later to the mission. Daisy even took up her guitar; regretfully, she would have to leave this behind, but maybe, she thought, young Rachel would play it one day . . . Anyway, it had belonged to her mother Anne, and Bay must keep it once more.

It was very late and dark when Daisy and Clemmie slipped into their bunks. Clemmie really was too big to cuddle up with Daisy in the top one now. She missed Pompom, curled on the rope. She heard the baby crying for, hopefully, the final feed of the day and the murmuring of Bay and Ruth's voices. Really happy *they* were now, Daisy thought sleepily, which proved that, given time, love could unexpectedly grow with the years. She mustn't forget her prayers for tomorrow. The hard bunk was a useful reminder of the primitive living conditions which would shortly be her lot. She wouldn't be lying alone *then*.

Clemmie whispered, "Are you nervous about tomorrow? I know I am, and I'm only playing a small part."

Daisy said, "You'll be all right, Clem, I promise. Truly everything will be fine." A single tear she wiped away, a tear for a lost love.

A coronet fashioned from rosemary she wore on her head, made by Juniper's worn fingers; a simple dress in ivory silk, with many tiny pearl buttons. She had not thought to wear anything so special but it had been sewn with love by Annie as a surprise. It had proved a perfect fit, to Annie's pleasure. Her gloves were borrowed from Mrs B, ruched above the elbow. Round her throat she wore a simple silver chain, with a tiny pearl.

Daisy walked surely down the aisle on her father's arm. Clemmie and Jem followed demurely, wearing dresses of palest blue, also made by Annie on her marvellous machine. She carried no flowers, just her mother's prayer book. That was very important to her. Would the mother she never knew have approved of her, on her wedding day?

They were all here, her friends. Eli and Gwennie, rocking Elijah determinedly, for he could be a noisy baby at times, more crowing than crying of course, but they were determined he should not interrupt the service. Gwennie wore a new dress to accommodate her even more ample figure. Both she and Eli dabbed emotionally at their eyes.

Here was Juniper, in the costume she had worn for her own daughter's wedding, with Molly fast asleep in her lap. Rose and Huw looked shyly at each other, held hands, no doubt recalling their own wedding day, not so long ago. It would be their anniversary next week and already Rose had whispered to her mother that there was another baby on the way – they must look in earnest for that cottage now! It had always been a sadness to Juniper that she had only the one surviving child. Rose was so pretty she made Huw's pulse race as he and she sat very close.

Ivor and Annie looked very proud and prosperous. Meg had declined an invitation for she had married her widower in March and had wasted no time for she too was already expecting a baby. Annie tweaked Clemmie's dress imperceptibly as she passed. Trust Clemmie to crease the skirt.

In the front row of chairs sat Ruth Owen with Rachel wrapped in her best shawl, and Mrs B with Eric's wife Margaret, who had wisely left her toddler at home with his grandmother.

Dick stood straight and tall, unfamiliar in his new suit, his silver hair bright in the light from the window above. Eric, as best man, felt nervously for the wedding ring in his pocket.

Then she was at Dick's side and he swallowed hard at the sheer radiance of her.

The service was conducted by a preacher who obviously thought very highly of Dick and said so in his address to the congregation. Daisy thought that he probably disapproved of her, just a little, being one of The Singing Barleys. But then she was suddenly aware that the preacher was now including *her* in his homily.

"In Daisy, I believe that Dick has the partner he richly deserves, a loyal helpmate who is prepared to travel with him into the unknown, to be receptive to his needs and tender towards those who seek spiritual guidance. From her mother-in-law, from the friends she has made here in Wales, I have learned that she can be most brave in defence of those in trouble, that she has been a most loving daughter and sister, so what conclusion can I come to other than that Dick is a most fortunate man?"

Then the wedding ring was sliding effortlessly on to her finger and Dick and Daisy were man and wife.

'They children, like the olive branches: round about thy table . . .' The words of the psalm were so fitting. Children here and surely to come?

She had asked him to select his favourite hymns and she was not disappointed. It made her happy to hear Bay's voice leading the singing and she smiled at Dick as they heard the little ones present joining in, with the underlying shushing from their parents.

They received Communion together; and the Blessing. Then the music pealed forth loudly; there was much clearing of throats, turning of heads as together they walked back up the aisle.

Outside in the flood of sunshine which greeted them, their way was strewn with sprigs of rosemary from Juniper's basket by the two lively bridesmaids, laughing as they scampered ahead. The fragrance from the crushed leaves and blue flowers was sweet.

"For Remembrance . . ." Juniper called after them.

Thirty-Six

M rs B, elegant in violet silk, as if to remind the others that she had a given name, Violet, which was scarcely used since she had wed the late Mr Bucktrout, escorted Ruth Owen upstairs to her bedroom when young Rachel's needs became more urgent than the cutting of the wedding cake.

"Here, Ruth, just let me move all these beautiful hats – my bed has become quite a millinery department it seems; the ladies seemed quite eager to divest themselves of all these plumes when we came back to the house . . . Put your feet up on my bed, my dear, you look so tired," she fussed kindly, as she had over Ruth the night they had first stayed here, and as she had over Jem when Dick and Daisy brought her to her new home. Mrs B gently removed Ruth's smart, tight shoes so that she could wriggle her cramped toes gratefully, and piled the pillows behind her to lend support so that she could nurse the baby in comfort.

"I *am* tired, I don't know why—" Ruth said slowly, "because this has been one of the happiest days of my life, seeing Daisy married to Dick."

"It is an anti-climax, as they say," Mrs B observed shrewdly. "You are just beginning to realise, I think, how much you will miss Daisy. As I am, with Dick."

"She is as much a daughter to me," Ruth said, shifting the tiny girl in her arms, "as Clemmie, or now, Rachel. Until she went away for the first time I didn't realise how much I - we - depended on her. There *were* good times in the early days when we were touring around you know: she was such an earnest little girl when she came to us but I think she learned to laugh then. I know you well enough to say that Bay was not

234

the easiest of husbands and fathers to live with; he did not allow himself to become close to his eldest daughter, which made me determined to compensate by loving her more myself."

"You succeeded, dear Ruth Owen."

"I'm glad."

A tap on the door and in came Gwennie. "May I join you? Eli the younger is hungry again and I only nursed him an hour ago!"

"I'll leave you mothers to your babies," Mrs B smiled. "I should join the guests. We'll keep the ceremony of the cake until you come downstairs again, eh?"

Ruth Owen obligingly shifted on the bed to make room for her friend and her baby.

They chatted of this and that, mainly the ceremony and what the guests were wearing; were changing the babies, commiserating one with the other over the posseted milk on their offspring's fronts and on their own shoulders, when Gwennie, serious for once, asked, "Had you heard that Drago is returning to the house with many steps?"

Ruth Owen was startled. Naturally, old friends had known or suspected Rachel Hughes's youthful affair and her own origins, she thought, but they had remained loyally silent on the subject until she learned the truth herself in her teens. "Why, I wonder?"

"He was abroad as you know. Last month he suffered a severe stroke – just like your Rachel! It is doubtful he will live long; he desired, we heard, to be brought home, to be in his own home when the time comes . . . Mari Evans is back there with some of the other staff to make ready: she thinks he will want to see *you*."

Ruth lifted her baby to her shoulder, wrapped the damp napkin and pushed it in her bag. Of course, everyone knew of her relationship to Drago now – it was inevitable. "I can't think about that *today*, Gwennie," she said, "but thank you for telling me. I *should* know . . . Are you ready? They will be impatient, with the knife poised over that wonderful cake you made!"

When the cake was cut and served, and the time was drawing

near for the happy couple to depart, Daisy took the baby from her mother, which was how she truly thought of Ruth on this special day.

Rachel obligingly dribbled down the wedding gown, and Pompom, jumping up in excitement, pulled a thread or two of silk with her claws. Both of them were dampened by Daisy's sudden flood of tears, and it was not because of the dress.

Dick, concerned, mopped her face with his pocket handkerchief. "Darling, whatever is it?"

"I don't know!" she sobbed, but she managed a smile at the same time to let them all know she was just being silly and how happy she was really.

"Me mam's comin' soon, for a holiday like, with Ted and our baby," Jem told her, scolding Pom and hugging her at the same time. "Mrs B said they could. It's all thanks to you two this is, and to Ruth and Bay and Clemmie for letting me come aboard *Pili Pala* in the first place. *I* wish I could come with you to Africa, but Mrs B says I'll no doubt be joining you out there one of these days but she can't spare me *yet*, 'cause she'll be missing Dick you see."

"I'm so happy for you, Jem," Daisy told her. "Love little Pom for me."

Ruth Owen stood back with Bay and Clemmie while the farewells were made. Their turn would come all too soon, she thought, near to tears herself.

Juniper, Rose, Huw and Molly came shyly forward. "Got to take *The Molly Kelly* back down the canal again, and it's time for Molly to go in her cradle." Quite a speech from Rose. She put out her slender brown hand. "I hope you'll be as joyful as we has been," she added.

"And as blessed!" Huw held Molly up for Daisy to kiss.

Juniper wasn't the hugging sort, but her smile said it all.

"Goodbye and thank you for coming – and especially for the rosemary – we'll take a sprig with us," they said.

Babies cut short celebrations it seemed. Eli and Gwennie were off too. Daisy passed Rachel to Dick, while she felt the weight of young Eli. "He can't hurt my dress, Gwennie!" When they had embraced she asked, "Keep in touch, won't you? Ruth

Owen will give you our address when we are settled – we just know that letters from home are going to mean *so* much."

Ruth, Clemmie, Bay and Rachel were staying overnight with Mrs B. "We're going to talk all night, Jem and me!" Clemmie assured her sister.

Margaret and Eric had left already. Friends from the chapel helped to pack up the remnants of the wedding feast to distribute at a mission supper to surpass all previous ones.

"We'll be glad to deliver it for you to the mission hall," Ivor offered. He and Annie were next in line for the kissing and hugging. "*Pili Pala*," he added, "will always be there when you want to use her. Even though she is only fit for a summer season nowadays."

"*Our* summer season," put in Ruth, "is one we will never forget, isn't it, Daisy?"

As she embraced Annie, Daisy's gaze met Ruth Owen's, over her shoulder. The message was: *she* would not forget . . . To Annie she said, "Thank you for my beautiful dress, Ruth is going to keep it for the next bride in the family!"

"Or it would cut down for a lovely christening dress," Annie sighed sentimentally.

Then it was time for Ruth to go with Daisy to help her change. She wondered if she was expected to give the traditional words of advice as the mother of the bride. Daisy stood there in her shift, while Ruth smoothed out the wedding gown, folding it carefully, exclaiming over the stains and flaws, hoping that dear Annie had not seen the same; then she put Ruth out of her misery.

"Don't worry about me – us, will you? Dick, well, Dick will be thoughtful, as he always is – take care of me always, you must be sure of that . . . Oh, dear Ruth Owen, I am going to miss you – you don't know how much! And Bay, and Clemmie, and the baby."

"You look so lovely," Ruth said, when Daisy was dressed in the neat, inexpensive costume for the short journey to the modest hotel in town. The overnight bags had gone ahead of them; their heavy luggage, for the boat, was already in transit.

237

Daisy unclasped the cheap necklace and passed it to Ruth. "Would you keep this for Rachel for me please? Perhaps I shouldn't have worn it today – Mrs B offered to lend me her pearls – but Dick said of course he didn't mind and—"

"I will keep it safe for her – and you – from Alun," Ruth said softly.

"I haven't said all the things I wanted to, you know, but I'll write them when I'm not feeling so emotional . . ."

Ruth Owen held her so tightly. "Be happy, be *loved*, Daisy."

Daisy lay still in the bed, waiting for Dick to come to her. Her trousseau, she thought ruefully, consisted of sensible clothes needed for the new country. Dick had spent what he had on canvas baths, netting, a travelling stove, a stout tent – they really were going into the unknown. It would be some time before they were provided with a house: the mission itself had been a priority. Together with local help they would build a school first.

Thanks to a last minute gift from Mrs B – "You must wear this tonight like a proper bride!" – she was not wearing one of the plain lawn nightgowns which she had run up so quickly on Annie's machine before she went to the mission school, but a softly sensuous satin slip which left her arms and throat bare and made her feel vulnerable, even though she knew there was no need. Aquamarine, the colour of the sea they would cross, she mused; how different from the canal waters it would be.

Dick sat on the edge of the bed, his hair disarmingly rumpled, his face freshly shaved. He smelled nicely of astringent cologne; so did she. There had been a bottle in the hotel bathroom. She smiled at the thought: neither of them were vain but both had wanted, needed to be a little different tonight . . . He must be nervous too, she realised, for he had paper on a razor cut. He smiled back. He took her unresisting hand. "Daisy, darling, I just want to say – I want you to be *sure*; I know how much you felt for Alun. I do love you so much, but I want things to be right for *both* of us."

She looked up at his earnest face, the bright eyes and she

sensed his yearning. He was strong and caring; she was so glad she had married him, for didn't she already love him? And she was confident that love would continue to expand. Loving Dick would be more pleasure than pain. He had the qualities which Alun had lacked. Here was someone for *her*, at last, to lean on when she needed to.

"You look beautiful," he told her as he touched a fold of the satin slip.

She said quietly, "You've waited long enough for me, you know." She was nineteen years old; she was a woman; she was full of love ready to give. Alun had awakened desire; made her aware of this. But she was glad that it was Dick who would fulfil it. She slid her arms firmly round his neck and held him very close. "I *do* love you," she murmured against his lips. Passion was as sweet as unexpected.

Thirty-Seven

S trangely, the sitting room at Ty-Gyda-Cerded was much as they remembered. The dust sheets had been removed from the furniture, the curtains at the open French windows still fluttered outwards in the breeze, but the garden beyond had signs of neglect, was already overgrown.

The sofa on which Eluned Drago had reclined had been replaced by a day bed on which her husband now lay, helpless. There were the requisites of an invalid placed on a small table nearby. Some of the ornaments had obviously been packed away. But the chess pieces were still out as if a game was in progress.

Only two of the servants had returned, the housekeeper and Mari; the others had been pensioned off or been fortunate enough to secure new posts. However, there were two nurses, who shared the day and night duties.

Clemmie, upset to see the man she had so recently been told was her grandfather – all these strange family relationships! – so much a shadow of himself, crossed the room to where the piano had been in place of honour. There was another shadow here, a discoloured patch on the wall, like a ghostly reminder of itself.

Ruth Owen sat in the chair beside her father, unwrapping the baby from her light shawl. She was still inclined to coddle little Rachel for they had taken such care of her in the early days. It had been imperative then to keep her warm: today, the baby wore a muslin gown, which she kicked up to reveal tiny feet, bare and rosy and on the go.

"Here is your newest granddaughter," she told Drago. "I think you will be pleased to know she is named for Rachel Hughes.

240

She is plucky, a real survivor against the odds, for she came much too soon, in the coldest weather of the winter. She can almost sit up, see, and, look, she is *smiling* at you! I know you can't tell me how you feel about us coming to see you after what I said, that last time, but I hope you are glad – I am."

The nurse on duty, her eyes lively with interest at this unexpected visit of what must be Mr Drago's family, although she had been told he had no close relatives since his wife died, slipped a slate under his hand and curled his fingers round the chalk. "He can write a word or two. We are positive he knows what is going on but his speech has not – yet—" she paused delicately, "returned."

Slowly Drago made some wavering outlines. Ruth Owen saw three uncertain words: 'Happy See You'.

"Bay," she called to her husband, who had stepped out into the garden, "take Clemmie and the baby to the summer house and sit in there for a bit. The air will do Rachel good."

He appeared, took the baby from her, motioned to Clemmie, then they went outside as Ruth suggested.

"I wonder, could you make us some tea please – and lemonade for Clemmie?" she asked the nurse. "I will watch Mr Drago for a few minutes."

"Of course," the nurse agreed readily, hiding her disappointment at not learning more. "Call me at once if you become alarmed," she added.

"I said" – Ruth took his nerveless hand in hers – "when we last met that I could not be a daughter to you, that you must not imagine yourself to be a father to me or a grandfather to my children, but I'm glad I said I hoped we would be able to be on friendly terms if ever we should meet . . . I was too ready to judge, too resentful of the past to be really forgiving, I'm afraid. I hope it is not too late for me to tell you how sorry I am to see you ill and that, if you should wish it, I will come to see you whenever I can. You see, I would like you to – be at peace with yourself. I have not had an easy life and perhaps I was too ready to put some of the blame for this on your shoulders. I am sorry. I do hope you can understand?" she ended anxiously.

His hand moved slightly toward the slate. She put it in place as the nurse had done. Just the one word this time: 'Glad'.

"So am I," she said softly, and she gently stroked his cheek before she bent and kissed him on his forehead. "We *both* loved Rachel," she added simply.

Drago had written his will before he was stricken. The house, some money, not much, for Eluned's inheritance had all gone on her lavish household expenses, was bequeathed to: 'my daughter, Ruth Owen Barley, to do with as she thinks fit.'

"I'm not sure I could ever live there," Ruth said, after the funeral which they had attended as a family. She saw the disappointment on Bay's face; after all, the cottage was cramped, it was only rented and *he* would like to live in style. Clemmie too, she thought wryly. "We couldn't afford to keep it up," she reminded them.

Ivor came up with the solution. "Why not rent it out for a few years until the girls are bigger?" he suggested. "This would pay for any repairs, for a small staff to keep it clean and the garden tidy, and what was left would still provide a useful added income for you. There is not a great deal to be made from the teaching of music in this area after all; there are many wanting to learn, but not the money to pay for it."

"I think you are right! Yes, maybe we could even help by taking on a deserving pupil or two who, as you say, cannot afford the lessons . . . And Bay, this would enable us to pay for Clemmie's further training when the time comes! I'm sure that is what Drago would have wanted." Ruth Owen sighed with relief. They were both convinced of their dream, as Daisy had said: 'Miss Clementina Barley, Concert Pianist'.

So was Clemmie. "At least I've got the piano here," she said, sitting down to play. Her touch was becoming sure and gentler, the precocious child was becoming serious, determined. She would succeed where her mother had not, Ruth Owen thought, and nowadays she was not regretful.

Life went on as before. Except that Daisy was in Rhodesia, and they all missed her so much, but by the next Christmas there was the news that she and Dick were expecting their first baby and they hoped they could complete the schoolroom before the event.

They never saw Alun, or heard from him at all.

Mrs B continued to encourage the young girl she had come to think of as the daughter she would have loved to have had. And Jem caught up with her schooling and made her friends very proud of her.

When the music swelled from Drago's piano, Ruth Owen would think of him, and Rachel, and sigh, just a little.

Epilogue

Ty-Gyda-Cerded, 1914

D aisy had grown her hair again since they returned from the mission field. She had grown in other respects, she thought ruefully, for she was heavily pregnant with her third child. The first two had come early in their marriage: Anne was fifteen and Bay fourteen. As Juniper had predicted long ago, despite the primitive conditions under which those first babies were born, Daisy had given birth easily with the women from the mission in attendance. The children had come home to school, for the climate was not considered good for the missionary families. This had been a great wrench for Daisy and Dick, to part with the daughter and son they adored, but they had accepted the inevitable. There were the grandparents for them to go to in the school holidays of course, Ruth Owen and Bay and Mrs B, and a youthful 'aunt' their own age in Rachel Barley, which amused the young Bucktrouts greatly.

"I shall enjoy this baby, even though it's unplanned, and I'm not as young as I was," Daisy told Dick. "I'll be about the same age as Ruth Owen was when Rachel was born."

The threat of war in Europe, now the world, had brought them back to Wales, to the canal at last. Dick was already back preaching at the chapel, for the younger men were joining up. He was forty-two and Daisy hoped fervently that he would not do the same.

Bay and Ruth had moved to Ty-Gyda-Cerded with some misgivings a few years back – still it meant there was plenty of room for homeless missionaries, Daisy smiled, and the children all loved being together. Mrs B was quite stricken with arthritis now and they had not thought it fair to descend on her – however they saw as much of her as they could.

Clemmie was home for a while now too; she had actually been in France in concert when war was declared. Daisy could hardly believe that her sister was twenty-four years old. "I wore *the dress*, as I promised!" she wrote jubilantly, after her debut concert, seven years ago. "As suspected, I never grew as tall as you, but Annie took the hem up. But I managed to fill it out – hurray!"

Jem, though, was still overseas. A wonderful born nurse, Daisy thought. She had married the mission doctor, a middle-aged German. This meant that they could not come back to Britain, where the doctor had trained, as a one-time refugee. They had no children of their own, but the mission children meant so much to Jem and her husband. All the family were very proud of Jem, especially Mrs B and Jem's own mother who had come to live with Dick's mother to help out when Nanny died. Elsie was now doing splendidly at school, following in her sister's footsteps. This was a base for Jem's brothers to return to, too, though Ted was now a policeman in Cardiff.

As for the canal friends, Juniper now cared for seven children in her cottage and the eldest, sixteen-year-old Molly, was already courting – the Midnight Grocer's son, of course! Young Eli was an only son and the image of his father. Gwennie and Eli still couldn't get up in the mornings! Ivor was close to retiring and he and Annie made splendid extra honorary grandparents to Daisy and Dick's two, which gave them great pleasure.

Daisy slowly descended the many steps, now pristine once more. "Meet him on your own, at the bottom of the steps," Dick had suggested when they heard he was coming. She had seen the children exchanging curious glances. All they had heard was that he had come to Ivor and Annie's and was to stay for a few days. Ivor had relayed the message: "He would like to see you all, especially Daisy, but will understand if she would rather not."

Dick had answered for her, "Of course Daisy will want to see him. And Ruth – all of us. Do tell him to come soon, and welcome!"

She stood now on the canal bank, breathing fast from the exertion, looking back up at the house. She could hear the faint shrieks and laughter of the young people playing tennis, over an improvised net, her two tall and strong like Dick and herself, fair haired, yet so compatible with Clemmie and Rachel, like twins those two, she thought, in looks and nature. Rachel Hughes and Ruth Owen all over again.

She felt the fear bubbling inside her, that this war would be still be raging in two or more years, despite what the politicians said, that eventually their son would be called upon to fight. The three girls, she was aware, were already talking of training as volunteer nurses – Clemmie was certainly the right age.

Here he came at last, walking fast along the grass toward her. His hair was as dark as ever, his figure just a trifle thicker, his dark Owen gaze fixed upon her. She hoped fervently that Ivor and Annie had told him of her condition. The autumn breeze mercifully cooled her treacherously burning cheeks, sneaked tendrils of red-gold hair from the coil in the nape of her neck.

"*Alun* . . ." Daisy seemed to hear another voice say, but it was her own.

"I said I would come back and you, Daisy, kept your promise too, eh, to be here, when I did. We've both been away so long. You look well," he told her, then he embraced her carefully, as a brother might his sister, so obviously pregnant. He kissed her cheek, murmuring, "I'm only sorry I waited all this time."

"How is your wife?" Daisy asked, breathing fast again.

His expression immediately became guarded. "Fine, I imagine. She is still in Cornwall. I have been in London for some weeks, prior to coming here, arranging things like. I am now an unofficial war artist; off to France, very shortly. Too old at present for the actual fighting, when so many young men have volunteered, but until my time comes I can do something, in my own way, I feel."

246

"Our son, our daughter, Ruth Owen's girls, they are all eager to be a part of it, but *I* hate the thought!"

"Ah, but you are a peaceable person, Daisy, you always were. Yet, I learn from Ivor and Annie that you have fought in your own way for the people in your mission, fought for the right for them to be educated, to receive proper medical care, fought for their souls . . . Did you pray for *me* over the long years – you and Dick, I wonder?"

He was smiling, but she took him seriously. "Oh Alun – we – I did!"

"You married the right man," he said solemnly, "but what a fool I was to let you go."

"Alun, surely you love your wife?"

"Do I?" he countered her question wryly. The sacrifice for him had not been worth the let-down.

"You have a family?" she asked. "You will know that I have two, well" – she glanced ruefully down at herself – "almost three, as you can see. A late blessing, just like Ruth Owen and Bay!"

"I have no children," he said shortly.

"But—" She seemed to see those words in his last letter to her. *'I have to marry Madeleine.'*

"It was a mistake," he added.

"Oh . . ." she said. Then, "We sometimes heard of you, Alun, over the years, even where we were, for when you were in touch with Ivor and Annie again they wrote of your successes, your acceptance by the Royal Academy. We, Dick and I, and of course, Ruth Owen and her family were so proud." She could not speak as warmly as she felt. His painting of the young Daisy had been out to Africa and back.

"Shall we go up to the house?" he asked. "I'm looking forward to seeing them all again and meeting the newer members of the family of course. Ivor tells me that dear Ruth Owen is as youthful and full of joy as ever and that little Rachel is growing just like Clemmie. What a career *that* young lady has carved for herself! You had some share in that, teaching her as you did when she was young, I'm sure."

He offered his arm and helped her to make the ascent.

They stood for a brief moment on the top step, just looking at each other.

"I never stopped loving you, Daisy." He looked searchingly at her now. "And you?"

"I love my husband dearly, I hope and pray I've been a good wife to him, Alun. He has never minded, always understood that there is, always will be, a special place in my heart for you."

"That is all I wanted to know – perhaps the reason I came back. I have no right to ask you for more, and I would not dream of doing so. That summer, Daisy, there was the best and saddest of everything."

"Love is as much pain as pleasure," she quoted Juniper's wise words of long ago.

Dick answered the door, at Ruth Owen's prompting, but she, all excited, stood just behind him.

He looked eloquently at his wife. Then at Alun. "Good to see you again," he said sincerely.

She released Alun's arm and went to Dick. His arm supported her tired frame protectively. She leaned against him, full of love. After all, she realised happily, theirs was a passionate, compatible relationship: she could not imagine life without him.

"I told Alun how very happy and contented we are," she said, "how pleased we both are that he has come back at last."

"Don't stand there, come in," Dick said warmly. "We always prayed you would come home to your family one day."

And Ruth Owen cried, as he hugged her as if he would never let her go: "If only Rachel Hughes were here!"

"All together," Ruth said proudly. She looked round her table. Clemmie, reminding them of Meg, now a proud matron with four children of her own, had insisted, "*I* knew him first!" making sure he sat by her.

He looked at young Rachel and smiled. "Oh, I seem to recognise those eyes!" He shook Anne gravely by the hand, for she was a reserved girl, not one for kissing long-lost cousins. "And you, Anne, you are Daisy Barley as I knew her, all over again." She blushed and brushed back her bush of curls.

Bay, really mellow now if not at the carpet slipper stage because Ruth Owen kept him on his toes and feeling young, not allowing delusions of grandeur now they resided in this splendid house, put in, "Young Bay, now, I hope you will say is also a chip off the old block?"

"He has your nose, Bay, like me," Clemmie grinned. Drago's piano, reinstated, would be brilliantly played to entertain them tonight.

In the Painted Room Ruth snuggled up to Bay in the grand bed. The room held no terrors for her now. They had moved in here when Daisy, Dick and their children returned. "You'll soon have to be boiling water again, I think," she said sleepily. "Daisy's baby will be coming—"

"Sooner or later, *I know* . . . But it's not nearly as terrifying being a grandfather as a father – *Dick* can boil the water! D'you think it upset *her*, Ruth, to see Alun again?"

"Perhaps, just a little. She married the right one, though, didn't she?"

"Didn't I tell you that, in the beginning?"

"You did."

"And *I* married the right one, too, Ruth Owen – but it took a summer season to prove it to me."

She had anticipated the knocking on their door. Daisy's voice: "Oh Ruth Owen – can you come?"

Instantly she was out of bed, followed by Bay, who insisted she put on a wrapper. "It may be a long night," he said, with the voice of experience.

"Go back to bed, Daisy dear – I'll be with you in just a second," she promised.

She turned briefly to her husband. "Summer seasons come and go, my old darling, but we've got *all* our family around us *right now* – that's all that matters!"

Pili Pala swayed at her moorings. The bright paint had long faded, the delicate butterfly was almost obscured, but she was not forgotten. Sometimes the young people came aboard and partied. Ruth suspected there was a romantic tryst or two, for war meant partings. Of course, Old William was no more and Pompom too, no longer skittered on the deck. Ruth Owen and Daisy brought the newest member of the family along one day. Maybe little Ivor Alun, too, would be an artist like his step-uncle who had gone to war.

Not only men but the canal horses were being recruited for the Great War. When it was all over the canal would never return to its former busy ways. The railways, then the roads had won the battle for carrying goods.

Just past the middle of the century, the waterways would again revive. The holidaymakers would journey in boats fashioned after *Pili Pala*, for was there ever a better shape for meandering along the canal and raising your voice in song, when you felt like it? Another Daisy, the first Daisy's granddaughter, would name a new boat *Pili Pala*. Long before the turn of the century the narrowboats would be powered by diesel fuel and the Lock Cottage would finally become a tiny museum, a shrine to days and ways past. Ty-Gyda-Cerded would be a haven for holidays, too.

But for *Pili Pala*, the butterfly boat, the summer season was long over.